CHASING TIME

BRANDT LEGG

CHASING TIME

BRANDT LEGG

VINCI
BOOKS

By Brandt Legg

Chase Malone Thriller

Chasing Rain
Chasing Fire
Chasing Wind
Chasing Dirt
Chasing Life
Chasing Kill
Chasing Risk
Chasing Mind
Chasing Time
Chasing Lies
Chasing Fear
Chasing Lost

*As always, this book is dedicated to
Teakki and Ro*

Vinci Books

vinci-books.com

Published by Vinci Books Ltd in 2025

1

Copyright © Brandt Legg 2021

The author has asserted their moral right to be identified as the author of this work in accordance with the Copyright, Designs and Patents Act 1988. This work is a work of fiction. Names, characters, places and incidents are the product of the author's imagination or are used fictitiously. Any resemblance to actual persons, living or dead, places and incidents is entirely coincidental.

All rights reserved. No part of this publication may be copied, reproduced, distributed, stored in any retrieval system, or transmitted in any form or by any means, including photocopying, recording, or other electronic or mechanical methods, nor used as a source for any form of machine learning including AI datasets, without the prior written permission of the publisher.

The publisher and the author have made every effort to obtain permissions for any third party material used in this book and to comply with copyright law. Any queries in this respect should be brought to the attention of the publisher and any omissions will be corrected in future editions.

A CIP catalogue record for this book is available from the British Library.

Paperback ISBN: 9781036705282

Chapter One

WASHINGTON DC

April 2nd - 2:42 am - Eastern Time

The strong scent of cherry blossoms filled the warm, surprisingly humid night. He pictured their beauty, wondering if he'd ever see them again when they were drenched in sunlight. *They want to kill me,* he thought, looking back into the darkness. Washington in the spring was a beautiful place, even in the middle of the night, but not if you were running for your life.

The Astronaut tried to calm himself, pressed up against the black granite wall of the Vietnam Veterans Memorial. Breathing in the perfume of the trees, he could almost pretend it was going to be all right. Yet The Astronaut knew better. He was an intelligent man; logic, odds, calculating the countless potential outcomes of his predicament, came easily.

The CIA referred to him as an 'Astronaut' even though he'd never even piloted a plane, much less a spaceship. The odd moniker was due to his "out of this world" mind. His brain came wired a little differently than most—capable of extraordinary feats, able to detect patterns and see answers normal folk couldn't imagine.

But as he ran from people intent on doing him harm, The Astronaut felt anything but special. He felt ordinary. So ordinary it was as if he was nothing. For years, he had worked with the CIA and other intelligence agencies around the world, helping them do what even the super computers and advanced AI could not. He—and a few others like him—was able to use his mind in ways that programmers were unable to force machines to do. Something about human intelligence, mixed with human emotions, mixed with instincts and uniquely human experiences, mixed with one other ingredient, perhaps the most magical (The Astronaut was on the spectrum, a neurobiological type, gene variant of autism), had formed a mind that was indeed exceptional.

The math savant did not like to be touched, yet embraced numbers, which to him were a secret language expressed in colors so numerous that even the most talented artist could not conceive of what he saw.

So as he crouched in the shadows of the wall, he knew there were originally 57,939 names at the time of the memorial's dedication in 1982, but now there were 58,318, each etched in chronological order of their deaths on 140 panels. He knew the wall was constructed at a cost of $232 million, he knew how many members of Congress had voted to allocate funds, he knew that it attracted more than 78,000 visitors every month, he knew how high each letter was and the total number of letters on the wall, and The Astronaut also knew that this was where he would die.

But how many are trying to kill me? It drove him crazy not to know that answer to input the critical data into his mind, so he could accurately calculate the odds.

The Astronaut was close enough to the cold, monolithic surface that his warm, panting breaths clouded three of four names. The black granite had been so highly polished that in daylight it acted as a mirror, but at night its ominous structure might swallow him.

His entire life, The Astronaut had known he was "unique." In some ways that had made him fragile and weak, but he'd always believed that in any fight, the smartest would prevail.

I am one of the smartest.

However, on this balmy night, on the National Mall, in the capitol city of the most powerful country on earth, there was no solution that he could see . . . no way out.

What if my mind is not going to be able to save me this time? He scanned the area, sure they were closing in on him. *Maybe it will be my lungs and my legs that save me . . .*

He heard shouts. There were so many of them. It didn't make sense that a single unarmed mathematician could attract that kind of force against him, but nothing in The Astronaut's life made sense. A strange, awkward man outside of his realm, he ran with spies, secret agents, assassins, brilliant scientists, rogue revolutionaries . . . his life had been extraordinary because he had something so rare. And people, both good and bad, were attracted to rare things.

The Astronaut didn't even know who was after him, who was going to kill him. He had been running from them for days, weeks—in fact, it had actually been *months* if he admitted to ignoring the earliest signs.

How did I let it come to this? I am not ready to go. I don't want to leave this world . . . I like it here.

The panic began to take him. He fought its greasy claws, knowing that if he got lost in the terror, there would be nothing left.

Chapter Two

ANOTHER PART OF THE WORLD

"It's the middle of the night there," a gray-haired man said. His expensive black suit added an appearance of importance. He studied the faces on a giant monitor occupying a section of wall surrounded by rich, red, floor-to-ceiling draperies.

Another man in a bright red necktie nodded. He, too, looked at the faces as though they were pieces on a chessboard. Although the large table could easily accommodate thirty-six people, they were alone in the vast room. An eight foot wide bronze sculpture of a hammer and sickle hung on the opposite wall, mounted on a slab of wood, also painted a deep red.

"Have we heard from Tolstoy?"

"Not since this morning," the gray-haired man replied. "But as I said, it is nighttime there now."

"There is a situation beyond them," the red tie man said, motioning to the pictures on the monitor. "This Astronaut could unravel Blackout."

"Tolstoy's operatives will have The Astronaut soon. This is not a problem."

"But Tolstoy has not reported."

"We have another contact through our embassy in Washington."

"That is risky."

The gray-haired man smiled slightly. "Life is risky. They have full surveillance, and twenty-seven minutes ago they located The Astronaut again. This time he is alone, and he is running. We have also discovered where he has been staying."

"In Washington?"

"Yes. We have people going there now."

"The CIA and the FBI could pick up on our activities."

"Yes, they could."

The red tie man looked at the screen and began to say something, but hesitated.

"What is it?" the gray-haired man prodded. "Speak freely."

"I don't know if we can kill all these people and expect to make each one look accidental."

"Of course not. They will figure it out, but it will be too late."

"Not too late to blame us."

"The blame will fall elsewhere. You worry too much."

Red tie man nodded. "I do, because I am a strategist. I get paid to worry." He frowned. "Worrying is my life. You are in espionage. Worrying should be *your* life as well."

The gray-haired man looked to the portrait of Karl Marx on the other end of the room. "No, my job is to make sure our country, and our philosophy, dominate the world. Our ways during the era of the Cold War were often ignored. We were behind times, even forgotten . . . Ah, but the world has changed so much."

"When do we meet with the full committee?"

The gray-haired man looked at the clock. We are more than forty-eight hours from the removal. Much can still happen. We have a full meeting scheduled for twenty-four hours prior to removal and again at twelve hours ahead of time."

"Two meetings so close?" the man in the red tie asked, still uncomfortable with using the term 'removal' to describe the attack, although he could not argue with the accuracy of the word. In just over forty-eight hours, an American city, along with a million of its inhabitants, would be removed from the face of the earth.

"As I said, things are moving smoothly, but as we get closer . . ."

"And how will the president be able to deny our country's involvement?"

"You forget, our country is not involved."

The man in the red tie looked at him skeptically. "But we are. You more than anyone should know not to underestimate the US intelligence agencies."

"And *you* should know better not to underestimate *our* intelligence agencies."

The red tie man looked back at the screens. Being a diplomat, he was wary of this plan for many reasons, not the least of which was that a good many of his friends and associates were going to die as a result of it. He worried intensely that they would be discovered. Yet it might also work, and then they would have a whole new set of problems.

He had been against this radical intervention from the start. He was *afraid* of it. But theirs was not a structure where one could voice opposition to a plan that was already supported by one's superiors.

"Don't be so nervous," the gray-haired man said again.

"I told you, worry is my business."

"You will have much less to worry about after Five-Fours. We will clearly be dominant . . . the most powerful country in the world."

The official name for the attack, the removal, the insanity, was "Five-Fours," since the strike would happen at 4:44 am, on the fourth day of the fourth month. The field ops only knew it as "Blackout," but the diplomat in the red tie sitting at the long table in that massive room believed it should be called "The End."

"But you said they will not know it is us," red tie man said. "And if we avoid the blame, how will we get the credit?"

"The United States will be reeling," the gray-haired man replied. "You saw what happened after 9/11. They were never the same again. This is a million times 9/11. Five-Fours will *finish* them." His voice rose. "The United States will be a wreck, a failed state. They will be scrambling to put some semblance of their former selves back together again . . . and they will be missing almost all of their leadership."

"Yes, but—"

"Remember, it's not just Washington DC that will be gone, not just the great symbol of their *perceived* greatness, but all the *people*. The president, vice president, the entire cabinet, your friend, the Secretary of State, most of the members of Congress, all those annoying senators, the majority of their intelligence apparatus—that you tell me not to underestimate—will all be gone. Who will be left to figure anything out?"

Chapter Three

WASHINGTON DC

April 2nd - 2:51 am - Eastern Time

The Astronaut had left clues behind so that those wondering what had happened, curious as to why someone deemed him such a threat that he had to be exterminated, those who simply cared, would be able to find answers. *Because the answers are worth more than my life*, he thought. *The answers are worth everything.*

His pursuers were getting closer now, but he had found his breath again, and although he didn't think he could outrun them, he had to keep trying. It was the only logical thing to do.

Maybe I will discover a place where I can hide. The Astronaut was good at hiding. Intelligence agencies around the world were always trying to find him. *Hiding is a science.* If he could just find a place, his brilliant mind might have time to work on the elusive solution.

The twist in his gift, the duality, the two sides of the coin: his intellect told him it was over, his human emotions still clung to hope. And his practiced mind could compartmentalize and navigate both.

There is always an answer.

The Astronaut had already hidden the papers, the flash drive, the key. Now there was one last clue to leave, but there might not be time. He ran along the wall in darkness, the humid night closing in on him much the same as the people after him. He heard several more shouts in Russian, which he could understand. *They are speaking Russian. . . that doesn't make sense. Maybe it's bigger than I think? Maybe Popov . . .*

He looked up and saw a figure at the other end of the wall, then turned around. Another was behind him, but they still didn't know he was there.

Now or never.

He touched the black granite, felt the letters, somehow hoping the brave soldiers who were honored there might protect him. Might take the bullet for him.

Keeping far enough away from the killers as to not allow them a good shot is my only hope.

Hope. How odd it seemed to him. The logic around which his life had always centered had now given way to hope. The one thing he had never invested much time in was what kept him running when he knew there was no point.

If I can get to the road, Constitution Avenue . . . even at this hour there is traffic. There might be one last chance.

Hope.

The Astronaut checked the distance to Constitution Avenue again. *I can make it,* he thought. *Only because it is dark, and they don't know exactly where I am.*

But you can't outrun a bullet.

The thought of getting shot terrified him more than it would an average person. A bullet entering his body would be the ultimate invasion of his personal space. The Astronaut could not stand to get injections, or even haircuts (he did them himself). In a strange way, he feared the bullet entering his body more than he did dying.

His heart racing, he silently convinced himself, *Go on two. One. I must protect the data on my watch. Two. Don't get shot, don't get shot, don't get shot!*

He bolted. With the wall to his right, The Astronaut ran to the left. The pursuers had yet to fire shots. He had decided that was because they didn't want to attract attention—at least not until they were sure they could hit him.

Picturing himself running through feathers, as if this might make him quieter, The Astronaut felt suddenly free in the open air, away from the cold, imposing wall.

Halfway there, he still hadn't been spotted, and he was grateful for his dark clothing. Then he saw two vans stop on Constitution Avenue and heard orders given in Russian.

They cut me off. He wanted to cover his ears and scream. *Get away. Leave me alone. Get away. Leave me alone! Get away . . .*

Knowing he was about to run into the arms of his killers, instead he turned sharply right, the only choice he had, and ran for the trees of Constitution Gardens.

The land on which the fifty acre park sat had originally been submerged beneath the Potomac River, but had been dredged at the beginning of the 20th century by the Army Corps of Engineers. A memorial to the fifty-six signers of the Declaration of Independence sat on a small island at the center of the Garden's six acre lake.

The Astronaut had visited the Gardens often, and agreed with its nickname as being an "oasis" from the bustling city. He recalled that in 2003, a disgruntled tobacco farmer, claiming to have explosives, drove his tractor into the center of the lake. He had dug up part of the island,

and kept the FBI and US Park Police at bay for two days before surrendering.

Maybe I can survive there.

At a bench on a heavily treed section of the trail, he stopped to listen. Just in case, he quickly wrote a text message and set it up to send to the two people who he thought might be able to stop the nightmare. He ended it with the words, *"a great many people will surely die, but even more important, your actions will determine the fate of the world."*

Chapter Four

CHICAGO, ILLINOIS

April 2nd - 12:57 am - Central Time

Daniel Wallace heard the noise, but at first he didn't react because he was in the middle of a dream that involved him riding some giant bull in a dangerous rodeo taking place on the moon. "No air," he said in the nightmare as he fought the bucking animal, having no idea how he'd wound up in the ludicrous situation. He didn't realize it was the creaking of their bedroom door, yet the sound brought him out of sleep just enough that an instant before the gloved hands went around his throat, he opened his eyes and saw the shadowy figure.

Panic struck. He kicked his legs as he felt the hands tightening around his neck, now actually living a nightmare.

His wife's furious scream added another layer of terror. She had made the mistake of trying to grab the man attacking him instead of running. The last thing Daniel saw was the silhouette of another intruder, and he knew his wife was also about to die. His final thought was not of her, but rather his work. He had known it was a risk, but never believed it would cost him his life, and that of his wife. In that final split-second when he knew the fight was over, he wondered if the others had been targeted as well. What he did not waste time on was guessing who was behind the attacks. That he knew.

As the two black-clad operatives double-checked that the lifeless bodies of Daniel Wallace, a Nobel laureate scientist, and his wife, a well-liked professor at the University of Chicago, were in fact dead, they knew the third member of their hit squad was starting the fire. They quickly joined him. It would be more efficient with three.

That went well, the man in charge thought. *No noise other than that annoying scream. Now the fire.*

The men had come prepared with portable equipment that would incinerate the breaker box, then with strategic placement of stored solvents for a hobby, which neither Daniel or his wife actually had, the flames would quickly spread through the house and burn the bodies of the sleeping couple.

Not a perfect crime, the man thought. *The authorities will eventually figure it out, but it will be too late. After tomorrow, the cause of death of these people will not matter.*

They had parked their vehicle half a mile from the residence as to not arouse suspicion. The streets were nearly deserted at this hour. They turned onto South Central Avenue and headed out of Beverly, a lovely area with nice homes, one of which was now engulfed in flames.

Once they exited I-190 onto the West Kennedy Expressway, heading to O'Hare International Airport, the man in the passenger seat dialed a number from his burner phone, which he would destroy before they got on their flight.

Tolstoy looked at the clock before answering. It was just after 4 am eastern time. Tolstoy was neither a heavy sleeper, nor one to indulge in long sleeps, especially this close to ignition. "Yes?"

"Chicago. Completed," the man said as they pulled into a rental car return area.

"Good," Tolstoy said, not allowing himself a smile. Although pleased, there were still too many holes to plug, and little time to do it. "Next."

"On our way," the man said, checking the itinerary. *Cambridge*, he thought, but didn't say out loud. Already contemplating the methods of eliminating the next problem on the list, he wanted to ask if the source of these leaks had been taken care of, but it was not his place. The call had already been too long. "Will report when completed."

"Good," Tolstoy said, ending the call.

Chapter Five

WASHINGTON DC

April 2nd - 2:58 am - Eastern Time

With no chance to still make it to the road, The Astronaut wove in between trees and shadows inside Constitution Gardens, hoping to avoid using the "cyanide pill" app on his phone. It would permanently erase all its data instantly, but leave the phone itself working for sixty minutes.

However, when he came to a giant willow tree at the edge of the lake, he realized his mistake. The water would trap him. He heard more shouts—accented English, Russian, and un-accented English.

I can't make Constitution Avenue . . .

The Astronaut ran as fast as he could around the lake, his feet crunching loudly on the pea-gravel path. Back out in the open, he sprinted toward the reflecting pool.

Having no idea how many were after him, he still clung to hope. *It's dark, I might slip through.* If he'd known they had already been to his apartment, he might have felt worse, but ultimately it wouldn't have mattered. He was never going back there again anyway, even if he survived the night.

Running along the reflecting pool, he realized the openness made him an easy target. *There's a lot of ground for them to cover.* His eyes, well-adjusted to the darkness, darted around. *They still seem to be searching . . . somehow they haven't seen me.* He saw men among the trees of the Gardens and more still around the Vietnam Memorial.

I might make it.

He debated for an instant whether to head to the higher ground at the Washington Monument, but it was too far. He pushed ahead toward the Lincoln Memorial until two silhouettes appeared behind him, and knew his chances of survival had just plummeted. Even distracted and scared, his extraordinary mind calculated the odds. He had a 4.8693 chance of living through the next seven minutes. The odds increased a little bit in the two minutes, eight seconds after that, and increased substantially after twelve minutes, nine seconds.

It's not good, he thought, tapping his phone to send the texts he'd written in the Gardens, then taking a deep breath before initiating the cyanide pill to wipe its data. He looked down at his wrist at an elaborate, custom smart watch made by a friend. It wasn't the sentimental aspect that now concerned him, it was the urgent contents in the watch's memory.

I have to hide the watch. It's the final clue I can leave behind. If I'm gone, it may help them stop it . . .

He worked hard to calm his thoughts. The idea of being "gone" made him dizzy. The Astronaut wondered if it could even be stopped in time. If he'd known that one of the scientists on the list was already dead, he'd have known it was lost.

Chasing Time

He frantically scoured the area for anywhere to hide the watch. Tired and as scared as he'd ever been in his life, The Astronaut tried to imagine other ways they might kill him. If he had to die, he just wanted it to happen in some manner that didn't involve touching, or knives, or bullets, or anything entering his body.

Since he was running across what was essentially an open field, there was nowhere to hide the watch. *Get to the Lincoln Memorial, find a hiding place.* He didn't care about anything but the watch. The watch, and how he was going to die.

Maybe being dropped from an airplane without a parachute, or made to jump off a high building would be the best method, he wondered. *That way the impact will take all the feeling and no one would touch me.* Unfortunately, there wasn't anything high enough around other than the Washington Monument, but he was running in the opposite direction.

"Washington Monument," he whispered to himself. "Five hundred fifty-five feet, five inches tall . . . Four-Fives . . . " An ironic twist, he thought, but then realized it was fifty-five feet wide at its base. "So really *six* fives."

He looked back over his shoulder at the giant monolith rising from the mall.

"More than thirty-six thousand stones used to construct the Washington Monument," he muttered, repeating it several times. "Eight hundred ninety-seven steps inside the structure, too many steps. Eight-ninety-seven, eight-ninety-seven . . . " Numbers were safe, and he suddenly considered switching course and running to the Monument. He knew it weighed an estimated 100,000 tons, and that it had been the world's tallest building when completed, eclipsing the then tallest, the Cologne Cathedral in Germany, and that a few years later the Eiffel Tower surpassed the Monument for the crown. Perhaps what fascinated him the most about the obelisk had nothing to do with numbers, rather that no mortar was used between the huge marble blocks in the Monument's construction, meaning it was held together with gravity and friction alone.

"More than thirty-six thousand stones held together by gravity. Gravity, no mortar." He looked at it again, almost stumbling. *I will be okay if I can just get to the top of the monument.* But he didn't change course. He kept heading toward the Lincoln Memorial. "Safe at the top. Five hundred fifty-five feet and five inches. I will be safe."

Chapter Six

ANOTHER PART OF THE WORLD

A sick feeling welled in the stomach of the diplomat with the red tie. His mouth was dry, his hands cold. However, he concentrated on making sure the terror surging through his body was not revealed on his face. He knew the plan, but now that it was less than forty-eight hours from actually happening, he had to admit his government was crazy enough to do it.

"It is perhaps more risky than you imagine."

The gray-haired man scoffed. "When you say risk, you act as though there is no risk in the present state of things. Imagine if the United States had not developed the atomic bomb first. The geopolitical landscape would be entirely different today. This is the new atomic bomb. We have gotten there first; it will change everything."

"Surely we could just announce it? Make it known?"

"No, they would catch up in a year, maybe less. And just as the Americans demonstrated the true might and awesome destructive force of their bombs on the Japanese, we must demonstrate ours."

The diplomat looked startled. "I understood the blame would fall on the US, and this would appear as some kind of accident that they inflicted upon themselves."

The gray-haired man smiled. "Yes. The first reaction, the early conclusions, to further erode confidence in their government." He paused and looked again at the hammer and sickle sculpture on the far wall. "You must recognize this as the most brilliant strategic offensive the world has ever seen. It's a shame, really, that we won't get immediate credit. Perhaps one day history will reveal the boldness of this strike."

"I hope not."

"They will know," he whispered. "Somehow, they will know."

"If we're caught, it will lead to war," the diplomat warned again. "The worst war."

The gray-haired man laughed. "If we get caught, it will mean that Washington DC was destroyed, and our new weapon changes everything. Believe me, no one will be in a hurry for war, not with us."

The diplomat nodded, realizing that his arguments would do nothing but jeopardize his career.

"It is brilliant, because we win either way," the gray-haired man continued. "If someone else gets blamed, we win, because the damage has been inflicted and we got away with it. If we get blamed, the world will fear us again—this time forever."

Washington, DC

Although she was a registered diplomat, Katiya Popov never went to the Russian Embassy on Wisconsin Avenue in Washington. Her credentials looked nothing like her. The thirty-two year old Russian beauty could have passed for a blonde-haired college student. Depicted on her passport and other official photos, Popov resembled a woman closer to her mother's age. That was by design. She had many identities, many aliases. She preferred not to be seen, and never properly identified.

Since the Russian Embassy was under constant surveillance, she had no desire to be anywhere near the building.

She also didn't particularly care for Boris Nemtsov Plaza, a section of Wisconsin Avenue in front of the embassy named in honor of the opposition activist and vocal critic of the Russian President. Nemtsov was murdered by assassins as he walked across a bridge near the Kremlin in 2015. It annoyed her that some hot-shot US Senator pushed for the memorial to serve as "an enduring reminder to Vladimir Putin, and those who support him, that they cannot use murder and intimidation to suppress dissent."

But she used them for that every single day.

Popov was not a real diplomat. She was an agent with the Russian Federal Security Service (FSB), conducting most of her business from a fancy K Street bakery and coffee shop. Her offices and small staff of operatives were reached through an "employees only" door in the back. Its four am to midnight hours provided good cover for their comings and goings.

Stairs led to another floor where she maintained a small flat. However, she mostly stayed in hotels paid for by the ill-gotten gains of Russian hacking operations. She did whatever necessary, wherever necessary.

Popov rarely took time off, particularly these days with so many projects underway and so close to fruition. She believed in her work: "I do it for fun." Her father had been in the KGB, a man who had animatedly pontificated dangerous and adventurous stories. The world was simpler then. Much of the action was in Washington and a few world capitals, maybe the occasional hotspot in the Middle East, Central or South America, wherever.

Now things were different.

In one of the bakery's back rooms, Popov clicked her mouse. In a few hours, somebody was going to die in California. She checked the list of targets on her screen. Next, she reviewed a summary of ongoing cyber-attacks. Another monitor brought up the whereabouts of scientists, people they were watching, technologies traded, patents being bought and/or infringed. She juggled it all in her mind, always cognizant of how each event, every move, would affect the ultimate end game . . . and in the meantime, what they meant to Blackout.

Her father knew how many people he'd killed. He had done it personally, and not as often as an American spy movie audience would have imagined. His daughter, though in the same business, albeit now much more sophisticated, could never quantify a number like that. She had been responsible for hundreds, perhaps thousands, of deaths. She changed the world as often as she changed her bed linens. Yet even with those facts, and all that she had done, what she did in the next forty-eight hours was going to make everything else seem as if she and her father had never been born.

Chapter Seven

MIAMI, FLORIDA

April 2nd - 3:04 am - Eastern Time

Wen rolled over, sensing Chase was awake. "What's wrong?" she asked, touching the Glock 19 pistol under her pillow.

Chase, used to even the faintest sound waking her, had tried not to stir too much, knowing she needed to sleep. "Sorry. I don't know," he admitted. "A dream woke me. I don't really remember what it was about . . . something agitating."

Wen wasn't surprised. Chase regularly had disturbing dreams—people after them, or him letting people down. It wasn't unusual, given their lifestyle. Ever since the billionaire had given up his old life and gone on the run with her, they'd fallen deeper and deeper into an international web of espionage and conspiracies. "Want to talk?" She instinctively scanned the hotel room, lit only by the glow from a digital clock and a few indicator lights from the flatscreen tv on the wall.

Chase sighed. "I just wonder sometimes what we're doing all this for. We risk our lives *constantly*. Why? Are we really making a difference?"

"Of course we are. I could give you a list. In fact, The Astronaut actually keeps a list. He has all the stats on the people we've saved, the difference we've made. You know we've been effective. Think about some of the things we have done . . . some pretty *big* things."

"Yeah." He turned on his side, softened his gaze on her muscled, svelte body, clad only in the thin sheet.

She touched his stubbly cheek. "So what's this all about?"

"We've had this discussion before," he deflected. "We should just go back to sleep."

"It's an ongoing conversation," Wen said, taking his hand and rubbing it gently. "It has to be. Our lives are somewhat complicated."

"We've got the MSS after us, multiple corporations have hits out on us, and then the damned shadow people . . . so many people are trying to kill us."

"We're still here." She kissed him.

"Yeah, but we don't know *why* the shadow people want us dead. They're the ones that keep me up. And we don't even know who they are. That's the worst of it. At least with the MSS we *know* why. We know which corporations are dangerous, which ones we've interfered with."

"We're hours away from finding out about the shadow people," Wen reminded him.

"You're assuming that Grimes knows who they are."

"No, I'm not. But he knows a lot more than we do. Either way, we're going to get closer after this meeting. We'll have new information we can get to The Astronaut and input into

SEER," she said, referring to the Search Entire Existence Result program Chase had developed in strict secrecy. It employed advanced photonic quantum information processors and utilized deep learning, AI, quantum algorithms, and virtually every data point in digital existence to predict the future with stunning accuracy. "What we learn in the Caymans will be the breakthrough we've been waiting for."

"You're right," Chase agreed wearily. "I just get worn down by the running. Now with Tu, it seems so much more is at stake."

Wen thought about Tu, the DNA-altered boy they had rescued from a Chinese lab when he was only seven. "I feel like a parent, too," she admitted.

"He's already been through so much, yet we keep putting ourselves in harm's way. One day we might not come back. What happens to him then?"

"Dez and Bull would take care of him," Wen said, referring to Chase's business partner and his girlfriend, a hacker who also worked with them.

"You never heard back from The Astronaut, did you?"

Wen shook her head. "No. But he's been working on something really big. It's taking a lot of his time."

"For who? WOLF?" The group of revolutionaries, also known simply as "The Cause," was a point of contention between Chase and Wen.

"He hasn't said, but it's definitely not WOLF."

"Nash could be in trouble," Chase said, calling The Astronaut by his real name. "He works for some dangerous people."

"You mean us?"

"No," he chuckled, kissing her again, "you know what I'm talking about."

"He's been working with the Mossad recently, and the Germans," she replied.

"I'm sure we'll hear from him this morning. He knows we're heading to the Caymans to meet Grimes."

"Yeah."

"You brought up WOLF," he said.

"No, you did." She pulled Chase in for another kiss.

"WOLF seems to be edging more toward the radical."

"They are still heavily engaged in their cyber-attacks."

"Sure, but I think they're doing more assassinations."

Wen felt differently than Chase concerning this subject. Although she did not enjoy killing, she believed things had gotten to a point in the world that strategic assassination was a far more efficient and safe way to bring about change. "They only remove people who need to be removed."

"I'm not sure I trust *them* to decide." Chase sought more nonviolent ways—exposing people through cyber breaches, compromising situations, even blackmail if necessary, using media as propaganda and a weapon. The Cause was good at producing fake news and manipulating events.

"We don't really have to go into all the issues with The Cause right now, do we?" Wen asked. "It's a big day ahead. I'd like to get some sleep."

"You just don't want to discuss WOLF because we usually end up arguing about them."

"Not arguing," she said. "I don't remember ever arguing with you." She winked.

"True." He kissed her again. "Let's see if we can get a few more hours of sleep before we go to face the people who've been trying to kill us for the past few years."

"Sweet dreams."

Chapter Eight

WASHINGTON DC

April 2nd - 3:06 am - Eastern Time

The monuments and memorials seemed to be protecting The Astronaut. He knew they couldn't *actually* be doing anything; his logical mind believed in not much beyond the power of numbers and facts. Yet knowing that Washington DC was going to be destroyed, that every single person within the historic power center was going to die a hideous death, he felt reality bend a little, as if trying to get his mind to accept the imminent tragedy, the proportions and cost of it, changed the way facts were establishing themselves.

If the reflecting pool had just been grass, I might've been able to escape that way. But they are funneling me in, trapping me.

He so desperately wanted to warn people, to stop the attack.

Wait, the reflecting pool . . . my watch is waterproof! The watch had been specially modified—it could hold four terabytes of data, and had many other special features. *I have to save the watch . . . it will live on and warn them.*

When he reached the end of the reflecting pool and could finally turn the corner and cut over to the Lincoln Memorial, he took off the watch. Well concealed by his stride, he moved into a shadow and tossed the precious watch, with its vital data content, into the pool.

Knowing it might be found by the right people, calculating the odds, he decided the chances were good that it would not be discovered by one of his pursuers. Then he heard a chorus of shouts and worried his actions might have been witnessed. Despair overtook him for a moment.

Keep going, he told himself, fighting the urge to go back to the pool to try to save the watch.

The Memorial glowed before him. He revered Abraham Lincoln, the great man who had issued the most famous executive order, known as the "Emancipation Proclamation." With his signature, he declared that effective on January 1, 1863, more than 3.5 million African American slaves—men, women, and children—would forever after be free.

Lincoln was his last hope.

The Astronaut kept having flashes of memory about August 28, 1963, when Martin Luther King Jr. gave his famous "I have a dream" speech at the Lincoln Memorial in front of a quarter million people.

I have a dream.

Finally, reaching those historical steps, he climbed the marble ledges. *I remember reading about tunnels underneath the Lincoln Memorial*, he suddenly thought. *If I can find those tunnels, I might escape.*

"Eighty-seven steps because four scores and seven years . . . " he whispered as a mantra. "Eighty-seven steps . . . " He knew the thirty-six columns represented the thirty-six states in America at the time Lincoln saved the union. "Who will save it now?" he asked, at the same time realizing with dread that *he* was their best chance.

Inside the building, two rows of four Ionic Columns caught his attention. He recalled that each of the giant columns measured fifty feet tall and was five point five feet apart from each other at their base.

More fives and fours . . . there must be a message in these numbers.

He knew these things because numbers were his core language. He saw them everywhere. All the great buildings in Washington had symbolic uses of numbers, and accidental equations occurred from there.

The imposing statue of America's sixteenth president was elevated on an eleven-foot high pedestal. The statue itself rose another nineteen feet high, but if standing, Lincoln would be twenty-eight feet tall. The Astronaut glanced up at the president, depicted as a warm, yet strong man. *The protector of the oppressed.* The Astronaut whispered a silent request for help as he passed the base of the statue, now frantically desperate to find a way into the tunnels that might lead him to safety.

However, that last remaining hope faded in a brutal instant as he looked over in horror at the bleeding, unmoving body of a security guard.

Bullets ripped through The Astronaut an instant before he heard the suppressed fire echoing through the marble edifice.

The Astronaut saw his own blood splattered on the polished white marble of Lincoln's throne. He watched the hard floor come up at him, not realizing that he was falling. The agony of his body being torn apart stole all semblance of logic. The turmoil and terror lasted only seconds, yet seemed like forever. It ended when his head cracked onto the stone floor.

His breathing stopped as all the numbers, colors, angles, and ideas inside his mind ceased to exist. At least on the earthly plane, the man was no more.

Chapter Nine

AN UNDISCLOSED LOCATION

April 2nd - 5:02 am - Eastern Time

They waited until five am to call Tolstoy, because there was no reason to wake the often cranky, and always lethal, operative in charge of the mission.

They didn't know Tolstoy had been awake for almost an hour. Sleep would not be enjoyed until Blackout was done. Tolstoy had been selected to coordinate the mission in the United States for specific talents that few possessed—an ease of killing regardless of whom or how many, great organizational skills, strategic thinking, vision, and a complete disdain for the Americans and capitalism.

"The Astronaut is dead," the man said once Tolstoy answered.

"When?"

"Little over an hour ago."

"Confirmation?"

"Yes. I sent you a photo. There is no doubt."

"Witnesses?"

"No."

"Did you recover anything?"

"We have his phone."

"Excellent. Leave it at the usual place."

"It's already on the way."

"And his residence?"

The man, a seasoned killer with nearly two decades of field experience doing covert missions in combat zones around the world, had anticipated the question, but still had not come up with an answer that was not going to bring Tolstoy's wrath. "We came up empty."

There was a brief silence. "Do you need a signal fire?"

He didn't really know what that meant. "No."

"Apparently you do not understand the scope and *importance* of this mission. Arguably your failure has become part of the mission that now the rest of us must overcome."

He decided saying nothing at that point was the best course.

"Are you anatomically incorrect?"

"Excuse me?"

"There is no excuse! Do you understand? There is *no* excuse."

"Yes."

"Yes, what?"

"I understand."

"You do *not* understand! Am I to believe that The Astronaut, who did not know we had located his residence, and did not know he was going to die, did not hide the materials we seek in his home?"

The man frowned to himself. "We ripped the place apart. Six of us covered every inch. There was nothing there. It must be at another location. Perhaps his workplace."

"And where is that, exactly?"

"We don't know."

"No, you don't, because you are an idiot."

The man didn't think he was paid enough to take this kind of abuse, and that's what he wanted to say to Tolstoy (a few other things as well), but he was actually being paid handsomely, and beyond that, he knew that just one word from Tolstoy and there would be a bullet in his head. As it was, he worried that after whatever it was they were planning—perhaps weeks, months, even years from now—he would be standing in line at a grocery store, sailing on his boat, catching a beer with friends, whatever, and that bullet would come. He'd heard stories of it happening. It was one of the reasons he worked so hard, that *all* of them did.

Fear.

Tolstoy started speaking again, but he missed the first few words. In his mind, he was running, fighting, desperate for a way out. Yet he only knew the ways of the warrior: honor, fight, survive.

"You need to go back to that apartment. You need to find what I need. This is not a little thing we are doing here. Lives are at stake. The Astronaut was the first casualty, but he is not going to be the last."

Tolstoy ended the call, greatly relieved that the biggest threat to Blackout had been stopped. Still, until The Astronaut's data was recovered, there was the potential for disaster.

Pulling up the list, Tolstoy looked over the names—brilliant scientists that, under normal circumstance, they would like to kidnap, but the clock was ticking. They had to die, especially if The Astronaut's data could be recovered somewhere.

Blackout, Tolstoy thought. *A fitting name for the removal of Washington DC.* However, officially the "project" was Five-Fours, since the programming had been set for ignition to occur at precisely 4:44 AM ET, on April 4th. That would be the exact moment that Washington would be destroyed, its people erased, and the United States would immediately fall from its place as lone superpower. *It might even be consumed by its own ashes.*

"Listen to how in English 'Five-Fours' sounds like 'By force,'" Tolstoy whispered to the dark skies. "Yes, by force at Five-Fours . . . I like that. Death is coming."

Chapter Ten

GEORGE TOWN, GRAND CAYMAN

April 2nd - 1:58 pm - Eastern Time

Wen looked at her phone. "Still nothing from The Astronaut," the former MSS agent said, concerned. Her natural ability to detect when something was wrong was seldom off.

"We're cutting it close," Chase replied as the private jet descended to Owen Roberts International Airport on Grand Cayman Island. Chase Malone, the thirty year-old billionaire and tech wizard, along with Wen, was *still* on the run. And he didn't know *why*.

He glanced at Wen, a beautiful woman a few years younger than he, waiting for an answer. She looked like a grad student, he thought. No one would guess she was one of the world's most lethal spies. In intelligence circles, by those aware of her presence, Wen was considered one of the top ten agents in the world. She had been trained by the Chinese MSS to be an efficient killing machine. And she was.

Wen Sung's fluency in countless accent-free languages, proficiency in numerous martial arts, and abilities with weapons made her a super spy. She could identify guns by sight and sound, was as accurate a marksman the MSS had ever produced, and had saved his life dozens of times. He often wished they could disappear together . . . forever.

The two of them were about to embark on another dangerous mission, and he knew one day, inevitably, their luck would run out. Chase just hoped that day wasn't today.

Wen, distracted by The Astronaut's silence, stared out the window, always checking for threats. The two of them constantly wound up in the middle of everything; partially because they wanted to save the world, and partially because they had made many enemies while trying to do so. "We'll make it," she said, watching the islands come into view. Grand Cayman, with its visible barrier reef and turquoise waters, beckoned to the beach lover in her. Yet she knew this tropical paradise could instead turn out to be a grand trap. "Anyway, I have a feeling they'll wait."

The "they" Chase and Wen were flying to meet were two of the world's top assassins. The deadly pair had been tracking Chase and Wen for years. Finally, Wen captured one of their would-be killers—Lena Shelby. As snipers went, male or female, Shelby was a legend—at least in the underworld of mercenaries, death merchants, and rogues.

"I hope we don't regret this," Chase said, for at least the tenth time.

"Grimes and Shelby are also taking a big risk," Wen said.

"Not because they like us," Chase said. "Because they like money."

Wen shook her head. "I've told you. They're scared."

"Not of us."

"No."

Chase fiddled with his multi-tool. Custom made by the Leatherman company, it was one of the billionaire's prized possessions. For a guy who liked to fix things, it was the Holy Grail of pocket devices. It also helped him think, soothed his nerves. It, or one like it, had gotten him out of many a tight spot. "People like Grimes and Shelby aren't scared of anything."

"Wrong," Wen said. "They know how ruthless their employer is, how brutal, how dangerous, how powerful . . . They realize, just like us, that they may not survive the shadow people." She noticed Chase's hand in his pocket and knew he was nervously fiddling with that damned tool. She smiled.

"What?"

"Let me see that thing," she said softly.

He handed it to her. She pretended to be impressed by all of its gadgets, and told him her favorites.

Like Q in a James Bond movie, he explained each tool. His voice relaxed and his anxiety eased.

She kissed him as she returned his prized possession.

"Shadow people" was the name Chase and Wen had given to the mysterious organization that had unleashed a seemingly never-ending stream of ruthless operatives against them.

"Remember, Shelby and Grimes are the only link we have," Wen said.

Chase knew. That's why they'd released Shelby, calculating that they might be able to turn her and Grimes to their side, hoping to finally discover who the persistent pair worked for, desperate to know who was after them and, perhaps even more importantly, learn *why*.

After parking their rental car, Wen surveyed the concrete park. They were surrounded by low walls, historical plaques, an honor roll of names, busts of great people from Caymans' past, an unused fountain in the pattern of a navigational compass, and two life-sized bronze seafarers at a ship's wheel.

"I don't like it," she said, standing on the brick, herringbone-patterned ground, framed by a patchwork of polished marble with white decorative rock at the base of Silver Thatch Palms.

Wen glanced at another life sized statue of a young girl carrying a globe in her right hand while her left held her mother's hand. Its base identified it as "Aspiration." She looked up at the hotels across the street, white three and four story buildings. *One may be an apartment,* she thought. *Traffic on three sides . . .*

"It's open," she said. "Too open."

"Yeah, but unless they've got snipers up in those buildings— Wait, *do* you think they have snipers up there?" Chase asked, suddenly concerned for an ambush.

"Stay close to this wall," she said. "The angles won't work for them if we stay here." At the same time, her head swiveled around, trying to take in all the possible points. "I think it's the roads I'm most worried about." She gazed up the streets, looking for trouble while keeping her hand on the Glock 19 concealed under her linen blouse.

As it turned out, it was both. Shots suddenly ricocheted off the bricks at their feet *and* the wall at their backs.

Chapter Eleven

LANGLEY, VIRGINIA

April 2nd - 2:15 pm - Eastern Time

Arguably, the three most important people in the world sat in plush leather chairs, their tense faces reflected in the polished conference table.

"We meet again," two of them said simultaneously, their standard icebreaker.

The CIA seal on one wall, a framed painting of the Washington, DC skyline on the other, gave the only hint as to where they were. The windowless space was sparse, but formal. "Bunker W," the most exclusive of bunkers located under the grounds of the CIA Langley, Virginia campus, did not officially exist.

The two men and one woman exchanged weary glances. If they were together *here*, things were bad.

"Critical level?" the woman asked.

One of the men stood and looked around, as if an enemy agent might materialize at any moment, although he knew it to be an impossibility. The room, equipped with every scrambling and anti-listening tech in existence, could only be accessed by its current occupants.

"Four," Skyenor, the director of DARPA, replied. His silver hair and matching close-cropped beard and mustache, made the slim, impeccably dressed man appear a dashing character from a noir film.

She nodded, relieved. The critical scale went from five to one, with five representing a major crisis, and one being "damn near the end of the world."

They could speak with confidence that their frank discussions, which often considered options that violated US and/or international laws and treaties, would stay within the room. The bunker's sophisticated construction also meant nothing would be overheard, as phones and recording devices did not work inside its thick walls. Other than an un-networked monitor capable of playing presentations from enabled flash drives, no computers or electronics were present.

"But don't let the number fool you—it won't stay there for long," he added. "This is an arms race that's going to make the Cold War look like a squirt gun battle between nine-year-olds." Dr. J. W. Skyenor had headed the Defense Advanced Research Projects Agency for eight years. DARPA, the Pentagon's emerging technology agency, had been formed in 1958 by President Eisenhower after the Soviet Union's surprise success with launching the first manmade object, Sputnik, into space in 1957. Since then, the agency had made "pivotal investments in breakthrough technologies for national security," at least officially. Unofficially, DARPA was leading the US into the future of high-tech warfare by spearheading hundreds of advanced technological developments with military applications.

The woman, Tess Federgreen, the director of CISS—

Corporate Intelligence Security Section—the CIA's most powerful and secretive division, hand wrote a note on a manilla file folder. As head of the fast-growing agency within the agency—actually a joint operation of the CIA, NSA, and FBI—Tess had almost unlimited power to pursue its mandate of preventing war between corporations and nations.

Skyenor pointed to a CGI simulation on a twelve foot wide super high definition monitor. The images could have been taken from the next installment of a Lucas Film space adventure. Instead, the stark views were predictive models of what the first volley of World War III would look like. The three were smart enough to understand what many in the general population, and even certain factions within the Pentagon, didn't fully comprehend. The next great world war would not be fought in the fields, towns, and cities of Europe, or even the wide waters of the South China Sea. Rather, it would be fought from space.

It had already begun in cyberspace. Russia, China, and the United States engaged in a constant battle for supremacy across computer networks and various slices of the Internet. However, the natural escalation that these three were constantly preparing for was in outer space. "*Cyberspace to outer space,*" Skyenor often said.

Tess Federgreen, the one with the least technical knowledge of the three, watched in amazement as lasers fired from satellites, destroying space stations, other satellites, manned and unmanned space vehicles. The precision was stunning, the destruction surgical.

"Somebody's leapfrogged ahead of us," Skyenor said. "They have this capability now."

"Five years ahead of what we expected," Tess clarified,

wiping a lock of wavy auburn hair away from her cutting green eyes.

"Based on this." Skyenor indicated a mock satellite launch being obliterated on the screen. "What you're witnessing is five, maybe even seven years away. However, someone has gone beyond this. They are at a place that our simulators have not caught up to yet."

"So this is . . . ?" Tess asked.

"Already out of date," Skyenor finished. "I have a team working on creating images to correspond to our enemies' new capabilities, but this couldn't wait."

Tess looked again at the science fiction erupting on the big screen, thinking if it wasn't so awful, so real, so *scary*, she might like a giant tub of buttered popcorn to go along with the movie, hoping Harrison Ford would burst onto the scene and save them all. "Who's moved so far ahead of us?" she asked. "The Russians? Chinese? Please don't tell me it's one of the Middle Eastern states, or North Korea, or some other rogue bad actor."

"That's just it," Skyenor said, his eyebrows pinching together. "We don't know."

Chapter Twelve

GEORGE TOWN, GRAND CAYMAN

Wen was right—the angles were protecting them, at least for the moment. However, the snipers had them pinned down, and Wen knew more trouble would be coming.

"Grimes set us up!" Chase yelled, crouching lower, looking for something close to shoot.

Wen, returning fire toward the windows, didn't answer.

Dozens of shoppers and visitors screamed and ran for safety as two silver SUVs squealed around the corner, while black and white SUVs barreled up the street. In an instant, they all converged at the little concrete park, one of them running up on the curb and knocking the Aspiration statue off its pedestal, snapping the bronze girl's hand from her mother's.

Five armed men poured from each vehicle. Three more appeared across the street, but it was the three that came over the wall that sealed their fate. While shooting at the SUVs, two operatives leapt for the wall and knocked Wen to the ground. She came down hard with them on top of her, unable to breathe. The fight was lost.

Chase was quickly surrounded, and seconds later found himself with his arms being zip-tied behind his back. He looked around, trying to spot Grimes, but didn't see him or Shelby.

They took his gun and patted him down. Finding his multi-tool, one of the men nodded approvingly. "Mind if I keep this?"

"*Yes*," Chase snapped.

"Too bad," he replied, stuffing it in his pocket.

Wen was cuffed while still on the ground, her face scraping against the bricks. Three of them held her down while a fourth kept a rough boot on her head.

After stripping her of all weapons, another walked up and stuck the muzzle of a pistol in her ear. "Want to live, princess?" he asked in a German accent.

She did not answer.

"I'll take that as a yes. After all, why would you shoot back if you didn't care about dying?"

"Let's go," another one said. "Cops have only been paid off for a delay. Time's up."

"Now we are going to let you stand," the German began. "If you try anything, they will kill your boyfriend first, and we will let you live just long enough to know he is dead before sending you to join him. Got it?"

She said nothing.

"This time I need you to answer."

Wen, calculating the odds and method of escape, paid no attention to him.

He kicked her hard in the ribs.

She groaned.

"Good, that sounds like a yes," he said. "Was that a yes?"

Nothing.

He kicked her again, then nodded to one of his men. "Slowly."

The men moved off of Wen, and in one swift motion, two of them yanked her to her feet.

Twenty-six men now surrounded the two high-value targets, pushing them toward one of the SUVs. Wen, who wore a small, jeweled ring that opened into a concealed razor, cut herself free as they shoved her. She spun and launched herself into the air, one foot landing on the shoulder of a man, the other hitting the second man in the neck. She sprang off them and ran across the gaggle, using the men's heads and shoulders as stepping stones as they tried to react. By the time they turned around, she was already gone.

In that same moment, Chase dove toward the SUV, rolling underneath and breaking the zip ties against the trailer hitch as he wriggled out the other end.

Realizing he had escaped, half the crew who had been pursuing Wen peeled off and went after Chase. At the same time, the few remaining tourists on the streets fled.

Wen grabbed the painted white support column of a Duty Free Center that catered to the cruise ship crowds and pulled herself onto the building's second story. The balcony extended half a block. At the end, she climbed a drainpipe and was now on the roof. Worried about Chase, she knew that her best chance to help him was to get distance first.

The roof opened a new avenue of escape options. The mistake the men had made was in not injuring her. *They obviously have orders to bring us in alive,* she thought without trying to figure out who could have given those orders. The number of agents, the ambush, the snipers and machine guns not taking them out were all clues that this was not a hit job. *They could have easily killed us many times, but didn't. They should have shot us in the legs, then at least we couldn't run. They could have brought a medic to patch us up.* Still, she wasn't sure if they would change their plans now that she was getting away.

The answer came quickly when two men appeared on the other end of the roof. "Stop!" they both yelled, aiming submachine guns at her.

Wen ran to another corner, smiling when they chased her. *They could have killed me again. It must be a firm order not to.* She was now less worried about Chase. *The worst that happens is they capture him again.*

She took a running jump and sailed fifteen feet across a side street, catching the railing on the second floor of a four story condominium building. Wen climbed the balconies like a ladder. It would have been a great escape, if it hadn't been for the three men waiting for her on the condo's roof.

Chapter Thirteen

LANGLEY, VIRGINIA

Holt Gatewood, the third person in Bunker W, was the administrator of the most secretive government entity in existence—HITE. Hidden Information and Technology Exchange was so classified that most US presidents usually didn't learn about it unless they got a second term, and perhaps not even then. Gatewood carried himself with the confidence of a Caesar, as if, with the flick of his finger, empires could fall. It may not have been much of an exaggeration.

Gatewood stood and paced. He never liked being in the Bunker, feeling trapped, an animal in a cage, scowling, defeated, yet strangely powerful. "Technology such as this has an origin point," he said. "It shouldn't be that difficult to ascertain *who* possesses it and whether it was developed, stolen, or . . . found."

HITE had been established after World War II to handle captured Nazi secrets, technology, and even metaphysical data and artifacts. If a UFO of extraterrestrial origin really *did* crash in Roswell, New Mexico, during the summer of 1947, HITE would have wound up with the wreckage and whatever it may have contained.

"I'll put a couple of IT-Squads on it," Tess said. CISS had, by far, the largest number of operatives of the three agencies. IT-Squad members, the elite CISS units, were made up of special ops proficient in both combat and technology.

"Put five IT-Squads on it," Skyenor said. "There is an apparent Russian operative, goes by the name Tolstoy, who may be involved."

"The name rings a bell," Tess said. "I'll pull our files."

"We've got to stop this," Skyenor added. "This could be the ballgame."

Skyenor, the only one with a public profile, may also have been the most purely patriotic. He often said, "*It is a near-impossible task, using technology no one has yet seen, to develop military applications for preventing or winning wars before the enemy discovers a way to destroy the country I love.*" He found it exhilarating, and exhausting.

"I'd like to look at the raw data used to make this simulation," Gatewood said.

Skyenor looked at his colleague and narrowed his eyes. "You want to construct your own simulations?"

"Perhaps."

"With what system? Something you might care to share?"

"Not particularly. Nothing you would need."

HITE's name, or at least the "E" part, was a bit of a misnomer because the hidden technology and/or information was never exchanged. Instead, a select committee made up of top US intelligence leaders—with security clearances *much* higher than the President of the United States—

decided who, where, when, and *if* the information would be released—though *never* publicly.

"You'll have the data in the morning," Skyenor said, not interested in sparring with Gatewood. At nearly sixty, Skyenor was the oldest of the three, yet the tall, lean man exuded power. His experience, and the nature of DARPA's work, combined to create an intelligent, mysterious persona that most found intimidating.

"Excellent," Gatewood said, his word of choice whenever he was pleased.

They all knew that HITE offered the ultimate strategic advantage because its cache of "wonders" could ignite huge shifts in power and wealth via the introduction of never-before-seen technologies—be it nuclear weapons, computers, satellites, pharmaceuticals, any number of other items, even whole new industries.

"We may have something to counter it," Gatewood said, his thinning black hair perfectly trimmed to make it appear as thick as possible. Graying at the temples was part of his "look," as was the tan that never faded, which he maintained year-round by spending his weekends in the Caribbean, Bahamas, or some other warm destination. He favored perfectly tailored suits and polished Cucinellis, maybe more befitting a business tycoon than a government worker, but HITE was not a "normal" federal agency, and its director's secret eight figure salary reflected that.

Tess smiled at Gatewood's comment. "Don't you always have something?" she said. While she had long liked Skyenor, she had never cared for Gatewood, whom she sometimes referred to as "the Godfather," since she considered HITE as close to the mafia as existed in the US Intelligence community.

Her collection of cowboy boots and love of the dusty

corners of New Mexico also seemed polar-opposite to Gatewood's refined approach to everything. Tess, the youngest of the three, a no-nonsense forty-something, had risen through the ranks of the NSA with an impressive list of Washington contacts. She knew more than her share of secrets.

With auburn hair (this week) and eyes the color of wet jade, she sometimes looked prettier than she was, but most described her as "a handsome woman" and "tough, but fair." A master with strategy and presentation, Tess could usually sum up a complex situation and bottom-line it while many of her peers were still sifting through reports, data dumps, and exhibits. However, the current crisis was an anomaly—trouble wrapped in whispers and hunches. She'd learned to anticipate based on accumulated scraps of information, somehow noticing a pattern, like knowing a hurricane was starting by seeing a few stray clouds over warm water and a burgeoning breeze.

"Who's taking point on this then?" Tess asked. "CHAD cannot let this get to a three."

CHAD, in the acronym loving town of Washington, was perhaps the least spoken of all the government alphabet agencies. Just knowing it stood for CISS, HITE, and DARPA meant you had the highest security clearances, but it did not mean you had any idea what CHAD *did*, or even what CISS or HITE *were*.

"It's you," Skyenor said. "CISS has the best operatives."

Gatewood shifted in his uncomfortable chair. "CISS has the *most* operatives," he corrected.

Tess smiled, not taking the bait. She looked back at the screen. "Then, to summarize, you believe that someone has found a way to triangulate space weapons in an undetected manner."

"Correct," Skyenor replied. "Meaning they could take down virtually any and all earth orbit satellites. There are currently thousands of active satellites in earth's orbit right now. Imagine what this destructive capability would do to everything—to the modern world as we know it."

Chapter Fourteen

GEORGE TOWN, GRAND CAYMAN

Wen looked at the three men facing her on top of the roof and could not help but laugh.

"What's so funny?" a man, at least a foot taller than her, asked as they formed an arch around her.

"That anyone imagined three of you could capture me," she said.

They looked at each other, smiling nervously. They knew of her reputation.

"We'll see," the man said bravely.

"See you on the ground," she said.

Before any of them could react, she sent the talker sailing off the roof. After a brief skirmish, another one was dangling from the edge. Wen backed up and stomped on his hands, causing him to plunge to his death.

The last man, apparently deciding to forgo orders by shooting her, wasn't quick enough on the draw. Wen kicked the pistol out of his hands and immediately cursed her overzealous attack as the gun went skittering over the edge.

"You should run," she said.

For an instant he appeared to be thinking about it, but the lure of a big pay day, machismo, or just stupidity, got the best of him. "You're dead!" he yelled, charging her.

In a move that seemed almost effortless, she rolled off his blow and allowed his momentum to take him soaring off the roof.

She ran to the hatch they had come out of and climbed into the upper stairwell of the building.

"There you are!" a man yelled, grabbing her.

She flipped him over her shoulder and dropped him down the center of the stairwell, not hearing his broken body bash the railings on the way down four stories, nor when he smashed head-first onto the concrete floor below, because she was hearing at least six more storming up the stairs.

She ran down the long hall. "It's a dead end," she muttered, then looked back and saw the men coming up fast. Bullets sprayed low against the doors and walls. *I guess they finally decided injuring me was easier than catching me.* Wen launched herself into the air, catching a ceiling beam just long enough to propel herself through the small glass window above the nearest condo door.

Inside, a startled elderly couple screamed, but Wen never stopped moving. She burst through the sliding screen door and flipped herself over the railing, counting on the pattern being the same as the ones she'd climbed to the roof on the other side of the building.

Going down was a little slower, but in less than twelve seconds, she was back on the ground.

Catching her breath while scanning the area, hoping to see Chase, all she saw was more trouble as one of the silver SUVs barreled straight for her. Wen jumped on its hood, ran up the windshield, across its roof, and kept going, landing on a slowing car's roof and rolling off the other side, where she crashed into two of her assailants. Another seven were charging from the street.

"You're done!" a big man barked.

She kicked his head, came down twisting, and snapped the neck of another thug. Wen grabbed his submachine gun and emptied its magazine into the seven operatives on the street. The carnage of seven dead bodies left the area looking like a war zone, locals and brightly dressed tourists fleeing.

She ran to get another gun from one of the fallen, but three police cars suddenly appeared.

Instead, Wen slipped between an abandoned delivery truck and a parked sedan. She headed to the ocean front, searching for Chase, but spotting another group of shadow people at a corner T-shirt shop.

She ran onto Harbour Drive and leapt onto the back of a Honda Accord. That's when she finally spotted Chase. To her horror, he was climbing to the top of one of two large dockside cargo loading cranes perched at the harbor's edge. Three men were following right on his heels.

Wen jumped from the Honda, rolled onto a sandy strip in front of a visitor center, came up, and took off toward the cranes. She estimated them to be fifty feet high, and wondered what Chase was going to do once he reached the top.

By the time she got to the base, Chase had less than fifteen feet of crane left. *After that, it's all sky,* she thought, but she had no doubt he was the best climber on the island.

She started up. Only a few feet into her ascent, four men appeared below her.

"We *will* kill you!" one of them said as they all pointed submachine guns at her.

She looked back up at Chase, and then down at the men, studying the face of the man making the threats. "I believe you," she said swinging down and simultaneously kicking him and another one in their faces. Crashing down onto one of them, it only took three lightning fast round kicks to disarm the other two. Once she had a gun, she killed them instantly. "Normally, I would have liked to question you," she said, climbing again. "But Chase is in a tight spot."

Chapter Fifteen

LANGLEY, VIRGINIA

Gatewood picked up the conversation of what life would be like without satellites. "It's not just our base-stationed pilots losing contact with armed drones over the Middle East. We will experience failed communications systems in the field, stranding soldiers, ships, and manned aircraft without the ability to contact command."

"Right," Skyenor concurred. "And internationally, general civilian communications will be severely limited. However, the major disruption will come from the loss of the GPS. We're talking about grounding *all* commercial aircraft worldwide."

"A genuine disaster like we've never faced," Tess said.

"We've run predictive models," Skyenor said. "We've phased in a series of transactions, taken into account all satellites, including the partially implemented and proposed mega-constellations, everything going on in low earth orbit, merged the data of all top scientists, even commercial patent applications, trade deals . . . we've looked at the *entirety* of the modern technological reality."

"What's the program?" she asked, wondering if DARPA had somehow gotten ahold of Chase Malone's most guarded secret, his SEER program, which allegedly could predict future events with startling accuracy.

"We call it DANN. DARPA Advanced Neural Network."

"New?"

"We've had it operational for eight years," he said with a sly smile. "Sorry. Up until now, it's been so secret that no one outside a handful of people at DARPA knew about it."

Tess and Gatewood were surprised, but not stunned. They each had their own projects that remained in classified cocoons within their agencies. Neither of them even needed to ask if the president was aware of DANN. They knew he would not have been informed. Tess often said, "*Presidents cannot be trusted. They're just politicians who have mastered corruption better than the other corrupt politicians and grabbed the ultimate prize. But they'll be gone as soon as the next one manipulated the system.*"

"We continually tweak and adjust the algorithms, deep learning, machine learning, and a super advanced AI," Skyenor continued. "We utilize RAI and other proprietary programs. It's quite something."

Once again, Tess thought of Chase, wondering if he imagined how far his invention, Rapid Artificial Intelligence, had gone. DARPA regularly utilized unlicensed versions of anything they wanted. They combined, dissected, and revised versions of software to accommodate their needs. "Why would Russia make this kind of move?" Tess asked. "And why now?"

"A chance to grab supremacy," Gatewood answered before Skyenor had a chance. "Whoever controls space, controls earth."

Tess nodded. "It really is that simple, isn't it?"

"Let me read you what a former NATO official said when the alliance was considering whether space should be declared a war domain," Skyenor said. "'Being able to control space warfare will be a vital position for any country or organization since it can almost dictate the outcome of armed conflicts. You can have warfare exclusively in space, but whoever controls space also controls what happens on land, on the sea, and in the air. If you don't control space, you don't control the other domains either.'"

"We're in deep trouble," Tess said.

Skyenor nodded.

"We still have a few ways we may be able to get through this," Gatewood said. "But we have to stop them. We have to put *everything* we have on this. Nothing else matters."

"There'll be targets," Skyenor said. "That's your department, Tess."

"Tell me who to kill, who to raid, what to steal, what to sabotage, where to attack, where to surveil," Tess said. "We will do whatever it takes. We will *not* lose this."

After more strategizing and dividing up the responsibilities, they adjourned.

"Shall we tell the president?" Skyenor asked.

Gatewood and Tess exchanged a quick glance.

"Not yet," Tess said. "It'll only leak if we do."

"I agree," Skyenor said. "Just wanted to make sure we addressed it."

This was the biggest crisis CHAD had ever faced. It was decided that Skyenor would liaison with the military. He knew who could get things done, who could be trusted. Tess would, of course, handle the intelligence agencies. Gatewood, as always, headed the strategic deployment of beyond advanced high tech equipment and weapons that no one had even heard of yet. Tess called him the Godfather, but Skyenor had another nickname for him: Gatewood the game changer.

Gatewood's driver left first. Tess and Skyenor lingered in the parking area for a few moments.

"You really believe they have the capability to wipe out all our satellites?" Tess asked.

"Yes."

"And that they'd really do it?"

"That and much worse."

"*Worse?*"

"Be prepared to be back in Bunker W again tomorrow," Skyenor said.

"Why? What else is going on?"

"It's related to this. Something . . . I really don't want to discuss it yet. Today, I'll be getting a lot more information. Tomorrow. This is enough for today, don't you think?"

"The complete breakdown of all modern communication, travel, and logistics? The Russians leap-frogging us in space so we'll likely never catch up? Yeah. That's why I'm terrified of what could possibly be *worse*."

"You should be."

Chapter Sixteen

GEORGE TOWN, GRAND CAYMAN

As Wen rapidly climbed the crane, she could see police involved in a shootout with some of the shadow people. She had been trying to keep a mental tally on how many were left. She had killed at least eleven, and there were two more above her on the crane that would soon be dead. Stealing quick glances at the action below, she noted two more bodies taken out by the cops, and it looked like three had been arrested. By her calculations, after she'd taken care of these three on the tower, seven would be left.

Wen still wasn't close enough to shoot the men once Chase reached the top. She had no idea if they would continue obeying their orders, or if they would kill him.

What is Chase thinking? she wondered. *Why would he climb up to where there was no escape? He must have had no choice.*

The burst of gunfire above her answered all her questions. They were shooting at him, and her!

With almost no cover, Wen had to rely on her return fire. She wedged herself between two thick metal crossbeams and shot above.

I've got to be careful not to shoot Chase . . .

It was a nightmarish predicament. She had to fire enough to keep them from picking her off, at the same time needing to conserve ammunition and not accidentally kill Chase. Unsure if it could get any worse, she saw one of the most horrifying spectacles she'd ever witnessed.

Fifty feet above the ground, Chase leapt off the crane.

"No!" she yelled. Wen spun to see how far the harbor was. He'd never make it to the water, and even if he did, there was no way it was deep enough to survive a jump from that height.

The men stopped firing, apparently as spellbound by the suicidal feat as she was. Her training took over. Wen swung out onto an outer crossbar and shot one of the men. He plunged past her while she injured another enough that he dropped his gun and clung to a rail.

This caught the attention of the final man. He showered bullets at her. Wen, back in her wedge, knew he had the high ground advantage and realized this was a losing battle.

I've got to get back to the ground.

She began working down, inches at a time, with almost nothing protecting her from the machine gun fire raining down from above.

Suddenly, the shooting changed. She looked up and saw he was now shooting at the neighboring crane. Following his bullets, Wen saw what he was shooting at. "Chase!" she shouted with delight. The shadow person had made a mistake. Chase was sliding down the rails out of range, and would soon be on the ground. Wen knew a good idea when she saw it, and mimicked Chase's method.

By the time she reached the ground, Chase was there. He picked up a submachine gun from one of the dead shadow people and flashed her a smile.

"Don't ever do that again!" she shouted.

"But it worked," he said, aiming above her, taking out the shadow person who had been trying to kill him.

Wen glanced up as the man fell. "Nice," she said.

"I had a good teacher."

She smiled, even though joking about killing people didn't sit well with her.

"What about him?" Chase motioned up to the injured man still holding on.

"Wish we could question him," she replied, pulling extra mags off the dead men. "But there are still too many out there, and the police are a problem. I have a feeling they're going to arrest anyone moving."

"Especially while we're carrying these." He motioned toward their guns.

"Right." Wen, already moving back to the road, checked a map on her phone.

"Any sign of Grimes?"

"He's not here," Wen said.

"Are you sure?"

"I would have seen him," she said, wishing she could conceal her guns and ammo, moving toward a street that, from her aerial view, had been clear of shadow people and cops.

"That coward."

"He may already be dead."

"I hope so."

"There's a chance he was compromised," she theorized. "Maybe someone found out about the meeting and killed him."

Chase thought about how powerful the group was that employed the shadow people. They always seemed to know where he and Wen were, a step ahead, an endless supply of weapons and soldiers to use against them, the latest equipment and technology. Once again, he asked the question that had been torturing them for two years. "Who the hell *are* they?"

"We aren't going to find out today."

"How many left?"

"I think seven."

"We could capture one, question them."

"Too risky," she said, moving between two hotels to another street.

"Then where are we going?"

"Our car," she said, pointing to the end of the street. They had routinely parked a couple of blocks away from the meeting place just to be safe.

"We're just going to *leave*?" Chase asked, surprised.

"Why, you want to stop for dinner?"

"Fish and chips," he said, pointing to a restaurant across the street.

"Funny."

Chase was surprised she didn't want to finish off the seven shadow people remaining, but he too had seen the massive police presence—at least six cruisers and two SWAT vans. He knew it must be every law enforcement vehicle they had on the island.

"I guess you're right," he said. "We don't want to get caught up in that."

They reached their car. Each took a quick look around, and Chase inched away from the curb.

"We might pull this off," Chase said, checking the rearview mirror. "Maybe the cops got them all."

Across from them, a black SUV suddenly came out of nowhere.

"Damn it!" Chase yelled as he floored it.

Chapter Seventeen
UNDISCLOSED LOCATION

Tolstoy stood in a moderately priced hotel room, staring out the eighth floor window, enjoying the surprisingly good view.

Years of work had gone into operation Blackout, its culmination a little more than thirty-six hours away. Tolstoy planned to survive the event. Yet, if need be, she would give her life to see it succeed. She wasn't fooling herself into thinking she'd go down in a blaze of glory, a heroic and noble death. No, Tolstoy did not want to die, and did not believe she would have to. However, she would make that choice not out of devotion to a cause, or even her government, but simply because she sought perfection, the completion of a task—in this case, a monumental achievement that would change the world. She would die if that's what it took.

"Now everything is the clock," Tolstoy whispered to her reflection in the large picture window. "I am chasing time."

Her phone rang. The call was expected. Yuri wanted an

update. Checking her watch, Tolstoy took a deep breath, preparing for her daily chat with her superiors.

Like Tolstoy, Yuri was a code name. Everyone involved had them, and they were strictly adhered to. Secrecy was the only thing between success and failure.

Having used a code name for so long, if someone had suddenly addressed Tolstoy by another name, confusion would be the likely response. Tolstoy had grown accustomed to the moniker. She believed it fit her, saying once to a colleague, "*I spin great works of fiction, only instead of doing it on paper, I do it in the real world.*" She also enjoyed the concept that she was always walking the fine line between war and peace. However, she'd never read the book.

This call, significantly more urgent than the hundreds of previous conversations with Yuri, would be their final communication before the culmination of operation Blackout. Tolstoy had to admit that skipping the evening call tomorrow was an added perk to the dangerous day ahead.

Unless there is a problem, she thought as she answered confidently.

Everything was in order. The familiar voice of her superior began sounding somewhat tense, somewhat distracted, and even a little warm. She was an expert at detecting slight shifts in mood and personality. However, Yuri was always a tough read. He was a lethal presence in the leadership, intelligence his domain, and, like Stalin, "Dissent and die" was his motto. Advancing the state was all that mattered.

Their communications, although encrypted with a combination 4,096-bit key, and 8,192 forge crossed photon curve, were always cautious.

"All indications look good from the technical side," Yuri said. "But there appears to be a leak."

Tolstoy smiled in an irritable way. *She* had been the one

to inform Yuri of the leak via an earlier digital communications. "Yes, as I stated in my last message, this Astronaut working on the DARPA program." She glanced over at a computer screen, open to a photo and biographical information of The Astronaut. "We have a team taking care of that problem."

"That may not be enough. If he's learned of our timetable, we must remove anyone else connected to him."

"Of course. It is our highest priority. All other preparations are in place, and we are sure that neither our identities, nor the details, have been compromised."

"Do not underestimate the Americans," Yuri said, echoing what the diplomat had said to him earlier. "If they know what city we plan to attack, they will find a way to defend it."

Tolstoy wanted to argue with Yuri, believing she knew more of the science than he did. Her mind filled with facts and figures to refute that claim. However, she simply said, "We are less than twenty-four hours away from the event reaching the tipping point. Once we are under twelve hours until ignition, the event will become unstoppable. Even now, it would be difficult, unless they knew the method." She tensed at the thought of the information The Astronaut had obtained.

"Tolstoy, you are good. This is why you were chosen to lead the most important undertaking in our history. It is almost done, yet do not become overconfident."

"Blackout is my life."

Chapter Eighteen

GEORGE TOWN, GRAND CAYMAN

Chase swerved onto Shedden Road, now going in the opposite direction of the airport, to avoid the SUV.

"Stay away from Mary Street, Main, and Cardinal," Wen said while trying to get a shot lined up out the window. "That's where all the police were."

He swung a right on Harbour Street—the road was closed the other way.

"Why aren't you shooting?"

"I'm not going to fire until I know I'll kill someone. We don't need *more* police attention."

Now on North Church Street, Chase had an idea. As spray from the high surf hit the road, Chase veered to the right inland lane and slowed.

"What are you doing?" Wen yelled. "They're going to catch us!"

Chase maintained enough speed so the shadow people would hopefully still believe he was trying to get away.

"Never question a professional race car driver while he's driving," Chase said.

"I'm serious. Here they come!"

Chase checked the road ahead and played with the accelerator to get just where he wanted to be. "Get ready to shoot!"

Wen dove into the backseat so she could fire from the driver's side. As soon as they were halfway parallel with the car, Chase tapped the brakes, causing the shadow people to be directly beside them sooner than they expected. Chase wrenched the wheel left hard, making the car slam into the SUV, sending it across the oncoming lanes. The driver overcorrected, and the SUV careened off the road, rolling down the large breaker rocks and into the crashing waves.

"Wow," Wen said, impressed. "You really are a good driver."

"Good?"

"*Really* good."

"*Great*," Chase corrected.

"*Maybe* great."

Chase laughed. He took a right on Eastern and headed back to the airport.

"Four unaccounted for," Wen said as their private jet took off.

"The police probably got them," Chase said, knowing how badly Wen wanted to question the shadow people.

She nodded. "I tried to contact The Astronaut to send him the data we got from the attack, but he still hasn't responded."

"Maybe he's having a late lunch. You know he doesn't like to be disturbed while he's eating."

"Does he eat?" she asked lightly. However, she was worried.

Chase saw the concern on her face. He was a little worried, too. "When did you last talk to him?"

"Two days ago. He was agitated. You know how he gets when he's consumed by a project. He doesn't like to talk to people."

"Yeah, seems as though talking is difficult for him."

"That's how he is."

"Then that's why," Chase said. "I'm sure we'll hear from him soon."

Washington DC

"What do we have here?" Popov asked the computer as she flipped through the windows, each showing a seemingly bigger revelation than the last. "It all seems to fit with the fallen Astronaut."

The news of The Astronaut's death was like a bittersweet conclusion of the first chapter of a very scary book. Popov had twice worked with him. Once a few years earlier when she gained his trust, and again, more recently, when she'd cashed in that trust.

He was a nice man, she thought. *But the world is filled with nice people.* Although she ultimately believed that didn't matter. "The world is only one thing," she once told one of her comrades. "It is a game. Good people and bad people are irrelevant. It comes down to only winners and losers."

"You really believe that?" the cynical operative, who only hours before had executed a good man, asked.

"Yes."

"God, you are a cold woman."

"There is no God," she said, smiling. "There is no do over. One life. That's it. Precious few years to play the game. *That* is the point of living."

"I thought the point of life was being loyal to the party?"

"My father believed in communism. Thought he was doing the right thing. He bought excuses of the leadership who told him the only reason Communism was not working in the Soviet Union was because the West, especially America, selfishly consumed more than their share."

"That's true," he said. "Have you been to a Walmart?"

"It's *not* true," she snapped. "I know better."

"Educate me," he teased, used to her rants.

"There have to be two sides. Winners and losers. It is all a game. Those winners make people believe there are good guys and bad guys, but there really aren't. It is circumstances that are made to appear good or bad. Circumstances make the man, dictate what he does. If you can manipulate the circumstances enough, you can bend the will of all the people in the world."

"Is that the prize?" he asked, sipping black coffee. "To make other people do what you want?"

She shook her head. "It is only the means to the end."

"What is the end?" he asked as she looked at the screen, scouring recent emails, dissecting the final needs in preparation for Blackout, hitting send on an encrypted message that would have key people evacuate the Russian embassy.

"The prize?" she said thoughtfully. "I don't know. Only the winner gets to find out what it is."

Chapter Nineteen

SAN FRANCISCO, CALIFORNIA

April 2nd - 1:02 pm - Pacific Time

Chris and Sanvay were colleagues at Stanford. They also had high-level clearances for their experimental work with lasers. Their research and patents had been utilized by several major defense contractors, as well as DARPA. They had taken a long lunch at their favorite Thai place because they planned on working into the evening.

Their discussions at lunch had been about the breakthrough they were close to cracking—a series of complex advancements with optics and photons. These scientific developments were at molecular levels, down to the most elemental points.

"We're there," Sanvay said, his Indian accent still heavy, as they walked out to the car. "The 3D photonic crystal lattice structure . . . "

"The improvements allow containment to streamline the application," Chris said, speaking of laser light the way a chef might talk about a new way to prepare steak.

Sanvay had driven. As the two colleagues approached their vehicle in the parking lot, a different pair of men approached. One of them smiled, asking, "Hey, that's the new Tesla, isn't it?"

"Yeah," Sanvay said proudly, used to people occasionally wanting to take a look at it.

"Wow, how's the range?"

"Five hundred miles," Sanvay replied.

"Amazing," the man said excitedly. "Can I see the inside?"

Sanvay looked at Chris. "Sorry, man," Chris responded. "I don't think so. We're in quite a bit of a hurry to get back to work."

"Sure," the man said, dejected. "But as luck would have it, we're also on our way to Stanford, so we'd appreciate if maybe you'd give us a ride."

Sanvay and Chris exchanged another nervous glance, clearly alarmed that the two men knew where they worked.

"I'm sorry," Chris said. "Did we say where we were going?"

"No need," the man said, no longer smiling. "Dr. Christopher Matthews, we know all about you and Dr. Sanvay Khatri." He motioned to Sanvay. "We're big fans." He smiled again, flashing a gun. "Really, I insist that you give us a ride."

The two scientists, so good at thinking about theoretical physics and molecular science, had no idea what to do in this situation. Before they realized what was happening, the doors opened and they were shoved inside. One man got in next to Sanvay in the front, the other sat beside Chris in the backseat.

"Sorry to be more of a hassle," the one in front began. "I know you're late for work, but we need to make one stop before we get back to Stanford. Take a right up here instead."

"What's this about?" Sanvay asked, suspecting this wasn't a regular carjacking. It was almost certainly related to their breakthrough.

"There's nothing to worry about," the man replied. "We work for some very important and friendly people who simply wish to ask you some questions."

"About what?"

"I don't really know, I'm not that smart."

He continued giving Sanvay directions. After a couple miles, Sanvay decided that this wasn't going to end well, and began trying to figure the best way to jump out of the car at an intersection. However, his plans fell apart when he saw Chris in the rearview mirror. His co-worker was slumped over, apparently unconscious.

"What happened to him?" he asked, now even more scared.

"Don't worry. Your friend was stressed out. We just gave him a sedative," the man in the back replied.

"This way we can both concentrate on you," the one in the front said. "We want to make sure you follow through. Don't do anything that would spoil our upcoming meeting. Understand?'

"Yes."

"Good. Almost there. Turn here."

"The people you want me to talk to are here?"

"That's right."

As soon as Sanvay pulled into a parking space behind what appeared to be a small, abandoned warehouse, he realized this was the end.

"A strange place for meeting."

"Not really," the man said, injecting something into his arm.

"Why are . . . " Sanvay started to say, but instead, everything went blurry. His words slurred and he quickly blacked out.

The two abductors poured fifths of whiskey down the throats of their victims, then moved Chris into the front passenger seat, and lowered all the windows.

One of them pulled out a special control box connected to a mobile device, while the other sprinkled the remaining alcohol over Sanvay's clothes, just in case they didn't make it to the water.

After adjusting the interior controls, the man used the special box they'd brought to hack into the vehicle's Autopilot system. The advanced suite of features was fed by cameras, ultrasonic sensors, and radar. The program utilizes all the data and deep learning to provide a semi-autonomous driving mode, but the hack allowed full self-driving.

"It's like a video game," the man said as he maneuvered the Tesla remotely. "Watch this." The car sped off the parking lot, across a narrow strip of grass, and then flew over a steep ravine, crashing nearly forty feet into the bay below.

The pair jogged to the edge and watched as the car floated for a few minutes. "Don't worry, it will sink."

Finally, the murky water closed around the sinking steel until nothing of the shiny red Tesla remained visible. They glanced around, satisfied that no one had witnessed the crash, knowing it wouldn't have mattered anyway. Sanvay and Chris would be drowned before any help could arrive.

Walking back to a second vehicle, which they had parked there a few hours earlier, one of them dialed a number on a burner phone that would be destroyed after the call.

"Yes?" Tolstoy answered.

"Stanford complete."

"Both?"

"Correct."

"Good," Tolstoy said. "Return."

"Yes, understood."

Tolstoy ended the call, then checked two more names off the list.

Chapter Twenty

CISS HEADQUARTERS, VIENNA, VIRGINIA

April 2nd - 4:19 pm - Eastern Time

Tess rushed into CISS Mission Control like a woman late for a meeting, because she was.

The lowest below-ground level of the secret CISS headquarters in Vienna, Virginia, which fronted as an insurance company, was filled with wall-sized monitors and computer terminals, making it look like a futuristic version of NASA's Mission Control—thus the name. After a quick check of the screens, populated with crisis points around the globe, which CISS was keeping track of and involved in, she dashed back out into the hall.

Tess's deputy, Linda, walked up behind her. "You're back?"

"Yes."

Linda tapped the touchscreen of her tablet. She knew Tess was aware that she was late for the last-minute meeting, so she didn't remind her. "They're waiting for you in conference room three."

"You should join us."

"Okay," Linda said. "While we're walking, can you tell me what we're going to do about Jie Shi, since you pulled almost everyone off the case." Before the laser space weapons revelations, Jie Shi had been the top priority of CISS during the prior weeks. "We can't just drop her?"

"We're going to punt it over to the FBI with a CIA oversight," Tess said. "That's what this meeting is about."

Waiting, seemingly patiently, was an FBI agent and a CIA official. "Everyone knows each other, and my attention is needed elsewhere," Tess began, "so let's get into this quickly. Linda, please bring them up to speed on Jie Shi."

"Jie Shi, a Chinese national, went to college in California and then attended grad school in New York."

"That in and of itself isn't a crime," the FBI man said.

Tess frowned.

"No," Linda said. "However, along the way she's made some interesting friends."

"Anyone we know?"

"Hal Condit, Executive Vice President, Silverton Dynamics."

"Never heard of him."

"But you know of Silverton Dynamics?" Linda clarified.

"Yes, of course. Major US tech company. Communications, robotics."

"Yes. Apparently Jie Shi is having an affair with the married Mr. Condit."

"Not what I'd like," the FBI man said, "but why is this a big problem?"

"Ever hear of PredCon Technologies?"

"No."

Linda looked at the CIA man.

"Me neither," he said, shrugging.

"Not many people outside of Silicon Valley have, but PredCon is a red hot start-up, a unicorn."

They stared at her blankly.

"'Unicorn' is a term venture capitalist use to describe a privately held company with a valuation in excess of $1 billion," Linda explained. "In this case, PredCon's most recent fundraising round put its value at $12 billion."

"And this connects to Jie Shi *how?*" the FBI man asked.

"She is also dating the CEO of PredCon."

"At the same time she's seeing the Silverton VP?" the CIA man said.

Linda nodded.

"Girl gets around," the FBI man quipped.

"Turns out PredCon has an impressive portfolio of patents, and they've accumulated an equally exciting pool of talent."

"And the FBI can't handle this alone because?"

"There's more."

"I assumed so."

"It seems Jie Shi is also having an affair with the governor of a rather populous state."

The FBI man groaned.

"Yes. The esteemed governor of New York is a member of the Jie Shi party."

"Now it's getting interesting," the CIA man said.

"Particularly when the governor is a rumored presidential candidate," Linda added.

"I believe you can remove the rumor. I don't think there's any question he's running in the next cycle."

"And there's one last wrinkle. Jie Shi has also been linked with Congressman Caldwell."

The CIA man raised his eyebrows. "*Another* presidential candidate."

"You begin to see the problem," Linda stated. "The fact that she's seeing all four of these men at the same time?"

"Yes. Wow," the FBI man said. "Why hasn't she been picked up or deported yet?"

"That's where it gets complicated," Tess said.

"I bet it does!" the CIA man said. "Having known you for so long, Tess, I can only imagine your motives for not yet pulling in this little honey trap."

Tess smiled. "We believe she's also involved with as many as three other prominent men."

"We have not yet ascertained their identities," Linda added. "We'd prefer to find out who the others are."

"Could be me," the FBI man joked. "Or the president. She seems quite proficient."

"Doubt it's you," the CIA man deadpanned. "She only seems to go for men with power."

"Gentlemen, please," Tess said, clearly annoyed by the continued banter from her colleagues. "We believe Jie Shi is one of potentially *hundreds* of young, highly educated, well-trained Chinese women working at the behest of the MSS to either compromise these men, blackmail and expose them, control, use, debrief, whatever. They're utilizing their natural 'assets' and any means necessary to learn secrets and gain influence over them."

"This is a major threat," Linda added.

"We know the most about Jie Shi," Tess continued. "If we arrest or deport her, or she gets wind of us and flees on her own, that source—our *best* source—is gone. Under any of those scenarios, we lose."

"And we'll never know if they have an objective beyond gathering intel and influences," Linda said. "We won't learn how deep they go, how many there are, or who else has been compromised."

Chapter Twenty-One

CISS HEADQUARTERS, VIENNA, VIRGINIA

The FBI and CIA men were silent for a moment. The images of Jie Shi and her "victims" stared back at them from the large monitors.

"There is a risk that if we leave her in the game long enough," the CIA man finally began, "a chance that she will further compromise her subjects, gaining more information that she may relay to her superiors."

"That is actually a real possibility," Tess said. "So what?"

"We would be allowing national security to be jeopardized."

"We'll keep her on a short leash."

"And what about the politicians?" the FBI man asked.

"We'll leak their identities and photos of them with Jie Shi as soon as we're done," Tess said.

"Because?" the FBI man asked.

"They are unreliable, compromised, weak men."

"Okay," he said. "Hope I don't ever get on *your* bad side."

"It's not hard," Tess said. "One simple rule makes everyone's life easier."

"And that is?"

"Don't do anything stupid."

"I'll try and remember that."

"He's already forgotten it," the CIA man said. "Now back to business. Let's say we play along. First, I'd like to know how Jie Shi does this. Does she date a different guy every night? And, I'm being serious here, how does she keep it all straight? What if two or three of them want to see her at the same time?"

"We're just getting into this," Linda said. "And unfortunately other priorities are now diverting our attention."

"Why are you pushing this off on us?" the FBI man asked.

"We are not pushing," Tess said tersely. "I am giving you my baby to take care of while I go kill a monster. *Do not screw this up*. I *want* Jie Shi."

"What monster?" the CIA man asked.

"Need to know only."

He nodded, dissatisfied.

"I can only spare a few agents," Tess said. "They will shadow this, keep on monitoring her, and provide your team with all background."

"You'll need to crosscheck everything," Linda added.

"We're all over it then," the CIA man said.

"Find out where the connections are going in China," Tess said. "We need to find a way to penetrate this ring on either side of the Pacific."

"I'll get our people over there lit up."

"Thank you," Tess said. "This is a big one."

"I just sent you the slice numbers in Heaven where you can see everything we've got," Linda said, referring to the

US's most highly classified intelligence network—codenamed "Heaven" because it "may or may not actually exist," and those who knew of the rumors of it often said, *"One can only get into Heaven by dying."*

The CIA man checked his phone and noticed another message asking him to stick around after the meeting. "Got it."

"Me, too," the FBI man said.

Linda adjourned the group a few minutes later. The CIA man excused himself to the restroom. When he came out, the FBI man was gone.

"What's up?" he asked Tess.

"You need to be overlooking the FBI on this one."

He raised an eyebrow.

"Jie Shi may have compromised an agent."

"So it goes even deeper?"

"Yes. Review every move the Bureau makes, triple check all their actions, assumptions, and methods."

"Got it," he replied. "I'm a little concerned about what's going down that it took you off point on this case. The Tess Federgreen I know wouldn't give up on something *you* broke. Knowing you have the experience and abilities . . . CISS is the perfect one to be handling this."

She nodded. "If we get lucky, and we all do our jobs, you'll never find out what has taken priority over this."

"And if we're not lucky?"

"You'll know about it very soon, and the aftermath will haunt us for the rest of our lives."

Once Linda and Tess were alone again, they returned to

Mission Control, now a full scale operational command center on the weaponization of space.

"China could be the force here," Tess said, looking at updates on the Peoples Republic of China space program. "They're launching a lot of satellites."

"They've just done a fifth unmanned moon landing," a technician volunteered, even though Tess had not been addressing her. "And they currently have a craft in orbit around Mars."

"Russia?" she asked looking at their screen.

"Nothing to lose."

"Which is why they may be the bigger threat."

"Yes," the technician agreed. "Russia has a lunar landing coming up, and they're keeping pace with the US and China in satellites."

"If you discount the constellation launches."

"Exactly. But the Russian president is determined to restore Russian greatness in space. They have the experience, and he seems to be finding the rubles somewhere."

Tess was aware of a recent CIA report showing the Russians were involved in many black market and secret tech deals to further their space program, and that they were obtaining funding from many dark sources. "Worrisome," she said.

Linda presented Tess with an objectives overview from the earlier CHAD conference.

1. Identify which country or group is arming the satellites.

2. Create a counter measure.

3. Cripple the offending party.

"And do it all before we lose communications and control over our military and intelligence assets, or they destroy the world economy," Tess said. "Should be easy."

She already felt hungover, though she hadn't had a drink in months.

Chapter Twenty-Two

WASHINGTON DC

Tu looked like a typical nine year old boy staying up past his bedtime to watch Star Wars Mandalorian. Yet, anything but ordinary, Chase and Wen had rescued him from a Chinese facility where the boy had been held since birth, and now acted as his surrogate parents.

Zǔ mǔ, Wen's grandmother, took care of him since Chase and Wen were almost always somewhere else, somewhere dangerous. Looking at him, tucked in bed under the covers, watching his favorite show, she could easily forget that the scientists, under direction of the Chinese Communist government, had modified his DNA prior to his birth. His tweaked mind was now generally genius-level, and in some areas reached far beyond that. At the same time, he was still a child.

"Time to turn off the TV," she said gently.

"But Zu-ey, it's *Mandalorian*."

She smiled. Their existence had been such an adventure since Chase and Wen swept them both out of China in the dark of night, dodging threats and gunfire. Now, after many attempts on their lives, they were finally safe, living in an ultra-secure and secret safe house in Washington DC. It was part of a major think tank which dealt with threats from the global rise of Communist China, as well as children's issues. Tu was now one of their top minds. The Astronaut had arranged for him to get the gig.

"You did a lot of thinking today," Zǔ mǔ said. "You need to rest that special mind of yours."

"Look," he pleaded, pointing at the screen. "It's baby Yoda!"

"He is cute," she agreed, sitting on his bed to watch.

"When will Chase and Wen be here?" he asked for the twentieth time.

"I don't know. Sometime tonight."

"I'm so excited. It's been a long time."

"Three weeks."

"A *long time*," he repeated. Then a fight scene took his attention. "The Mandalorian is so tough!"

"Tougher than Wen?" Zǔ mǔ teased.

"No one is tougher than Wen!"

By the time Chase and Wen arrived, they found the little genius fast asleep.

"He's so peaceful," Wen said. "I love to see him like this."

"Hard to imagine what's going on in that brilliant mind of his," Chase whispered.

"No it isn't," Tu said, surprising them as he opened his eyes. "All you have to do is ask me. My mind is very busy today."

"Have you been awake this whole time?" Wen asked.

"Only since I stopped sleeping." He reached up to hug her, beaming. Chase took his hug next. "I wanted to see you," Tu said, turning on the light. "And to hear all about how it went with the shadow people in the Caymans."

Chase and Wen and Tu had made a deal a long time ago that they would always tell him what they were working on and, if possible, where they would be. Tu, with his unusual mind and unique way of looking at things, had helped them solve many of the challenges they faced. Their deal eased his tendency to worry and took away his reason to complain about not going with them.

"It didn't go too well," Wen said. "Grimes and Shelby were not there."

However, they did tell him the bare minimum of the danger they encountered. Tu had already witnessed enough violence and death in his young life.

"Then it was a trap," Tu said, having warned them before they left that he thought it might be one, but he did not remind them of his prediction.

"Yes," Chase said. "You were right. There were some other men waiting for us."

"But you took care of them," Tu said proudly, knowing the answer, even if they weren't standing right in front of him.

Chase sat on the bed. "We did. Now we still have to find Grimes again. Wen thinks he didn't set us up, but that maybe somebody found out."

"Belfort," Tu said, looking at Wen.

"One way or another, it's always Belfort," Wen agreed.

"We will find him," Tu said. "The Astronaut and I were working on a new data sort the other day. We're going to try it next time he comes over. It will give us more tools to lock-in on Belfort."

"Good," Chase said. "We appreciate your help. We'll all have dinner tomorrow and talk about it."

"Maybe," Wen said quickly, shooting Chase a disapproving glance. Chase knew she didn't want him promising Tu something that might not happen, since they didn't know where The Astronaut was, or even what tomorrow would bring.

But he smiled and covered it. "We have to make sure The Astronaut can come, but we'll be here."

Wen nodded. "But now you need to get to bed."

"I'm already in bed!"

"I mean to *sleep*," Wen said, kissing him and tucking him in.

"I know." He winked at her, then laughed.

Chase turned out the light. "Sweet dreams. See you tomorrow."

Wen set a special shell on his shelf that Tu would find in the morning. They had picked it up for him in the Caymans to add to his collection.

As he walked out of the room, Chase tried to shake off the nagging feeling that tomorrow might not happen at all.

Chapter Twenty-Three

WASHINGTON, DC

April 2nd - 9:39 pm

After a shower, Chase joined Wen in bed. The hotel room was nice, but he hadn't felt secure in a hotel room for quite a long time.

"I thought I lost you back there on the crane," Wen said.

"Like you are with a gun, I'm safest when I'm climbing."

She handed him a little wrapped box.

"What's this?"

"Apparently it's a gift," she said. "You can usually tell by the ribbon and fancy colored paper."

"I meant what's the *occasion*, funny girl?"

"Because you are still alive."

"I didn't get you anything . . . I didn't know."

"You didn't know we were still alive?"

"I didn't know it was a custom . . . "

"Custom?"

"Tradition?"

She teased him with a confused look.

"Never mind."

"You do know that presents are generally meant to be opened by the recipient?"

"I think I'll do that."

"Good idea."

"A new multi-tool! When did you—?"

"I have my methods."

"But it's custom . . . just like the one they took from me on Grand Cayman. But it's not that one, it's brand new."

"I'm tricky."

"Yeah." He kissed her. "Thank you."

"You're going to need your multi-tool," she added.

"Because?"

"Shadow people will track us to Washington."

He also knew they would. It was the reason they didn't stay in the same place with Tu.

"Grimes betrayed us," Chase said.

"We'll see . . . I wish we could get ahold of The Astronaut. I'm starting to get worried."

"Me, too."

Washington, DC
April 3rd - 4:38 am
24 hours 6 minutes until 4:44AM on 4/4

Trained to sleep lightly, Wen woke violently. The darkness greeted her like an angry animal. Something was wrong—dangerously, deadly wrong. Relying on muscle memory, she reached up from her slumber and grabbed, finding something solid where there should only have been air. She twisted, rose, and snapped, not knowing she had gotten him an instant before the man was going to pull the trigger of the 9mm pistol he was pointing at her head.

He did manage to get the shot off, but not according to plan. In their struggle, the bullet exited the chamber, the suppressor dulling its sound, lodging somewhere in the wall above the bed.

The man yelped in pain and immediately cursed at the miss.

Wen, without releasing his arm, flipped him onto the bed. In the same motion, she escaped the covers and found her own gun under the pillow. At the same time she heard two more shots, confirming what she'd already suspected—that there was at least one other intruder in the room. Through the blur, in the murky darkness and rapid movements, she did not believe Chase had been hit, but couldn't be sure. The only light in the room came from a couple of LEDs on the flatscreen and spilled over from the edge of a sock she'd put in front of the digital clock.

She now had her hand on the gun that had been meant to kill her and used it to shoot her intended assassin in the chest. In a fluid motion, she flipped the light switch with the barrel of her gun in her other hand. An ambidextrous shooter, she had once fired a gun with her nose.

As Chase was diving off the king-sized bed, she fired again. The sudden light surprised the second man, as did Wen's shot, which caught him in the arm as he retreated to the bathroom.

Wen quickly scanned the room, looking for any others and for Chase.

"I'm okay," he said from the floor on the other side of the bed.

She handed him her Glock, preferring to use the other man's gun since it had a suppressor, then crept around the other end of the bed toward the bathroom. She stayed low, but could now see in the mirror where the man was waiting. Doing the math in her head, she instantly knew the angle wasn't right. Instead, Wen fired two shots through the wall. The 9 mm rounds exited the barrel traveling at 1,400 feet per second, and entered the plastered-pattern sheetrock. They blew out the other side and hit the man before he even knew they'd been fired.

Wen raced into the room. "We got lucky," she yelled to Chase as she kicked the man's head and stepped on his wrist. "He's still alive."

She shoved the still warm suppressor end of the gun in his mouth. "Tell me who sent you."

She could see from the blood on the floor he wasn't going to be alive for long. With her free hand, she picked his gun up from the floor, knowing a dying man could be the most dangerous. Then she pulled the barrel out of his mouth. "Tell me who sent you and I'll call 9-1-1. If not, I'll watch you bleed out."

Chapter Twenty-Four

The bleeding man on the bathroom floor moaned in agony, desperate for help.

"Who?" Wen repeated.

"Belfort," he said without hesitating.

"Call 9-1-1," Wen yelled to Chase. She checked his body for additional weapons, looking for a phone or ID. She found nothing but a key fob and two 15-round magazines. "What are you driving?"

He wheezed, but managed to give her the make and model. "It's a rental, Maryland plates."

"Where is it parked?"

"G-3." He also told her the row and space number, then coughed some blood.

"Anyone waiting for us down there?"

"No."

"Thanks. Ambulance is on the way," she said, leaving the bathroom after a quick search for tattoos.

Chase pointed back to the bathroom.

"He's not going anywhere," she whispered. "Did you

check that one?" she asked, pointing to the man she'd killed on the bed.

"Yeah, no tattoos, and nothing else except a couple magazines."

"Grab them. You can never have too much ammo."

"Don't we want to be out of here before the cops come?" he asked as she went back to the bathroom.

"Ambulance will be here soon. Now tell me, who does Belfort work for?"

"I don't know."

She stepped on his hand.

"I swear I don't know!"

"*Where* is he?"

"No idea." He wiped blood from his mouth.

She believed him. Belfort wasn't that dumb to let some worker-bee know anything other than who to kill.

She pressed his finger against the screen of her phone. An app would record his prints. Back in the bedroom, she did the same to the other man. "Get the land line," she yelled to Chase.

He ripped the phone out of the wall, yanked the cord from the base, and shoved it in his pocket.

She parted the curtains and looked out the window, happy to see no action below. "Let's go."

With her gun ready, Wen opened the door slowly, checking the hall both ways.

"Let's take the stairs," she said. "Police and paramedics will use the elevator."

"You really think that guy is going to live?"

"For a few more minutes," she said. "Ten at the most."

"What about us?"

"Depends on who's waiting in the parking garage."

Chasing Time

Wen looked at the big brass number eight hung on the hotel stairwell's wall. She wanted to get down to the parking garage fast, but knew a killer could be waiting for them on each floor.

Seven.

"Why did they only send two?" Chase asked softly.

She shook her head. He wasn't sure if that meant "shut up" or that she had no idea. *Both*, he decided.

Six.

An old woman in a white robe suddenly appeared on the stairs below them, strangely silent. Wen could have easily shot her by accident, and then considered shooting her on purpose just to be sure, but let her pass.

Five.

"How do we know there aren't ten guys waiting in the parking garage?"

"We don't."

Not the answer he wanted, but the one he expected.

Four.

Wen glanced up at one of the security cameras and wished they had time for The Astronaut to tap into the hotel's surveillance system so they could see each floor and the parking garage.

Even if there was time, where is The Astronaut? she thought.

Three.

The sound of walkie-talkie static broke through the din of their footsteps on the stairs, and she stopped for the first time. It was hard to tell exactly where the noise was coming from in the rebounding echoes of the stairwell. Chase pointed up. Wen nodded and began moving again—faster.

Two.

The door to the third floor, which they had passed seconds before, opened. Another walkie talkie. This one sounded like police. "Code-3, shots fired."

One.

Chase was about to grab the doorhandle, but Wen pointed down, reminding him they had to go to the parking garage. Two hotel security guards burst through the door, almost knocking into Chase. Wen managed to conceal her gun.

"Hotel guests?" one of them asked.

"Yes," Wen said. "What's going on? We heard gunshots."

"Room number?" the other asked, ignoring her question.

"Five-ten," she answered.

"Last name?" he asked, pulling up a computer tablet.

"Denkensly," she said.

"I'm sorry, could you repeat that?"

"No, we aren't waiting around to get shot," Chase said. "You shouldn't be harassing guests, you need to be concerned about our safety instead."

Wen and Chase started moving again.

"Stop!" one of the security officers yelled.

Chapter Twenty-Five

UNDISCLOSED LOCATION

Tolstoy looked at the technician, trying to decide how competent he was. She generally didn't like weaselly, brainy people who looked as if they never exercised or encountered the sun. Although she appreciated and utilized their skills, Tolstoy did not believe that they were as loyal to the government as they should be, instead seeming more interested in advancing science and technology.

"We've replicated and dissected it," the technician said. "It's all been done under strict conditions. I think we can power it on now, if you agree."

She blinked. Other than some brief training, she didn't know about the inner workings of cell phones. "It's not going to explode or emit some poison gas, is it?"

The technician was amused, but also nervous. A smile tried to form, but retreated in a few quick flashes before he recovered. "No, nothing like that. Hopefully there will be data."

She nodded, having more important things to do, but

glad to finally be able to find out what was on The Astronaut's phone.

As soon as the phone completed its start-up cycle, she could see stress on the man's face.

"What?" she asked.

"No . . . no, that shouldn't be."

"*What?*" she repeated more urgently.

"It's sending."

"Sending? Sending what?"

"I don't know, a message."

"To who?"

"I don't know."

"Stop it!" she demanded.

"It's too late." He powered the phone off.

"Did it send?"

"I don't know."

She looked at him as if he were a fly that had just landed on her cupcake. "Find out *if* it sent, *what* it sent, and *who* it was sent to!"

"I'm sorry Tolstoy, that will take time."

"We don't *have* time!"

"This was unanticipated."

"I certainly hope it was unanticipated!" She could barely contain her rage. They had killed The Astronaut to prevent him from disclosing Blackout to anyone, and now, from the grave, he may have done just that. "You solve this problem and get that information to me immediately, or you are going to lose much more than your job."

Washington DC

The security guards ran down the stairs after Chase and Wen. One of them grabbed Wen. "I said stop. I need some—"

In less than a second, both men were crumpled on the ground, unconscious.

"Was that necessary?" Chase asked.

"Apparently."

"Are they—"

"No. They should wake up with bad headaches soon enough."

"Good. Just doing their jobs."

"Yeah, they'll be fine . . . unless they had some underlying medical condition."

G-1

"Which floor?" Chase asked.

"The vehicle is supposed to be on G-3."

G-2

"Here," Wen said.

"I thought you said G-3? Why are we getting out on two?"

"To get us out of the stairwell sooner, and because it's better to come down the ramp. Lots of cover."

"I heard the guy say no one was down here."

"He was lying."

They entered the parking garage as if walking into a surgical suite inside the library of a church. The musty air felt gritty, and smelled of rubber, oil, and fried food. Scanning for threats, they stayed close to the open end of the switchback concrete ramp and made their way down to G-3. Wen had memorized every detail of the G-2 layout, which she knew would be identical on the level below.

"That's why we yanked the phone? So he wouldn't call his buddies?" Chase whispered.

She nodded, touching a finger to her lips. They came around the corner and G-3 opened in front of them. Chase spotted the car, tapped Wen, and pointed. Eight vehicles up the row.

"That one. Dark blue Ford," she said, talking about another sedan four cars down on the row across. "There's the backup."

"Can you see if one of them is Grimes?"

"He won't be here."

"Why?"

"Grimes is running, too."

Chase still wasn't convinced. "Okay, what's the plan?"

"You get to play decoy."

"Don't you think they know what I look like?"

"Yes. I'm sure they have a nice collection of your photos. Probably staring at them right now, thinking about how cute you are."

"I am cute, but—"

"Don't let them see your face. Act like you're just walking through, looking for your car."

She crept into the row behind them, determined to take at least one alive before the police showed up.

Chase picked up a green beer bottle someone had left next to a concrete column and stumbled out, gazing around, confused, pretending he had misplaced his car.

One of the shadow people pushed his window down to get a better look. The two men chuckled at the drunk, but an instant later Wen pounced, slitting the throat of the driver and shoving her gun in the face of the passenger.

"Don't even move," she hissed. "You are the last one alive. I killed the other two upstairs. Unless you want to join them, drop your gun out the window."

"Okay," he said, seeing Chase was now sober and

standing by his window, pointing a gun at him. The man slowly dropped the gun, which Chase kicked under the car.

"Now, tell me how you communicate with Belfort," she said. "Chase, backseat."

Chase looked in the back and saw the thugs had brought duct tape. He grabbed the roll.

"Don't know nothing," the man replied bitterly.

"I wouldn't bother tying you up if I planned on killing you," Wen said as Chase opened the car door, pulled the man's arms behind his back, and began taping his wrists together, "so make this easy on yourself."

"I don't communicate with him."

"Who does?"

"Carl."

"Who?"

"The guy you just killed," he said, nodding his head toward the dead driver. "He was the one in charge. Got the orders from Belfort."

Chase taped his legs.

"I don't believe you."

"That's too bad."

She shot him in the thigh. "Too bad for *you*."

He screamed profanities.

"I've got more bullets."

"No, no, wait . . . Belfort calls us, we don't call him."

"Which phone?"

"In my pocket."

Chase carefully extracted the phone from the man's coat.

"When is he calling next?"

"In like fifteen minutes to check on the job."

"To see if we're dead?"

"Yeah."

Wen aimed her gun at his other thigh. "Tell me your password."

He told her. She unlocked the phone, quickly changing the password.

The sound of sirens echoed through the garage.

Chapter Twenty-Six

WASHINGTON, DC

The sirens wailed louder. "We've got to go!" Chase said.

"Gonna kill me?" the man asked.

"No."

"Then I owe you one. It won't be me that kills you, but you're never gonna be safe until you're dead. Belfort has an army, and they're all looking for you."

"Yeah, well, I'm looking for him."

"Won't ever find him," the man said, wincing as he adjusted himself in his seat. "Dude's too careful. They got money to throw around like they print it up themselves."

Wen pointed the key fob at the other rental car to unlock it, half expecting it to explode.

Chase ran over and found two cell phones in the glove box.

"Looks like we're collecting these," Wen said, pulling one out of the dead man's pocket. "You don't happen to have his password? And don't lie to me."

"No. Not exactly friends."

She nodded, snapped a photo of both men, and took

their fingerprints. "Okay, I need you to get in the trunk." She cut the tape securing his legs.

He suppressed a grunt of pain as he limped to the back of the car.

She looked at him closely as he leaned against the trunk. "You an ex-cop?"

His face registered surprise. "Former military police."

Wen nodded tightly. "If I see you again, I won't just put a bullet in your thigh."

"You won't see me again. You'll be dead by then."

"Maybe," she said, securing his legs again, taping his mouth, then shooting two holes in the trunk before slamming it shut.

She jogged over to Chase. "You drive," she said.

"This one?" He pointed to the shadow people's rental car.

"I don't think we have time to call an Uber."

"All right."

Chase pulled onto New York Avenue as two white Washington Metropolitan police cruisers passed them.

"Probably going to the front entrance around the block," Wen said. "It'll take them a few minutes to realize they should also be checking the garage."

"And they'll find the guy in the trunk, and eventually the two dead bodies in our room," Chase said as an ambulance raced past them. "Good thing you're wearing vIDs," he said.

They both had a large selection of false identities complete with credit cards, passports, driver's licenses, and assorted other documents. However, vIDs was something else. The virtual Image Deviation system was an incredible collaborative invention jointly created by The Astronaut and Chase. Its purpose was to fool the algorithms that powered facial recognition cameras. The ingenious, spray-on application covered a subject's face with hundreds of nano micro-processors, each thinner than a human hair. The translucent gold specks were virtually undetectable to the naked eye.

"We were wearing it when we checked in, but I don't know how much is left on our faces now," Wen said. "Cameras could've picked us up."

"We'll need The Astronaut to do a quick scrub then."

"Three and a half dead bodies?" Wen said. "If we can't reach him in time, we may need to get some help from Tess."

"Try him," Chase said, stopping for a red light at the intersection of New York and Florida Avenues. "Tess might be able to help us with identifying the bodies of those shadow people back there."

"Why? She's never given us much help with the shadow people before."

"This time she's going to have a live body. Assuming they find the guy in the trunk before he bleeds out or suffocates."

"I don't think he knows much more than he told us," Wen said. "But you can never be sure. Maybe they can connect some dots. Or maybe Tess will let me question him again when we aren't so rushed."

"I'll call her after we reach The Astronaut." Chase checked the time—just before five am. "He's certainly awake." They knew The Astronaut had odd sleeping schedules, but he was almost always up for the day by four am.

"Voicemail," Wen said, frustrated. "I hope he's all right."

"No one can find him," Chase assured her. "He's a magician."

"At least he's in the city. How many times have we needed him when he's on the other side of the world?"

"Yeah, but we don't know *where* in the city."

"I'm calling again. This time I'll leave a message. Meantime, we need to get rid of this car."

"Great, let's go get breakfast. I'm starving."

"Aren't you always?"

Wen left a detailed, yet cryptic message for The Astronaut, and Chase found a bakery just opening.

"This isn't a breakfast place," Wen said.

"What?" Chase scoffed, offended. "They sell cinnamon rolls, doughnuts, cheese filled croissants—what are you looking for, Eggs Benedict?"

"Real food, not pastries."

Chase gave her his best confused expression. "Okay, how about we get a couple bags of cinnamon buns and whatnot, then we'll go find some place for a 'real breakfast'?"

Wen checked the sideview mirror and scanned the area before they got out of the car. "Make it fast."

Chase ran inside while Wen paced the front sidewalk, recalling the parking garage man's warning.

Belfort is out there, with an army, hunting us.

She looked over her shoulder, back up New York Avenue. "They're getting closer," she whispered. "But so are we."

Chapter Twenty-Seven

WASHINGTON, DC

Chase kept the steering wheel steady while munching on the best cinnamon rolls he'd had since Mexico. "See how much better I drive with cinnamon buns?"

"We're only going thirty," Wen muttered as the morning traffic began to increase around them. She was looking through the phone she'd taken from the man in the parking garage. "This guy *did* have a lot of pictures of you. Oh! And here's a cute one."

"What about the others?"

She shook her head. "You look kind of goofy . . . as usual."

Chase laughed.

"Actually, this is horrifying."

"Now that's mean."

"Not you," she said, "but he has photos of us in the Caymans, Miami, Mexico, San Diego, these are from Barcelona, Amsterdam, on and on. They're everywhere we go."

"How are they finding us?"

"Money," she replied. "It's hard to hide in the modern world, but it can be done, unless someone is willing to spend whatever it takes to find you."

"Yeah. Still . . . they're good."

"We're alive."

He finished the center bite of a cinnamon roll. "After the Caymans and this morning, I think we need to move forward with assembling our own team."

"Speaking of spending money."

"I don't care what it costs. We need our own army."

Wen's phone vibrated. She looked at the series of numbers displayed. "It's Nash!" she said in gleeful relief.

"Finally," Chase said.

"Nash, are you okay?" Wen asked. "We've been very worried."

"He's dead."

"What? Who? Who's dead?"

"They killed him."

Wen looked at Chase questioningly, as if he might somehow know *who* had been killed. He shrugged.

"Who?" she tried again.

"Hayward. They killed him."

Wen knew that if Nash Graham had a best friend, it would be Hayward Hughes. They were both Astronauts of similar ages, backgrounds, and abilities. Although Nash exceeded Hayward in mathematics, patterns, and concepts, they had similar gifts. The two had worked together many times. Tess Federgreen sometimes referred to them as 'brothers from different mothers.'

"Who killed him?" Wen asked slowly.

"The ones planning the attack. Hayward found out. He was working with DARPA. It was code-word classified, and somewhere in there he found out about Blackout. Then they found out he found out."

"Who?"

"Then they just . . . he's dead . . . they ambushed him. I don't know. I don't know. I don't know."

"Wait, slow down. What is the attack? What is Blackout?"

"Blackout is the plan . . . the attack . . . It's big. They're going to kill a million people."

"What?" Chase asked. "Who's going to kill a million? Where? When? What are we—"

Wen squeezed Chase's arm and signaled with her hands for him to shut up, knowing how fragile The Astronaut was when he became agitated. "Where are you?" Wen asked. "Let us come."

"Not safe."

"Why? Are the same people after you?"

"Yes. Hayward sent me a message. The encryption should hold, but I don't know what the status of his phone is. Or his watch. I *made* him that watch. If they have that watch, it can link with the phone, and they can find me. They'll kill me, too."

"No one is going to kill you. People have tried to get you before. You're always running, just like us. You're the best one at hiding and—"

"Hayward was good at hiding, Hayward was better at running than me, and now he's dead. They killed him, they *killed* him."

"Listen," Wen began, calming her voice with each syllable. "I will not let anything happen to you. Chase and I will protect you."

"I don't know. I don't know. I don't know."

Chase reached over and muted the phone for a second.

"You have to find out where Hayward was killed. Who did it. And what's this Blackout attack on a million people?"

"I know. But I can't let him just shut down." She unmuted the phone. "Are you safe right now?"

"I don't know. I don't know," he repeated.

"Nash, you have to breathe. You have to know that the more upset you are, the harder it is for your mind to work . . . your beautiful mind. Your mind can do anything. We're going to find who did this, and we will make them pay. But I need your mind to be working."

"Mind . . . Hayward's mind got him killed."

"That's not going to happen here. Not to you."

"Hayward sent me a message. They know."

"Can you send the message you got from Hayward to me?"

"Yes. He sent it after . . . The message just came, but they killed him yesterday."

"Can you do it right now?" Wen asked, not sure how a dead man could send a message, but she'd worry about that later.

"Yes. I can send it now."

"Good. We'll come get you."

"No. Once you get the message, they will want to kill you, too. Everyone is going to die."

Chapter Twenty-Eight

WASHINGTON, DC

April 3rd - 5:23 am

Chase couldn't digest the message and safely drive at the same time. The million people dead, the talk of an advanced weapons program, DARPA—

"This is crazy!" Wen said to Chase. "Find a place to pull over."

Chase pulled into a loading zone.

"Look," she said, pointing to the message.

As Chase scanned it, adrenaline started to flow. "Is this for real?" he asked The Astronaut.

"Yes."

"But what city? How come he didn't tell us the city?"

"He may not know, or maybe the full message didn't get out, or maybe it's more than one . . . I don't know."

"Nash, we need to see Skyenor at DARPA right away," Wen said gently. "Can you help us get a message to him? Maybe hack into something and find out where he lives?" She looked at her watch, wondering if he'd still be home.

"I think I can."

"I *know* you can do it. Get us a meeting as quickly as possible."

"Okay."

"Tell me, where was Hayward staying?"

He gave them the address.

"We're going there now. I need you to focus on getting us into Skyenor."

"I will."

"And Nash, where did it happen?"

"What?"

"Hayward," Wen clarified. "Where did they get him?"

"They killed him at the Lincoln Memorial. It was bad." He stopped talking for several seconds. "But I traced the origins of the message . . . I've been working the traffic cams and other security cameras. I saw . . . I saw the shadows after him."

Wen thought of the shadow people, the ones that almost killed them in the Caymans and again this morning. However, she knew these weren't the same shadows he was talking about. "Okay, we'll go there, too."

"I looked at the crime photos. He didn't have his watch on. You have to find his watch."

"We'll look for it."

"They killed him. Hayward is dead. *Dead*."

"I know, I'm so sorry . . . "

"Find the watch. Find watch."

"We will. Where are you?"

"I don't want to say."

"Are you safe?" she asked.

"No one is safe."

"Don't move. You stay where you are. After we see Skyenor—"

"I have to set up a meeting."

"Yes, then after we see him, we'll come get you. You be ready. Tell us where you are."

"Okay, maybe. They're looking for me, too."

"But we're looking for *them* now."

"Okay. Find watch."

"I love you."

She heard him sigh, maybe crying. "Find watch."

He ended the call.

"Unbelievable," Chase said. "If this is true, we've got less than twenty-four hours to prevent the single worst terrorist attack ever. A million people exterminated in an instant."

"I don't know how they could do this without nuclear weapons."

"That's where Skyenor comes in."

Wen nodded. "Right."

"But why don't we just call Tess and have her set up the meeting?"

"Two reasons," Wen replied. "First, I want to keep Nash busy. And second, I don't want Tess pushing us out until we know what's going on."

Chase looked at the message from Hayward, an Astronaut he had never met, and shuddered. "What city?" he asked Wen again. "How are we going to stop this if we don't even know *where* it's happening?"

"Nash will figure it out."

He scoffed. "Maybe not this time. Even if he pulls himself together, he's also a target."

"Then Skyenor at DARPA will know. He was working with Hayward. He'll *have* to know."

"I missed what Hayward and Nash were last working on together."

"Some sort of deep fake detector for the NSA with some other algorithm to make it more complex." Wen frowned. "Do you think there could be some connection to this?"

"Depends on if DARPA was involved with that project as well."

"Wouldn't Nash have mentioned that?"

"If he knew, and if he was thinking straight."

"Then again, Skyenor will know."

Chase sighed. "Let's hope Nash gets that meeting."

"Your big question though, 'what's the target?' is only a third of our problem," Wen said. "Who is behind it, and how are they doing it? We have less than twenty-four hours to answer those questions and figure out a way to stop it."

Chase stared at her, fear in his eyes. "How can we stop it when we know nothing?"

Chapter Twenty-Nine

WASHINGTON DC

April 3rd - 6:02 am

Popov studied the screen in front of her, checking the details, thinking again that Blackout was the most impressive plan she'd ever seen. "Blackout is going to destroy America," she said to her comrade.

"If it works."

"Do not doubt it," she said. "Can't you already feel it in the air?"

He wasn't sure what she meant. While Popov lived and breathed espionage, political intrigue, conspiracies, attacks, and counterattacks, he was just doing his job. "I don't understand why we haven't evacuated all our people from the embassy."

"We've done as much as we can without raising suspicion," she said, thinking that she didn't particularly care for anyone in the embassy.

"They should not have to die."

"Soldiers die in war."

"They are not soldiers."

She glared at him. "We are at war. *Everyone* is a soldier."

He nodded, knowing that too much protest could cost him his life.

Popov, unconvinced of his agreement, continued, "Imagine when Blackout is complete . . . the massive death . . . unimaginable destruction. Even before they begin to pick up the pieces, the Americans will be looking for revenge."

"So?"

"We don't want anything that could remotely point them back to us."

The man's skeptical expression made it clear he still did not agree, but he'd already lost this battle with Popov. "Once the weapon is publicly known, the entire world order will shift."

She smiled. "Yes."

"A new phase in the arms race," the man said.

"It has already begun." Popov had been working on a report that would help protect against any Russian city from suffering the same consequences.

"Vilification," the man said. "Do we really want to live in a world where four or five countries have the ability to destroy entire cities in an instant?"

"I think for a long time it will be held by just three countries with that ability. Even that will depend on how quickly the United States recovers. I believe the Americans will be a distant third position—powerful, yet perhaps no longer a super power. We shall see. However, once the element of surprise is removed, this kind of attack will be much more difficult. Remember, with lasers, it all gets down to the power source."

He nodded. The man didn't know too much about lasers, and only understood the broad complexities of

Blackout, but it definitely made him nervous. "The world's moving very fast," he said, revealing a cloaked admission of his anxiety. "Just when we figure out how to maneuver and advance our country's objectives, to protect ourselves, suddenly it's a whole new technology. Blackout will be the power move today. Next it could be sonic weapons or some kind of AI takeover. It's always something new to learn. This is a young man's game."

"Man?" she echoed. "You mean a young *person's* game."

"Maybe."

"Yes. It's another change you speak of. Yet another one you are apparently behind on. It is women running things now."

"Wasn't that supposed to make things better?"

"Oh, we're not done yet. We've got thousands of years of men's mistakes to fix. That'll take us at least a few more years."

He looked at the clock. "We're going to be in a different place in twenty-two hours and thirty-seven minutes."

"Yes, tomorrow will be much more than different. But first, today. And that will be quite eventful, especially in Washington."

"I would think they want to keep things quiet today."

"We don't always get what we want, do we?"

Jie Shi waited. The updates were resetting. They had been constant during the past two days.

"They know about you," a man wearing thick glasses said.

"That is unfortunate," she replied. "What agency?"

"CIA."

"This is not new."

"It isn't about your efforts to gain approval for the telecom mergers," the man who, in his fifties, was almost twenty years her senior.

"And this from the Department of Justice?"

"There will be six indictments unsealed tomorrow."

"The congressman, or me?"

"It appears you are safe for now, but when the DOJ squeezes those six, it is likely they will, as the Americans like to say, roll over and give you up."

"So the technology transfers?"

The man smiled, always amused at the official term the Chinese government used for intellectual property theft. "They have begun to unravel. After the indictments, they will have a complete understanding of the damage."

She nodded, lost in thought for a moment. "But they will not discover the spyware installed in all the devices."

He shook his head. "How could they?"

"Then they will never catch me."

Chapter Thirty

WASHINGTON DC

April 3rd - 6:10 am

Wen easily picked the lock of Hayward's apartment. With their guns ready, she slowly pushed the door open. As soon as she and Chase got inside and saw the place in shambles, they knew it was too late.

Wen pointed for Chase to take the kitchen while she moved to the back of the one bedroom flat. Two minutes later, they decided it was clear.

"They may have been here last night," Wen said.

"Or right after they killed him."

"Probably at the same time," Wen said. "They were looking for something, and I don't think they found it." Her eyes flashed all over the disheveled flat.

"How do you get that?" Chase asked, unsure what method she'd used determine that the killers had left empty-handed when they had no idea what it was they were trying to find.

"The place is too ravaged. They killed him because he

knew something they didn't want anyone else to know, and they were here for something very specific." She picked up a couch cushion. One of its sides had been slashed open, foam and synthetic materials strewn around the room. "If they had found it, they would have stopped." She pointed to the contents of the freezer and refrigerator, thawing on the kitchen floor. "Just look at this place. They didn't stop, they gave up."

"So it may still be here?"

"Or it never was. Maybe he hid it somewhere else."

"Where he works?"

"Maybe," Wen said, feeling around the underside of the kitchen counter.

Chase checked behind the wall-mounted flatscreen television. It extended out on a swinging arm bracket. "Nothing."

"Bathrooms are a favorite hiding spot," Wen said, entering the surprisingly large room.

"It would help if we knew *what* we were looking for."

Using his multi-tool, Chase took apart the two ceiling light fixtures the earlier team had missed, but found nothing. Finally, after ten minutes without anything interesting turning up, he decided to check the news for mentions of Hayward, their morning hotel encounter, even the Cayman massacre.

Earlier, Chase had seen the television remote control in a scattered pile of books, pictures, and hundreds of colored pens. He retrieved it, but it didn't work. Knowing you could roll or rotate the batteries and get another few hours of service from a remote, he opened the battery compartment.

"We-en," he sang. "I think I found something."

She came from the bedroom, a framed photo in her hand. "What?"

Chase held up the remote. "No batteries. Instead, our Astronaut friend kept a flash drive in the battery compartment."

She smiled. "Nice work."

"See? I may not have been trained for search and surveillance by a top intelligence agency, but . . . "

"Can't wait to find out what's on it."

"We'll take it to Nash right after we meet with Skyenor."

Chase took one last look around the room and felt a wave of sadness for what had happened to this Astronaut. His brutal death, ripping apart his home . . . He imagined how easily it could have happened to Nash, or one of them. He thought of his own father's tragic murder. "There are always bad guys," he said quietly to himself.

Wen heard him, and knew where his thoughts were. "That's why we do what we do," she said, taking his hand and leading him toward the door. "We're the good guys."

Chapter Thirty-One

WASHINGTON, DC

April 3rd - 6:14 am

DARPA Director Skyenor knew it was going to be another long day, and this new, unwelcome wrinkle was surely going to make things worse. He called the one person that might be able to explain it, or at least make it go away.

Already at the office, Tess answered her private cell phone. *Crisis and turmoil never sleep* . . .

"Chase Malone wants to meet with me," Skyenor said, sounding agitated.

"Do you know what this is about?" Tess asked, pulling up a screen with the latest details of Chase and Wen's exploits. It was almost unnecessary, as she had most of the information memorized. More than her "pet project", as Linda sometimes called Chase, he was often the difference between success and failure. As much as he stymied her, she had come to rely on him more than she liked.

"If I knew what he wanted, I wouldn't be calling you for advice."

"How did he reach you?"

"He texted me. I don't know where he got my secure DARPA line, but he got it."

"When does he want to meet?"

"Right now."

"He's in *Washington*?" Tess asked, frustrated that she'd lost his trail again, but she was getting closer after the reports of an American man and an Asian woman killing more than a dozen mercenaries in the Caymans.

"Apparently."

"Did he say anything to peak your interest?"

"It was a *text*, but he said he needed to tell me something, and wanted some information about Hayward Hughes."

"The Astronaut?" Tess asked rhetorically. "He's dead."

"Dead?"

"I just got the report. Murder on the mall."

"My God . . . He was . . . He's *dead*? Wow . . . Hayward was working for me."

"Maybe that's why they want to meet you."

"They?"

"Chase *and* Wen."

"Right, how could I forget." Chase and Wen had been involved in an international plot to use weather controlling technology in which Skyenor and DARPA, along with Tess and CISS, played key roles. "Okay, I'll squeeze them in." He flashed on his incredibly tight schedule. The only possible opportunity without canceling something else was to see them at 7 am, when he was getting his morning coffee. He quickly replied to the text while still talking to Tess. "What do we know about Hayward's death?"

"Nothing yet. His body was just identified. But he was an Astronaut, and the protocol is fairly established. It won't be just us digging into this. The big six, maybe a few others, will be all over it."

Skyenor knew the big six in intelligence circles meant the US, China, Russia, Germany, Israel, and the UK. The thought of all that attention into the final works of any Astronaut was disconcerting, but adding the top intel minds in the world focusing on what Hayward was doing made Skyenor suddenly nauseous. "The timing couldn't be worse."

"What was he doing for you?" she asked, looking at another screen, trying to figure out who would kill Hayward Hughes. Astronauts were always targets, but it had been quite a while since the last assassination.

"Same thing we talked about yesterday." He hesitated. "But it's the deeper part."

"Right, the blanks you told me you would fill in later."

"Yeah. I was hoping to have more information from him first. Obviously, I'm not going to get that now."

"Can you give me a hint?"

"I'd rather go over the whole thing with you in a few hours. Let me collect the rest—"

"Give me *something* to get started on," she pressed.

"The space-based weapons. You need to look into specifics—NPL, that's nuclear pumped lasers, DEWs for direct energy weapons, chemical lasers, nuclear induced plasmas of gas mixtures. Airbase lasers, space-based lasers, and COIL, chemical oxygen iodine laser. Get up to speed on all that. Then our dialogue will be easier for you to grasp."

"Is this all as horrifying as it sounds?" she asked.

"Worse . . . much, *much*, worse."

"So nothing to worry about then," she said sarcastically.

"Why did they kill him?" Skyenor mused, ignoring her quip. "He must have found something he shouldn't have."

"What if I told you we've got increased Russian activity all over the place?"

"Then I'd even be more nervous."

"The Russian president is facing considerable domestic pressures. You know what that means?"

"Right, classic distraction. International crisis takes the pressure off the domestic front."

"Exactly. He may be about to launch something."

"I have a bad feeling," Skyenor said. "There's real evidence that it's much more complex than that. But I have to go right now. Don't forget, look at the lasers."

"Call me the minute you're done with Chase?"

"Absolutely."

"And then you have to lay this whole thing out for me."

"Promise."

Chapter Thirty-Two

UNDISCLOSED LOCATION

The technician looked at Tolstoy. She was pretty, if not for the fury in her eyes, lethal enough to kill him, but he knew it wouldn't be her stare that ended his life. It would be an arranged "accident". There was still hope, just not too much. "We've analyzed the number where The Astronaut's message went. Unfortunately, the recipient ID is . . . encrypted."

"Of course it is."

"We have programs working on it, but it will likely take . . . weeks to crack."

"*Weeks?*" Tolstoy shouted.

"If ever," the man admitted, then looked down at the floor, away from those beautiful-horrible killer eyes.

"We don't have *days*, let alone weeks. I need this in *hours*! Who has that information?"

"We will try."

Tolstoy wanted to execute the man on the spot. "What was in the message?"

The man smiled weakly.

"You think something is *pleasant* about this situation?" she asked, as if her words were daggers.

"I think there may be a solution. The message will have been preserved. We can use the phone to unencrypt that."

"Then why haven't you done it?"

"We have to power the phone back on."

"Turning it on is what got us into this mess."

"Yes, but it did not explode or make poison gas," he said, alluding to their earlier conversation as if trying to bring levity into the tense situation.

"It sent the message! An explosion or gas would have been far less damaging." She strangled him with her eyes. "Can you assure me it won't send anything else?"

"No, but if it does, we will be able to follow."

"Follow?"

"We will be ready to trace it immediately."

She wanted to ask why this precaution hadn't been taken earlier, but it would've been a wasted question. The damage had already been done, and she never wasted time —especially not today. Anyway, as soon as she was finished with the tech "expert," he would be removed from her world permanently. "Could there be another message waiting to send?"

"The chances are extremely low—almost zero percent —that it would actually send another message. I say this because if there *was* something, it should have sent simultaneously when the other went out. But we must turn the phone on to finally decipher the earlier one."

"Do it."

He opened a large briefcase, revealing several installed banks of wires and blinking LED lights. The technician carefully inserted Hayward's phone.

The instant the sequence completed, the phone emitted a "sent" chime.

"Does that mean it just sent another message?" she asked, instinctively reaching for her gun before deciding this wouldn't be the best time to kill the man.

"Yes, but it's okay. We will know where it goes."

"We better know *everything*."

He ran through the encryption. "Here it comes. Take a look." He swiveled the readout screen so she could see.

As Tolstoy read the message scrolling across the screen, she knew she could not let the technician leave the room alive. He had seen too much. But that was a small problem compared to the astronomical damage The Astronaut had done.

The mission had been compromised. Protocol dictated that she should notify Yuri. After years of work, Blackout was now a known operation to the enemy.

But there still might be a way to save it, she thought.

"Is this . . . true?" the technician asked, his expression flashing between fear and regret. As soon as he uttered the words, he seemingly realized he should never have asked, that the consequences of what he had seen were world-ending not just to the residents of the target city, but to himself. This was too big of a secret to know.

"I want that number," she said, ignoring his question.

"I already told you, it will take weeks."

"Not that one. *This* one." She pointed to the screen. The message remained there, blinking, as if taunting her.

It took them a couple of horrible minutes, but in the end, he succeeded. "It belongs to Dr. J. W. Skyenor, the director of DARPA."

"DARPA?"

"Yes, the Defense Advanced Research Projects Agency."

"I know what it stands for," she said, bristling. "Now, if you want to keep your job, get me that other number. It's more important . . . *very* important to you . . . understand?"

He did. It was clear that by 'keep his job,' she actually meant to keep his *life*. He believed the task impossible, especially since he had never encountered encryption such as this. However, buying time was what they did in his business, so that's what he started to do. The technician began tapping keys, hardly knowing what to do first, just hoping something good might happen. Maybe Tolstoy would drop dead by some other means.

It's okay, she thought, *I already have Skyenor covered. This part is actually good news. But the other one could be anybody . . . the director of the CIA, the NSA . . . who knows who this Astronaut knew. Given the work history of Astronauts, it could even be someone in a foreign intelligence service . . . What a nightmare.*

She sent an alert to the field team she had on Skyenor, raising the priority. Because of the DARPA director's push into the laser weapons area, he had gotten too close to Blackout. She had given an elimination order yesterday, but now it was critical, particularly since he had just received the message.

Tolstoy's coded message stated: "*Kill target immediately without regard to collateral damage.*"

Chapter Thirty-Three

WASHINGTON, DC

Skyenor's mind was working overtime. This was nothing new for the director of DARPA, who constantly juggled dozens of critically important technology-based weapons and related espionage projects. The events surrounding the constant search for supremacy among the major military powers of the world and, in recent years, the increasing threat from rogue nations and terror groups, kept him immersed in adrenaline and stress during his waking hours. Those terrorists and rogue nations who were finding it easier in the days of drones, autonomous weapons, and cyber warfare, to compete with the big boys, were a growing headache. However, on this day, he was even more distracted.

Firefly, DARPA's top secret space weapons program, had been surpassed. The revelations he'd received from various immediate intelligence reports had caused him to invoke CHAD. The urgent meeting of CISS, HITE, and DARPA had been a day early just to get Gatewood and Tess in the game. Later today, he would have enough information to absolutely terrify them.

The heated competition for laser space weapons worried him more than anything else in his career. Now, with The Astronaut's death, everything seemed to be closing in. The meeting with Chase and Wen, while an annoyance, could help. The pair of fugitives were looking for answers, but he hoped they could actually provide *him* with some. If they had any new information that would affect Firefly, he needed to know it.

Normally someone else got Skyenor his daily ritual of sugar and caffeine, but since he was meeting Chase and Wen there, he did it the old fashion way and ordered it himself. While waiting, he texted an assistant and demanded a complete review on the classified work Hayward had been doing for DARPA. Skyenor knew the basics, The Astronaut answered directly to him after all, but now he needed to understand the intricacies of his work, the parts that had gotten the gifted savant murdered in the middle of the capital of the free world, in the middle of the night, in the middle of the start of the space wars.

Sipping a Caramel Cocoa Cluster Frappuccino® Blended Coffee, as he walked out of the Starbucks, his phone sounded a chime that told him an encrypted message had arrived. He paused on the sidewalk, moved out of the flow of pedestrians, and placed his fingerprint on the biosensor so the message would present unencrypted. "Hughes," he muttered, shocked to be getting a text from a dead man.

Since Hayward had also been working on Firefly, he was anxious to read it. Yet as he did, the final words of the deceased Astronaut made the color drain from his face.

Suddenly, Firefly took a different priority. All his worst nightmares had been surpassed.

"Hell is coming," he breathed.

He glanced up absently, trying to make sense of it, and saw Chase and Wen coming toward him, recognizing them from photos Tess had sent. He stared back at the screen, reading the message again. *I've got to call a CHAD meeting immediately*, he thought. He looked up again, this time making eye contact with Chase, who was now less than twenty feet away.

Chase was the last thing Skyenor saw as the bullet blew apart his nose and entered the temporal lobe of his brain before exiting between the occipital and parietal lobes, taking a chunk of his skull with it. His body crashed onto the sidewalk, splattering coffee and blood. Pedestrians scattered, screaming, as two more bullets hit his torso, making sure the job was done.

Wen, witnessing the event as a trained marksman, quickly assessed the angle from which the sniper was shooting. She returned fire and watched as the man fled across a nearby low roof. Without hesitating, she ran toward the building, until more shots pinned her down. *A second shooter.* She knew there would be more. After spotting the sniper's nest, Wen found a way out.

Chase dove toward Skyenor and made a show of checking the dead body while reaching underneath to grab Skyenor's phone. He looked up just in time to see a man with a gun rushing toward him. Chase recalled Wen telling him months earlier that assassinations of high value targets would often utilize as many as four gunmen.

The billionaire pulled a gun out of his jacket, grateful he had been practicing the move, and pointed it at the man. "Federal agent, stop!" Chase hoped he sounded convincing.

The man fired anyway, but not at Chase. He pumped two more bullets into Skyenor's body, then turned and ran as Chase fired at him.

Chapter Thirty-Four

UNDISCLOSED LOCATION

The technician knew that if he could get the phone that had received the second encrypted message, he might be able to reverse engineer his way into figuring out who had gotten the first one.

"Any chance an operative could retrieve Skyenor's phone?" he asked Tolstoy.

She looked at him as if he were a dunce, impatient at having to do his job, clean up his messes. Tolstoy didn't answer. Instead, she tapped commands into her own phone, then worked the touch screen on a tablet as if she were casting a spell.

"The first and second messages were similar, but not the same," he said when she did not respond. "The first recipient received a shorter version. Like it might have encountered a glitch. Perhaps when we turned it off, or more likely, there was a type of cyanide app installed and deployed which distorted part of the message."

This seemed to please her, as her tone was softer when she replied. "What was missing?"

"Give me a minute." He compared the exposed aspects, syllables, character length, line spacing, duration, and numerous other factors. The technician smiled, relieved he finally had some good news to share. "The second message omitted the city, parts of the sender's theory of source, the perpetrators . . . and the pyramid schematic."

"Better," Tolstoy replied. "I still need to know who received the first message," she said, but there was hope now, as long as Skyenor was dead.

"I can't break the encryption yet, just the echoes and patterns. These are also three extra sentences in the first message that did not go to the second recipient, but that doesn't appear to mean anything."

"Obviously they mean *something*," she said, her tone turning sour again. *Idiot.*

"Of course. I meant they don't fit the other encryption. It's another code."

"I need to know what those sentences say."

"I know you do," he said, and he was desperate to decipher them as well, because he understood that they might be the only way he could identify who the recipient was— meaning the only way to save his life.

Washington, DC

Chase pursued the man who'd fired the last shots into Skyenor's already dead body. The shooter suddenly disappeared into an office building. Unbeknownst to Chase, he had just been ordered to make sure he obtained the target's phone, and hoped Chase would follow. The killer had seen Chase at Skyenor's body and thought he might have taken the phone, which had been in the target's hand when the first bullets hit. Anyway, going back to the crime scene wasn't going to happen, not in Washington DC, where one in six people walking the streets were some sort of federal agent.

Chase ran into the lobby of the building, hoping there would be a security guard. All he found was a maze of hallways and a bank of elevators. It turned out to be one of the older structures in the area. He cautiously went toward the main hall, having no idea where the shooter had gone.

A handful of early commuters were arriving. *More workers are probably caught up in the excitement down the street*, he thought. Moving carefully, he went around the corner, assessing the area as Wen had taught him, looking for the best paths of escape that would've appealed to a criminal trying to disappear.

What he should have been looking for were points of ambush. It had not occurred to Chase that the killer would be waiting for *him*.

He won't be in there, he thought glancing at the restroom doors. *He wouldn't be dumb enough to get himself trapped knowing authorities will be all over the area in minutes.* He scanned the area. *The most likely scenario is this guy found the back door.*

Chase was wrong.

The man burst out of the men's room behind him and shoved a pistol into his ribs. "Give me the DARPA phone, and I will not kill you," he said in accented voice that sounded to Chase to be Russian, or at least Eastern European.

Chase immediately doubted the proposition. The man could have just shot him, then searched his body for the phone. Maybe the shooter was being careful because the building was starting to come to life. Several more workers had arrived, a few were hovering around the elevators, waiting. A woman was walking down the hall nearby, and another man was heading toward the restrooms and them.

The killer's gun was concealed, but Chase knew the professional wouldn't hesitate to shoot him and everyone else in the lobby. In an instant, he relived all the lessons he'd learned the last couple of years on the run—trying to stay alive, trying to evade and then catch the shadow people . . .

Either way, I'm risking death, so here goes nothing!

"What DARPA phone?"

"Sorry, no phone, you die."

Spinning, Chase threw his elbow up hard and fast. He got lucky and caught the man's chin. The firm blow was only enough to throw him off balance for an instant. Chase could have taken the opportunity to run away, but the fate of a million innocent people was at stake and he needed every bit of information. This man was the only link.

Chase tackled him into the wall while screaming, "Call the police, call the police!"

"You fight like a little girl!" the man barked.

Chase thought of Wen and wished he could fight like her. The big man was like wrestling a bear.

The two of them slid to the ground while Chase tried to keep the man from aiming the gun at him. Finally, he jammed his knee into the Russian's wrist. On the third pump, the man released the gun, but his other thick arm snared Chase's neck and squeezed.

Chapter Thirty-Five

ANDROS, BAHAMAS - BRIGADIER'S RESTAURANT

Mumford Grimes squinted out toward the ocean, wondering if the small craft between the sandy beach and the horizon was packed with killers, or explosives, and if it was coming for them.

His career had been made by always making the right choice and avoiding mistakes. But then Chase Malone and Wen Sung had come along, the assignment of a lifetime, the one everyone dreams of—that last big score and then retirement on a beautiful tropical island. He'd known in the beginning that the pay was a little too much, the client a bit too mysterious, but he'd gone forward and ignored the things about it that didn't make sense. He wanted to be done. *Take the money and run.*

Turns out he had been hired to kill the only two immortal people on earth. Chase and Wen simply *refused* to die.

"Probably nothing," he mumbled to himself. He recalled more carefree days when he'd operated from Aruba. If not there, then from some other tropical island or at least a warm water beach. *There was a place in North Carolina on the Outer Banks . . .*

"We can't just stay here," Shelby said, not meaning the extended pier where the restaurant was housed, but the Bahamas as a whole.

"I know." If there was one thing he had learned in all his years in the trade, it was don't stay in one place too long, move as much as possible. But in this case he was stumped, not used to being hunted, particularly when someone so powerful wanted him dead.

He turned to Shelby, trying not to scowl. Grimes wasn't really mad at her, even though some of the blame certainly belonged with her. He loved her too much, and besides, anger was never healthy or profitable. Love and avoiding anger were two of the three things he considered most important—strange principles for a hitman. The third was even more surprising, but Grimes always lived on the edge of death—his or someone he was sending to the grave. If pressed, the thing that kept him tied to the good part of life were those amber flecked brown eyes staring back at him.

"I guess I've sort of known for a long time that, one way or another, Chase and Wen were going to be the death of me," he said, holding her gaze for a moment, then looking back at the boat.

"Don't say that."

"One way or another," he repeated. "I mean, it's hard to believe Wen hasn't already gotten a bullet into me. It might be better money betting on one of Belfort's goons to finish me off." He turned back to her. "You might be able to get away Lena," he said, calling Shelby by her first name, something he only did when they were alone.

"He's got a contract out on me, too," Shelby said, touched by his attempt at chivalry.

"Yeah . . . but . . . we both know it's me he really wants. Maybe if I'm gone, they'll let you go." He sipped his drink as another diner squeezed past their table. Grimes appeared casual, but he was ready to go for his gun. Always ready.

"Nonsense, Grimes." She rarely used his first name, didn't like it much. "Fake identities, an island somewhere. We've got enough to live on for quite a while. Maybe we'll open a little seaside bar, a real cool joint. I know a couple tiny towns in Mexico where we could just be invisible."

"We'll always be looking over our shoulder," he said, loving her ideas, but too practical to ever believe they could get away with it—at least as long as Belfort was alive.

"Then we should go talk to Chase and Wen."

"Ha!" He took a swig of beer. "That's what got us *into* this mess."

"And it can get us out."

"You really think they'll talk to us after what happened on Grand Cayman? I wouldn't."

"We weren't there."

"They think we set them up. No other way someone could interpret it."

"We'll just explain."

"Yeah? Would *you* believe anything that we said under the circumstances?"

She frowned back at him. "It's the *truth*."

"What's that?" Grimes laughed. "Do you think they even understand the truth anymore?"

"Chase is a tech wizard. I'll explain that Belfort had us under digital hard-tap basket surveillance. He'll know better than me what that means. Then, of course, Belfort found out about the meeting . . . "

"You're assuming that Chase and Wen survived the Caymans."

"Aren't you?"

Grimes stared out to sea, as if their ghosts might be there. "Probably still alive. More than two years, we've never been able to nail them. You think Belfort found someone better than us?"

"There's no one better than us, but he sent numbers. I'm sure at least twenty or thirty. Chase and Wen were expecting to meet friendlies—you and me. Instead, they walked into a trap, a full-on military operation . . . war waiting for them."

Grimes nodded. "Sure he paid off local law enforcement to ignore or delay response."

"Standard procedure for Belfort. But Chase and Wen don't go quietly. Those cops wouldn't've been expecting the kind of fury they unleashed," Shelby said.

His face turned to an expression that somehow conveyed both pain and awe. "Yeah. Remember Cyprus? That time in Colorado? What about Barcelona? Every time they got away and left a trail of bodies." He let the lapping waves relax him for a moment.

"Chase and Wen got away again in the Caymans, and you know it." A cruel reminder.

"Yeah, I do," he admitted. "The question really isn't are they going to trust us again, the question is can *we* trust them."

Chapter Thirty-Six

WASHINGTON, DC

Wen raced across the street, barely avoiding being flattened by a Metro bus. Crowds of people were moving in all directions, some going toward Skyenor's fallen body, others fleeing from it, afraid they could be the next victim of a mass shooting. Still more seemed oblivious that the event had even occurred as they stared into smart phones or listened to their air-pods.

In her rapid movements, Wen surveyed the area. Even before, while walking to meet Skyenor, prior to the fatal shot, her training had forced her to check every angle, always looking for threats and escapes. Silently furious at herself for not having seen, or at least anticipating the DARPA director's assassination, Wen knew there would be time later to assess her failings. Right now there was a killer to catch.

She considered scaling the old marble edifice; its many ornamental accents could easily be used as handholds. However, he would be on the ground any second, and she'd be waiting.

The problem is, he's a professional. He won't leave the building carrying a sniper's rifle or anything else that says 'hitman,' she thought. Fortunately, most of the workers were going into the building, with only a few exiting. *I'll have to get close enough to assess the snipers face.*

Still on the other side of the street when the man emerged from the building, Wen was sure it was him because he looked both ways upon stepping on the sidewalk. He had obviously left the rifle on the roof. The disposable asset would be free from fingerprints or any other identifiable marks.

She sprinted across the street. There was no time for a stealthy approach. Bolting in front of yet another metro bus, she wondered how many chances she had left, and told herself to avoid the big diesel monsters in the future.

Where is Chase? She hadn't seen him since the shooting.

The bus driver hit the horn. The blaring sound caught the sniper's attention, and led his eyes straight to Wen. He took off, weaving in and out of the streams of pedestrians. Wen assessed him as she followed.

He is fit, his legs are longer than mine, makes catching him unlikely. In an open field I'd never get him, but in an open field I'd be able to shoot him down.

She plowed into a business man stepping up onto the curb. He fell backwards, stunned by the force that had hit him.

I want him alive, Wen thought, gripping her Glock 19, concealed in a light jacket carried in her hand. *I need him alive.*

Jammed between the hard, shiny floor and the polished brick wall, Chase could feel the battle lost. His lungs burned, desperate for oxygen, as he clawed at the big man's arm. Chase's legs kicked, struggling for any advantage, but it was wasted energy.

His eyes began to blur. In a fleeting thought, he wondered where Wen was. *Could it be possible that she'll save me?* The flash of hope spurred him to twist and contort his body in a final effort at escape. The Russian maintained his stranglehold. *Wen's rescued me so many times before.*

The next instant consumed everything he knew when he realized she'd run off to pursue the others and did not even know where he had gone. Chase summoned what remained of his strength, released his clawing grip from the killer's arm, then with all his might, pushed both elbows into his attacker's body. But what he imagined to be the herculean movements and power of a heavyweight boxer, was little more than a limp whimper of a dying man. His actions had no effect.

In the malaise of that defeated moment, he thought he heard cheers and then a loud clap of thunder. Nothing that happened afterwards made much sense until, after an impossible to define amount of time, he discovered new strength, and threw the man from him.

"Calm down," a man's voice said.

Chase's eyes darted. His arms flailed. He could breathe again.

The man he'd pushed away wasn't the Russian, it was someone younger, thinner. In a fuzzy second he realized the person had been trying to give him CPR.

Chase gulped in breath. In still-grainy focus, he saw the Russian lying next to him, blood puddling under his dead body.

"He shot him," a woman said, pointing to another man, a pistol still in his hand.

"The guy was going to kill you," the man said. "For a second, I thought he had."

"Thanks," Chase managed to say, trying to understand it all.

"I'm a Special Agent with the EPA."

"I wasn't aware the Environmental Protection Agency employed armed personnel."

"Well, now you are," the man said. "Why was he trying to kill you?"

"He just murdered a man on the street," Chase said. "I was trying to catch him."

"You're just a citizen?" the man asked.

"Something like that," Chase said, getting to his wobbly feet.

"What's your name?"

"Federgreen," Chase said. "Tim Federgreen."

The man holstered his weapon, gave him one more piercing look.

"You sure you're okay?" he asked.

"Yeah. Yeah, really, thanks man." Chase smiled and dusted off his clothes. A crowd had now gathered and several people had called 9-1-1. Chase slipped into the knot of onlookers and a second later was back out onto the street.

Where's Wen? he wondered as he ran back toward the coffee shop, patting his pocket to make sure he still had Skyenor's phone.

Chapter Thirty-Seven

NEW YORK CITY

Belfort loved his job. He stood in front of the breathtaking glass walls of a hundred million dollar Madison Avenue penthouse. Spread across the top five floors of a gleaming tower next to the Empire State Building, the gloriously stunning twenty-thousand square-foot space featured eleven bedrooms and fourteen baths, a private rooftop pool, and three thousand square feet of outdoor terraces.

The penthouse wasn't his, but he lived and worked there many months out of the year. And it wasn't even his favorite, nor the largest of the many mansions where he spent his time. The Circuit spared no expense to achieve its goals.

Belfort's official title was "Coordinator," which was a way of saying he kept track of all the people the Circuit and their members wanted dead.

This line of work didn't bother him, mostly because it paid so well, but also because he believed in what they were doing. "People need to die," he told his director.

The director, a lanky man with a metal mechanical

hand, had heard this before, but he let his boss continue. This kind of reflection usually occurred after a failed job, and always after a Chase and Wen miss.

"Seven and half billion people . . . that's a lot," Belfort said. "Obviously there are going to be quite a few in the global overpopulation who are bad, in the way, causing trouble of some sort, an obstacle to human progress . . . " He looked at the director, waiting for an agreeable nod, maybe even a verbal confirmation.

"Child molesters," the director added. "People who are mean to animals . . . "

Belfort shot him an icy glare. They didn't kill *those* types of people—at least knowingly. "How many bad people who need to be removed? What's that number?" Belfort asked.

"One percent?" the director said rhetorically. "Something like seven million."

"Perhaps. Either way, it's a lot," Belfort repeated. "And we do our part."

"Yes, we do," the director agreed, looking at a screen with a list of hundreds of targets on it, knowing he could click on any name, and it would tell him everything there was to know about the person who would soon be dead.

Chase and Wen were far from the only targets of the "shadow people." True, they had been on the list longer than all but a few, and they were the only ones who had escaped more than four attempts. However, there were a handful who had never been found for even a first attempt, and at least seventy who had escaped a hit and were never found again. Killing people wasn't as easy as it sounded, even for an organization with such vast resources. Still, thousands had been successfully terminated. Belfort ran a tight ship, and Chase and Wen were constant thorns in his side.

The director didn't much care one way or the other except for how the Chase/Wen failures affected his boss's mood and, more importantly, took the focus and resources from other targets, making those hits more difficult.

Chase and Wen had certainly reduced the available talent pool. Somewhere on Belfort's computer was another list—the lost list—containing the names and profiles of all the people Chase and Wen had killed. But this meeting wasn't about the hit list, the lost list, or even about Chase and Wen—at least not directly. Today, Belfort wanted to talk about his latest obsession.

"Grimes and Shelby are bad people," Belfort said in a way that made it sound as if he were discussing child Nazis. "I don't just want them to die, I want them to suffer."

Washington, DC

Wen ran as fast as she could, but the distance between her and the sniper kept increasing. There were too many people on the sidewalk for her to safely get a good clear shot at his lower body. "I need him *alive*," she repeated to herself.

Inflicting injuries that would drop a target but not kill them was a particular talent of hers, but with these already panicked pedestrians between her and him, she would need more than talent.

I don't have the luxury of not taking the shot. The stakes of losing an American city and a million of its inhabitants are high enough, she thought. *Unfortunately, any collateral damage is a price I have to pay. Injuring a few innocents is too bad . . .*

Wen raised her gun, still hidden under the jacket. Calculating the odds on the fly, she realized more than likely the people would be human shields, and the sniper would get away.

I have to get closer.

Then she realized the solution. Wen fired two shots into the air. As expected, about half of the people between her and the sniper hit the ground. The rest scattered, providing her with a clear shot. She took it, and the fleeing man crashed to the ground.

By the time Wen reached him, he was crawling, trying to get away. From a distance of less than three feet, she pointed the pistol at him. "Not another inch," she said.

He turned his head and stared into her eyes. "You have no idea what you've done," he said through gritted teeth. That's when she saw the explosive vest. Wen dove for cover, knowing it was already too late.

Chapter Thirty-Eight

ANDROS, BAHAMAS

The warm salt air relaxed Grimes like nothing else (other than Shelby) could. He wanted to close his eyes and lay on one of the plush double chaise lounges down on the beach with her at his side. It wasn't going to happen. Not yet, anyway . . . maybe never . . .

"I don't know that we have much of a choice," Shelby said, continuing their conversation. "Chase and Wen may be our only chance against the Circuit. They're the only ones that have proven they know how to beat them."

"Or at least survive."

"Same thing."

"Not really."

"No," she agreed. "Not really, but a damn good start."

"Yeah."

A woman jogging on the beach in a bikini caught Grimes' attention. Some women might've been jealous of the bikini-clad beauty, but Shelby knew Grimes had no interest in the young woman.

Grimes' eyes tracked the bikini woman's movements,

scanning the beach, making sure she wasn't being followed. She disappeared somewhere on the beach below them. A few minutes later, the woman reappeared up on the wooden planks of the pier, and headed to their table.

She sat down and took a sip of Grimes' beer. "Belfort sent twenty-eight to George Town," the bikini woman said. "None came back."

Shelby smiled. "Told you."

"How many dead?" Grimes asked quietly.

"They don't know for sure . . . somewhere around twenty. The others were arrested."

"They'll be out soon," Shelby said.

The bikini woman shook her head. "I don't think so. Two dead cops, and more injured."

"Thanks, Jen," Grimes said, sincerely appreciative of the information. Jen, who worked with a hacker, had become a reliable messenger. Belfort and the Circuit knew nothing about her—at least he hoped they didn't, but he knew that could change any moment. He scanned the beach again, confident that if he was being watched, he'd be dead. And although he *felt* dead, looking across at Shelby, he knew he wasn't.

She'd probably be a tad more upset if I were.

The hacker had long ago cracked a line into Belfort's network after a buddy of his was killed by the Circuit. When Grimes started looking for information on his employers, he eventually connected with the hacker—a friend of a friend, a contact, a guy who knew a guy. But in the world where Grimes navigated, populated with rogues, smugglers, and assassins, that was hard stuff . . . *extremely* dangerous stuff.

Washington DC
April 3rd - 7:07 am

The force of the explosion threw Wen nearly ten feet, slamming her into the side of a parked BMW, tipping its security alarm, sounding an annoying pattern of sirens.

What happened?

For a moment, she fought to regain reality. Mentally checking her body, Wen thought she'd cracked a rib, but as she struggled to breathe, decided it was only the wind knocked out of her.

A man's hands reached for her.

An instant from shooting him, she realized he wasn't a killer. Instead it was a rather normal looking businessman. He helped her to her feet. "Are you okay?" he asked, but the ringing in her ears made it sound more like one word.

"Yes," she said, nodding, having read his lips. Then he saw the gun still in her hand. The jacket she'd been using to conceal it lay nearby.

He backed away, his concerned eyes suddenly filled with fear.

"It's okay," Wen said. "I'm a federal agent." She picked up her jacket, once again hiding her pistol, and quickly scanned the area as the man went to check on other victims. The impact of the blast had been relatively small.

The explosives weren't designed for a terrorist attack, rather to keep the sniper in line, she thought. *And to make sure he wasn't caught alive.*

Wen saw part of the man's bloody hand laying ten feet from where he had been crawling. Strangely, parts of both his legs had landed right next to each other. A foot, still in his brown leather shoe, remained attached to a fleshy femur.

The other one was more complete, but also more mangled. There wasn't anything else left of him.

If she'd been closer, Wen might have grabbed the hand for finger printing. However, now the crowd was too large. She needed to disappear.

A block later, she spotted Chase jogging towards her.

"I heard the explosion," he said. "I was afraid . . . "

"It was the sniper," she said as they both headed the opposite direction from the blast. "His employers fitted him with an explosive vest. They must've been nearby. It was detonated remotely as soon as I caught him."

"How would they know?"

"He must've had a body cam," Wen said as they walked as fast as they dared without attracting attention. "A camera would verify the shooting and show if he was in danger of being apprehended."

"It's scary sophisticated."

She nodded. "*Very.* What about you? What happened to the other one?"

"An EPA agent killed him. Saved my life. But he was most likely Russian."

"The sniper only spoke a few words before . . . But I'm almost sure he was also Russian."

"So the Kremlin's making a serious move?"

"It would appear that way."

"Did you know the EPA had agents who carry guns?"

"I did. Seventy-three federal agencies have armed agents, including the Department of Education, the FDA, the Social Security Administration, and many more that seem excessive. The average American might be surprised to hear that even agents for the Railroad Retirement Board carry guns."

"And the MSS has files on all of them?" Chase asked, knowing the answer.

"The MSS knows what schools the agents' children attend, how much is in their bank and retirement accounts, what cars they drive, *everything*."

"The world is scarier than most know," Chase said. "Crazy!"

Once they were a good distance from the action, they started walking faster. Wen checked her phone. "There's a car rental place three blocks from here."

"You don't like the shadow people's car anymore?"

"Too risky. A few shootings is one thing, but when a bomb goes off this close to the White House, they're going to start locking down, checking everyone."

"We're only twenty-one hours and thirty-three minutes until a city gets wiped off the map," Chase said after checking his watch. "What if it's Washington?"

"It would be the hardest city to target, especially when it's on high alert. The Astronaut's running all the parameters. We'll know soon."

"Not soon enough."

Chapter Thirty-Nine

WASHINGTON, DC

With the rental car lot in sight, they stopped for a moment as Chase's phone vibrated.

Still catching his breath, Chase checked the name on the incoming call. "Unbelievable," he said, not really surprised.

"Tess Federgreen?" Wen asked, scanning the area, still anticipating another attack.

"Funny hearing from you," Chase answered suspiciously.

"Well there's nothing funny about this," Tess said.

"Make it quick," Chase snapped.

"We've been through a lot, the three of us," she said, referring to herself, Chase, and Wen, "but I'm not sure you've ever been in this deep before."

"Tell us what you know," Chase said, figuring she had already heard about the head of DARPA, recalling that Skyenor and Tess were old friends and their professional relationship went back even further.

"You know that's not how this works." Tess stormed

around Secure, an enclosed glass room at the end of mission control where technology made it impossible for conversations to be overheard, her scuffed cowboy boots making her sound even angrier as she moved across the hard tiled floor.

"That's how it's going to have to work, because we're not exactly lounging around the pool," Chase said. "We're in the middle of some real trouble."

"Aren't you always?"

"Three seconds, Tess."

If the phone in her hand had been a living thing, she would've squeezed it to death. As it was, she would've liked nothing more than to have found a way to crawl inside of it to assault Chase. "Okay, I'll go first. You were about to meet with JW Skyenor, the director of DARPA, and now . . . he's dead." The reality still shook her. "You were within shooting distance of one of the most important people in America. Meanwhile, I've got a covert space weapons program on my plate, and it turns out that The Astronaut who was centered on the technology was close with *your* Astronaut . . . and he's dead, too. You're a common denominator."

"I could say the same about you."

"Ask Wen if she knows Jie Shi."

"Wen is kind of busy at the moment."

"No need. I happen to know that Jie Shi is an MSS operative in the United States, and she's an old friend of Wen's. Or at least she was another one of Rong Lo's favorites . . . I know you remember Rong Lo."

"I remember killing him," Chase said, looking at Wen, trying to hear her silent response.

"I assure you, Jie Shi is no friend of mine," Wen said. "And if she's involved, your plate is filled with poison."

"She's not involved with the space weapons program,

but before this fiasco dropped into my lap, Jie Shi was occupying quite a bit of my time."

"Who has she compromised?" Wen asked. "A Congressman, or a governor?"

The question surprised Tess. "Both. How did you know?"

"That's what she was trained for."

"There are an awful lot of coincidences hitting my desk with your fingerprints on them," Tess said.

Chase, already tired of the conversation, interrupted, "We had nothing to do with Skyenor's death."

"What were you meeting him about?"

"That Astronaut who was working for him sent Nash a message. A warning, really. There's some group ready to unleash a terrorist strike like nothing the world has ever seen before."

"Details," Tess demanded.

"A million dead."

"A *million* people?"

"That's the claim."

"That could only be nuclear."

"Well you're the expert on that," Chase said. "But we don't have a lot else to go on. No target. No group. Just a name. 'Blackout.'"

"How do we even know it's real?" But as Tess asked the question, she knew the answer already. They had killed that Astronaut in order to silence him, and now Skyenor.

"I don't know," Chase said. "Do you want to risk it?"

Tess, digesting the new pieces of information Chase had provided, ran through a series of scenarios in her mind. *Why had Skyenor employed the dead Astronaut?* She thought of the commonalities—Skyenor, The Astronaut, The Russian space weapons, Chase and Wen. *What was Skyenor working on?*

"I need to talk to Nash," Tess said.

"I'll bet you do," Chase replied dryly.

"I'm serious. If there are a million people in harm's way, I need to talk to him, and it needs to be *today*. If the people planning this kind of attack believe we've discovered their plot, there's no telling how soon they'll act."

"Oh, I forgot. 4:44 AM, April fourth."

"That's tomorrow," Tess said, sounding more agitated than she would've liked.

"It's actually in twenty hours and fifty-six minutes. Don't plan on sleeping."

"We've got less time than that to find out where the target is, who's behind it, and what they're using!" Tess looked at the monitors showing the status of various CISS operations and live feeds displaying US and enemy agents in the field. *Everyone in the US intelligence community is about to be working on the same thing—Blackout.*

Chapter Forty

WASHINGTON DC

April 3rd - 8:02 am

On their way to the Lincoln Memorial, Chase and Wen made a quick stop to see Tu. Housed in a fortress-like building, the blandly named World Affairs Institute had become a behind-the-scenes force in US government policy, particularly in the intelligence arena, although the think tank also regularly lobbied Congress on matters of international trade and security as it related to the Institute's mission of global peace, freedom, and democracy. The secretive group had avoided the spotlight, yet still attracted controversy by refusing to disclose its contributors or annual budget, thought to be in excess of $100 million.

Through The Astronaut's connections, Tu had become a resident and fellow at WAI. Sepio, the elite security force employed by Chase to protect Tu and Wen's grandmother, had also been given an in-house barracks.

Tu beamed when he saw them come into his "office," a

room about the size of a convenience store. "Chase Bank! Wen!"

"Sorry," Chase said, giving Tu a hug, "but we're going to have to cancel dinner tonight."

"Why?" he asked, alarmed, knowing something horrible must have come up. " Did you find Grimes?"

They filled him in on what they knew, avoiding the part about an Astronaut getting killed, and leaving out Chase almost getting strangled to death and Wen getting blown up. Even with their deal to always tell him what they were working on, he didn't need the gruesome details. However, they did tell him about Skyenor, since it was already on the news, and in the case of Blackout, they told him all they knew. Since the clock was ticking away, they decided to tap into one of the best minds they knew.

"A whole city of people," Tu said. "This is terrible. I will get to work on it right away." He gave them a fierce look. "Who would do such an evil thing?"

"That's one of the three questions," Chase said. "Where is the attack going to happen? What kind of weapon? And who's behind it?"

"This is so big it can only be a few countries. I think China, Russia, maybe North Korea, possibly Iran. I believe it's probably China."

"It doesn't look like China's the bad guy this time," Wen said.

"Chinese Communist Party is *always* the bad guy," Tu said angrily.

"That may be true," Chase said. "However, I think they would be crazy to inflict such damage on their best customer, especially one with the most powerful military on earth."

"He's right," Wen said. "Too risky for China. They're already winning. Russia, on the other hand, is desperate."

"And we've got Russians all over this."

"It could be Russia," Tu said, appearing in deep thought. "Who else is working on this?"

"We just informed Tess, so I suspect the entire US government and all seventeen intelligence agencies are now fully engaged."

"What did Tess think?"

"We didn't talk at length," Chase said, "but she's already working on leads."

"How did we find out?" Tu asked.

Chase and Wen exchanged a quick glance. Tu noticed. "Something bad," Tu said. "You found out in a bad way, and you don't want to tell me. You *have* to tell me."

"A man was killed last night, but he managed to get a message out to Nash," Chase told him.

"He knew The Astronaut?"

"Yes."

"How?"

"He was working for DARPA."

Tu nodded, as if this satisfied him for the moment. "Perhaps they are not going to destroy a city. That is very hard to do. This could be a big scheme to distract the US military and intelligence agencies while they do another kind of attack."

"That is possible," Wen said, "but we can't take a chance it's not real."

"They know that."

Chase smiled. "Don't overthink it."

"Overthink? Is such a thing possible?"

"Playing out all the different scenarios in your mind can

make you crazy," Chase said. "It's usually the simplest of the possibilities that turns out to be correct."

"Oh, you mean Ockham's razor, the law of parsimony. I know about the problem-solving principle that states 'entities should not be multiplied without necessity.' Which is what I believe you mean."

Chase nodded, always impressed by Tu's sharp mind.

"The axiom is attributed to William of Ockham, a Franciscan friar. He was a fourteenth century philosopher and scholastic. I understand his premise that when facing differing hypotheses about a singular prediction, it is wisest to go with the solution that makes the fewest assumptions. However, in this case, we are coping with espionage, acts of war, strategy, and consequences too catastrophic to ponder. I assure you, this is more complex than you or William of Ockham could imagine."

"It's tomorrow," Chase said. "Knowing the time of the strike should help us figure it out."

Tu looked at him. His eyes suddenly appeared far wiser than his years. "Yoda says, 'Difficult to see; always in motion is the future.'"

Chapter Forty-One

WASHINGTON DC

April 3rd - 8:49 am

Chase turned the car onto Constitution Avenue. "We better call Nash. He might be able to get into Skyenor's phone."

"If only we *had* Skyenor's phone," Wen said, then paused and looked at Chase. "Wait, we have his phone?"

"We might."

"Why didn't you tell me?"

"I just did. We've been kind of busy since I took it from his body *while being shot at*." Chase slipped it out of his pocket and handed it to her.

"It's not a standard phone," she said excitedly.

"Wouldn't think so." Chase found a parking space.

"What secrets this must contain . . . It may tell us the city, the weapon, the people behind it . . ."

"The everything."

"Well, look at that," Wen said, looking at her phone. "It's The Astronaut."

"Do you think he was listening in on us somehow?" Chase asked.

"You never know with The Astronaut," she said, winking. "Hi Nash, how are you?"

"I'm alive," he said in an emotionless tone. "I called to tell you that Hayward's watch is there."

"Where?"

"On the National Mall."

"That's where we are," Chase said, glancing up at the sky, and then at Wen, as if to say, *The Astronaut already knows exactly where we are.*

"Where on the Mall?" Wen asked.

"I'm not sure exactly, but I've enhanced the footage from the National Park Service surveillance. In the first images, he was wearing the watch, and then at the end . . ." The Astronaut's voice cracked. "At the end, it wasn't on his wrist."

"Maybe the killers took it," Chase suggested.

"No," The Astronaut snapped. "Hayward would never have let them take the watch. I'm certain that he hid it somewhere between the gardens, the wall, and the Lincoln Memorial."

"That's a lot of real estate," Chase said. "It won't be easy to find. If Hayward did manage to hide the watch, he must have done a good job, assuming no one else discovered it yet."

The Astronaut sat in a dark room surrounded by a circular array of screens. He had hacked into the traffic and security cameras around the National Mall and followed the last steps of his friend's life. He cycled through images, knowing how afraid Hayward would have been in those final minutes. New images continued to come in, and one of them provided the key evidence he needed. "There,"

Nash said again. "I see Hayward entering the Lincoln Memorial." Nash paused, frozen by the horrified expression on Hayward's face as he saw the guard. "He doesn't have the watch on. The watch is not at the Memorial, and the killers didn't get it." A slight trace of relief returned to Nash's voice. "He got rid of it before he arrived at Lincoln."

Chase looked at Wen, and then around at the vast National Mall they were walking across. "So many trees," he said, trying to imagine where Hayward might have hidden the watch on that dark night, pursued by assassins. "The Vietnam wall, various statues . . . This is going to be a daunting search."

"It's there."

"Can you give us a little more to go on?" Wen asked. "We've got to narrow it."

The Astronaut continued scrolling through more windows and data. "Hold on . . . " He zoomed in on a new clip. "Hayward's arm moves. That's when he did it."

"Where?"

"The reflecting pool. It's hard to tell, because even with the layers and filters I'm applying, I'm dealing with shadows in the dark, but I think he threw the watch in the water."

Chase and Wen jogged forward. "Can you give us an approximate location?"

"Near the northwest corner, closest to the Lincoln Memorial."

They reached the spot and immediately began scanning the water. The sun's glare cast thousands of reflections, making identifying a little watch difficult. After several minutes, Chase thought he saw something almost ten feet from the edge. "What do you think?" he asked.

"I think that's it," Wen agreed.

Chase took off his shoes and socks, rolled up his khaki

pants, and waded in. "Cold. Cold. Cold!" he said, as the water came up to just below his knees. Finally he reached the thing they'd seen, and was able to use his toes to lift it out of the water. "Got it!" he yelled triumphantly to Wen.

"Is it the watch?" she yelled back.

He nodded.

"We have the watch," she told The Astronaut.

By the time Chase reached her, Wen had ended the call. While Chase put on his shoes and socks, she explained that The Astronaut wanted the watch, the flash drive from Hayward's apartment, and Skyenor's phone as soon as possible. They'd arranged to meet at The Astronaut's favorite pizza place.

"Pizza, this early?" Chase asked.

"We're meeting him at nine. It's a twenty-four hour place. You know how much he loves pizza."

"I do, too, and I'm hungry, but nine still seems too early for pizza."

"Might be our last meal." She was joking, but neither of them laughed.

Chapter Forty-Two

VIENNA, VIRGINIA

After immediately briefing the White House and the Director of National Intelligence, Tess called an all-hands-on-deck meeting of CISS.

"This is going to take a massive effort," she told them. "CISS is the elite of the elite. We can hope another agency stops this horrific attack, but we are in the best position to do it."

After some questions, she sent them all to work. "Do whatever it takes," Tess said. "The only rule is Do. Not. Let. This. *Happen*."

Walking back to Mission Control, several close aides updated her.

"It's bad," Linda said. "Six top scientists have died under mysterious circumstances in the past twenty-four hours."

"And we think it's related to Blackout?" Tess asked. "What do they all have in common?"

"Lasers."

"Of course. Who's behind it?"

"It appears to be Russian agents operating inside the US, but we're still in an early, *early* stage in the investigation. Each case has been carefully orchestrated to appear accidental. Pros are doing this."

"Where are the scientists based?"

"All over. Two from Stanford died in a single vehicle crash. One from the University of Chicago, apparent home fire, University of Colorado, University of Maryland—College Park, Cal-tech."

"They must all be working on something more specific than just lasers . . . Factor in space and see if that gets us to a common thread. They're being killed because they can somehow stop the attack by stopping the weapon. There must be more to know. Find them."

"On it."

"And don't forget, Skyenor knew something," Tess said, wondering again what the DARPA director was going to tell her. "He's the key. Get the Deputy Director on the phone."

Tess checked the clock, then joined the team trying to narrow down the target. "The big question, *what's* the target?"

"We're throwing darts in the dark," one of the analysts admitted.

"Not good enough. Find out if there have been any unusual movements anywhere. An exodus."

"Of Russians?"

"Of *anyone*. This is too big an operation. People know about it. Our enemies are not better than us. They only operate under the protection of secrecy, but that protection has cracked now thanks to Hayward Hughes. He died to give us this chance."

One large screen on the wall was playing out destruction scenarios of city after city. "The AI is trying to find the most likely target," a woman explained as they all stood in silent horror while a simulation wiped out Philadelphia.

"We can't evacuate every city," Tess said. "And we can't let that happen."

She walked away, her mind distracted by the images.

It must be nukes.

This could be the last day . . .

Tess didn't have time to travel to Bunker W at Langley. She and Gatewood held the first ever CHAD meeting outside the secret CIA underground via video.

She sat in Secure, looking out at Mission Control, the large room buzzing with more urgency than it had ever operated under. The meters on the screen showed the level of encryption and protection meant no one could intercept her communications with Gatewood, but she didn't really ever trust that. She knew too much. *Today there's no choice*, she told herself.

"Who is the terrorist?" she asked as Gatewood came on screen. "Who is doing it? What is the weapon? Where is the target? And how do we stop it?"

"Good questions," Gatewood said, his normal smugness completely absent.

"I keep asking myself those questions over and over." Tess pointed to a wall of monitors. "It could be any of the cities. It might be impossible to narrow it down."

"It seems DARPA has progressed farther than we thought on lasers," Gatewood said, now appearing self-conscious.

"Do you have something?" Tess asked, pouncing on

what she perceived to be a weakness, rare for the secretive HITE director.

"Possibly," he admitted. "I have enough information to know, or, at least, to *suggest* that Skyenor was near the final phases of a substantial laser weapon."

"Who else has it?"

He shook his head. "Tess, I believe they can destroy a city."

She had never seen Gatewood look so pale, so threatened, almost defeated. It scared her. If the man who held the keys to the most advanced weapons and technology on the face of the earth was *this* worried, then it was even worse than the apocalypse she'd been imagining. "How would they deliver such a weapon?"

"I have a team working on it. I'm not certain, but it must involve space. My best and brightest tell me it *is* possible if there's enough power."

"Where would they get power like that?"

"Humans are good at producing power. There are plants all over the world, and there are extraordinary new technologies—mass battery, Low-Energy Nuclear Reaction, E-Cat, nanotubes, fusion, solar sails, expanded kilo power, and . . . " His hesitation made her even more nervous.

"What?" she prompted.

"Nuclear power."

She looked at him aghast. "Are you telling me they can deliver nuclear through *laser*?"

"Yes."

Chapter Forty-Three

WASHINGTON, DC

April 3rd - 8:53 am

Anatoly, a stocky Russian, who was still arrogant over his successful killing of the most prized target, The Astronaut, made sure the incoming video call was encrypted.

The assassin was strong as an ox, and someone once said he looked like one, with his pockmarked face and thick neck. The person who'd made that observation had died painfully very shortly after uttering the insult.

"This is good job I did," he said upon seeing Tolstoy's face on the small screen in his large hand.

"A little messy," Tolstoy said curtly.

"Some time death is not pretty."

"There are now three jurisdictions investigating the death because it took place at the Lincoln Memorial—US Park Police, Washington Metropolitan Police Department, and for some reason the FBI," Tolstoy said.

"But man is dead. That was what you wanted. He is dead, and we have his phone."

"Yes," Tolstoy conceded, having no intention of engaging in a debate with the thug she didn't even like the sight of, and certainly didn't consider worthy of any more of her valuable time. "However, we have a new problem."

"New?" the man asked, as if he were a cat and there might be a new mouse to "play" with. "Tell me this problem and I will solve it for you. I am the problem solver."

"There is a couple—an American man and a Chinese woman. I sent you the dossiers. He is Chase Malone, a wealthy tech entrepreneur, she is a former MSS agent, extremely dangerous."

"As you know, I am former KGB. We sometimes laugh at MSS agents."

"Things have changed," Tolstoy said. "Back when the KGB still existed, maybe you could take the MSS lightly, but that would not be wise today."

"It's no matter. I am to kill them, and without caring who they work for, or who they used to work for."

"That's what I like to hear."

"I'll show you what KGB does to MSS."

"Yes," she said, annoyed. "These two could be a real problem though. They have resources, weapons, training."

"I'm not afraid," Anatoly said.

"I know you're not afraid. That's why you were given this assignment, because you are fearless," she said, while thinking *stupid and reckless*. However, there was no arguing with the results that Anatoly had provided thus far. "You are to spare no resources."

"Perfect."

"There will be a sizable bonus if these two are eliminated by the end of today. I repeat, eliminated by *the end of the day*."

"Then they will be." Anatoly had more than thirty

personnel available. "I can take over a small country with my men."

"I've transferred another twenty."

Anatoly laughed, surprised. "Then you want me to take over the medium country."

"Just kill Malone and the woman." Tolstoy did not like the unplanned appearance of Chase and Wen. However, every contingency had been anticipated.

After the unpleasant development of that Astronaut breaching their secrets, causing them to have to eliminate the scientists, the final hours were going to be messy. "Nothing can go wrong, do you understand?"

"Yes. Of course. I am professional."

"I don't care how many die," she said as she thought of Chase, the Chinese woman, the director of DARPA, and the others. Tolstoy's superiors may have been concerned, but Tolstoy knew there would be surprises and unknowns to deal with. That's why more than two hundred sleeper cell agents and mercenaries were on alert and now in action.

Tolstoy was one of the best because every detail was planned for, and the ones that could not be planned for were addressed by throwing large numbers at any issue that might arise—numbers as in plenty of cash and plenty of operatives.

Anatoly checked his tablet. "I see the dossiers. This pretty girl does not look so dangerous to me."

"She is *beyond* dangerous."

"I will take your word for it. But this Chase Malone, he looks like boy scout. Surely he cannot be dangerous."

"Surprisingly resourceful for someone out of his element."

"We will remove this problem for you."

"I have complete confidence."

After finishing the call with Tolstoy, Anatoly reviewed the last known sightings of his new targets and mumbled, "Hell is with me," to their pictures, as if this might intimidate his prey. He stared at the photos a little longer, perhaps thinking they might deteriorate under his threat, but really he was memorizing every detail. To some, Anatoly might have seemed to be a big clumsy Russian oaf, but he was, in fact, a stunningly efficient operative who had an uncanny ability to recognize his targets from far distances and under any disguise. He liked to think of himself as a wolf, able to track and hunt his prey from miles away, then kill them in a blinding moment of terror.

"They will not be a problem." He picked at his face, "No," he chuckled, "not a problem."

He called his second in command with orders of where to place units around the city. The dossier indicated it was unlikely Chase and Wen would be leaving Washington before the end of the day, but if they did, it would be to Baltimore, Philadelphia, or Virginia Beach via helicopter.

"I have helicopter, too," Anatoly said to the file. "You are already dead."

Chapter Forty-Four

VIENNA, VIRGINIA

April 3rd - 9:00 am

Tess studied the stream of reports coming into Mission Control. "It doesn't make sense," she said to Linda. "We've got three previously unreported Russian cells killing American scientists. Does the FBI have anything on this?"

"Just what's in the reports," Linda said.

Tess scrolled through a few screens. "I'm talking about prior activity for many of these?"

"Nothing, this is the first."

"How do you explain that, then?"

"We got another one," one of the technicians announced.

"Four cells now," Tess said, frustrated. "A couple more and it will be a full-fledged invasion."

"Could the Russians really be planning to take out an entire city?" Linda asked.

"Get me Tim Hyland in Moscow, and I want Ren

Havens in Belgium. If the Russians are doing something this drastic, our CIA operatives must have something."

"Nothing is in the report," Linda said.

"After what we've learned from the reports, these incidents, and sightings, perhaps now something will come into focus. They're going to an awful lot of trouble to make sure we don't unravel the particulars of whatever Blackout is." She flipped through another screen, bringing up live images of the top ten potential targets based on their AI algorithms. "This is after processing inputted data and projecting strategic advantage results."

"Too broad with the time we have left," Linda said, checking the clock.

"They don't seem too intent upon maintaining secrecy," an analyst commented, as he pointed to a screen indicating a fifth cell.

"This is indeed bold action," Tess said. "The Russian president is definitely looking to shake his domestic trouble."

"Taking a page out of the old Soviet playbook?" the analyst replied. "Trouble at home tends to go away once there's trouble abroad."

Tess stared at a map of the United States, projected on Mission Control's largest screen. "Study the cities most likely to be targeted," she said. "Cleveland, Cincinnati, Baltimore, Philadelphia, Norfolk/Virginia Beach, Manhattan, Newark, Indianapolis, Raleigh, Houston. That's the most likely bunch, but there are dozens more just below that, and the percentage difference in probability between them and the primary is in the single digits."

"It could be anywhere."

"It's difficult to know what to do," Tess agreed. "And I

alone cannot authorize the evacuation of an American city, let alone ten or more of them. The economic fallout, public relations disaster, international sign of weakness and embarrassment, means that's *not* going to happen."

"The Russians must know that," the technician said. "We're screwed either way."

Tess thought of the president. It was an impossible decision. "There must be a weakness," she said, a sudden surge of inspiration in her voice. "They're trying too hard to cover it up."

"How?"

"By killing all those scientists."

Linda reappeared. "Hyland is holding from Moscow."

"I'll take it in Secure," Tess said. "In the meantime, I want a list of any related scientists that might be the next targets. Crosscheck everything they're working on. Whatever the Russians are doing, the link is the scientists. Find out *why* they're killing these people."

"Anything else?"

"Yeah," Tess said, a dire expression on her face. "Protect the ones that are left. Get IT-Squads, FBI special teams, the secret CIA domestic dark ops out there. The next scientist that dies is on us. Make sure it doesn't happen!"

Once closed inside Secure, Tess took a deep breath.

Tim Hyland, the CIA station chief in Moscow, was one of the top people in the agency. *"Average doesn't get you an assignment in Moscow."* However, more than that, Tess had always liked him; a nice guy and straight shooter who reminded her of a Midwest farmboy. Not the typical type you saw in espionage, but it worked for him. Hyland had earned the loyalty of those above and below him with ease. She didn't know anyone who *didn't* like Tim, and she wouldn't be surprised if some of his counterparts on the Russian side likewise enjoyed his friendly, mild-mannered ways and easy sense of humor. Hyland was also a brain. If the Russians were making a move, he would have a sense of it, particularly a move that hadn't been made since the days of Brezhnev.

"Tess," the warm, raspy voice greeted her. She could tell he was smiling. She was, too.

"Timmy," she said, "I wish I had time to catch up, but we've got a big one kind of shaking things up around here."

"What can I do to help?"

She gave him the background of the cells, the scientists, and sent him photos and data files of who and what they had. "We're coming up empty. Can you shed any light?"

"I talked to Jane Ramsey earlier," he said, referring to a deputy CIA director who was coordinating the agency's response. "I reviewed the initial reports, but it's grown since then."

"I'd say."

"Jane Ramsey is holding now. I'll let it go to voicemail. I don't know, Tess . . . this is concerning."

"That's understating it a little, don't you think?"

"Yes, but this kind of aggression . . . It seems way off base."

"Domestically, is there anything threatening the Russian president?"

"There's always *something*, and I'd say he's quite a bit more defensive than we've seen in recent times, but nothing to warrant this."

"We're missing something."

"If the Kremlin wanted a distraction, they'd be looking at Ukraine, Eastern Europe, maybe even Central America.

This is far beyond that. If this is accurate, this could be the hottest we've been since the Cuban missile crisis."

Tess shook her head. "It's so much worse. That was a show down, and we had the clear advantage. If they have *this* weapon, they're about to erase an American city and write a new future for the world, one where Russia is in charge."

Chapter Forty-Five

WASHINGTON DC

April 3rd - 9:02 am

Wen kept a small duffle concealing an MP7 submachine gun on her lap as she scanned the patrons in the busy pizzeria just off the National Mall. Although she saw no overly suspicious people, under the circumstances, everyone bothered her for one reason or another.

They found The Astronaut sitting nervously at a table in the back. Normally, Wen was the only person Nash would let hug him, but as she approached, he shook his head.

"I'm very happy to see you," she said, knowing that whenever he was agitated or upset about something he could not take affection, even from her.

"It's busy," The Astronaut said, as if this were a personal attack against him. "I already ordered for us." The Astronaut was always efficient and, in this case, Chase and Wen were quite hungry, so they didn't even care what he'd chosen for them.

Chase placed three items on a napkin in front of Nash.

The Astronaut studied them one by one—the flash drive from Hayward's house, Skyenor's phone, and then the watch. Nash picked up Hayward's watch and held it lovingly, as if it were a sacred artifact.

Chase relayed brief details of each item, but Wen watched, and could tell The Astronaut wasn't really listening. She tapped Chase's thigh under the table. He met her eyes and understood. Chase stopped talking for a minute. Not all The Astronauts were friends (and they certainly didn't all get along, or even like each other), yet they shared a bond. An understanding similar to what military veterans found in the camaraderie of others who had survived the same battles they had. However, in this case, Hayward and Nash had been close, and had worked together many times.

As Nash held his old friend's watch, they could see him mourning the loss. The waiter approached and placed two pizzas on the table.

Nash quickly folded the three items into the napkin and pocketed them. Then his face fell as he looked at the pizzas.

"What's wrong?" Wen asked.

"There are forty-nine and a half pepperonis on my pizza," he replied, rapidly tapping his finger on the table as if working an imaginary calculator.

Chase and Wen looked at each other. Chase almost asked, *'What's the difference?'* but then remembered that these types of things were a big deal to Nash, particularly when he was already distraught about his friend.

"I was *very* specific in my instructions," The Astronaut said, looking at the pizza as if it might be dangerous. "Usually they do it right here. I have been here seventeen times over the last thirty-three months, and it is always right. Why would they do it wrong this time?"

"Can't we just take one off?" Chase asked.

Nash looked at him as if he'd just proposed pouring skunk's blood on it. "No! A pizza must be a certain way: eight slices, six pieces of pepperoni per slice, for a total of forty-eight pieces of pepperoni. This is not difficult math."

"But—"

"The numbers *matter*," The Astronaut continued. "Additionally, Chase Malone, you are incorrect, removing one pepperoni would not rectify the situation. There are forty-nine and a *half* pepperonis. . . This pizza is ruined." The Astronaut looked befuddled again, as if discovering the fiasco for the first time. "How did that half a pepperoni get on my pizza?"

"Perhaps you could just eat the slices that have the correct six pieces of pepperoni on them," Wen suggested.

The Astronaut looked at her warm eyes. Her face and her very presence soothed him. He looked back at the pizza. "Those are the two offending slices." He pointed them out.

Wen rotated the pizza so they were farthest from him. "Is it okay if I remove them?" she asked.

"Yes. I don't need them . . . they do not have the correct number."

Chase glanced at the other pizza (artichoke hearts and red onions), happy there were no incorrect numbers on his.

Even after the offending slices were off and out of sight, Nash still looked hesitantly upon his potential lunch, but after a nod from Wen, he tried one. "It is not as good as usual, but I think it is probably safe to eat."

With the 'crisis' averted, Wen gave him a smile, and then, ever vigilant, scanned the room and main entrance again.

The discussions moved to the items they had brought. The Astronaut retrieved them from his pocket, unfolded the napkin, and then took out a small cable which he connected to Skyenor's phone, plugging the other end into a custom computer tablet that he had made.

"This will download all the contents of his phone."

"Will it get past the heavy encryption?" Chase asked. "Will you be able to get into it?"

The Astronaut looked at him as if this were the most ludicrous question he'd ever been asked—at least since Chase had asked if he could just take the extra pepperoni off—but answered calmly. "It may take a few hours." Next, he picked up the flash drive and pushed it into a slot in his tablet. "Since presumably Hayward configured this drive, I should be able to get into it sooner."

While the drive and phone were busy, The Astronaut picked up the watch.

"Finally, the watch."

Chapter Forty-Six

WASHINGTON, DC

April 3rd - 10:18 am
18 hours 26 minutes until 4:44AM on 4/4

Chase and Wen headed back down the Mall towards their car. "So if The Astronaut made the watch for Hayward, how come he couldn't tell us what the contents were?"

"I think he wants time," Wen replied.

"We don't have time."

"Time *alone*."

"Oh," Chase said.

"He promised he'd call us soon."

"So where are we going now?"

"DARPA."

"And they'll just let us in?"

"If Tess tells them to, and if The Astronaut gets something from the phone, and . . . " Wen changed her stride. "Those aren't shadow people."

Chase turned his gaze in the direction she'd been

looking and saw at least ten operatives heading toward them.

"Who are they?"

"I don't know, but I'm pretty sure they work for whoever's planning operation Blackout."

"Then we must be getting close to something. Otherwise they wouldn't be sending the whole army after us."

Wen nodded tightly. "Right."

"Either way, we're sure keeping the DC police department busy today."

"At least The Astronaut got away," she said.

"At least *our* Astronaut got away," he amended. Chase looked back over his shoulder down the mall. He couldn't see the Lincoln Memorial anymore, but he thought of Hayward dying there.

They jogged past the Smithsonian Castle, named for James Smithson, a French-born British-raised man who had never even been to Washington. Smithson had left a substantial fortune to his nephew under the condition that if the nephew died without heirs, the money would go "to the United States of America, to start a national museum in Washington, under the name of the Smithsonian Institution, for the increase and diffusion of knowledge."

"Got your gun?" Wen asked as they jogged.

"Always."

The nephew did, in fact, die with no heirs, and the money was used to found the Smithsonian in 1846, and to construct its first building, the distinctive Seneca red sandstone castle, completed in 1855. It remained a mystery as to why Smithson left such a large bequest (estimated to be as much as $200 million in today's money) to start a museum in a place he'd never been, although his body was now entombed inside the Smithsonian castle.

"They're trying to hem us in!" Wen yelled.

"Run!" Chase shouted as more men appeared.

Today, the Smithsonian's collections include 154 million items held in the Institution's nineteen museums, twenty-one libraries, nine research centers, and a zoo, which are collectively visited by thirty million people each year, and has an annual budget of $1.2 billion.

"Where are they all coming from?" Chase yelled as they ran from now more than fifteen pursuers.

"We can't fight that many out in the open," Wen shouted.

"And we'd risk killing lots of innocent tourists," Chase answered. Many people were already fleeing in panic at the sight of the armed men.

Several of the operatives opened fire. "Apparently the people after us don't care about innocent bystanders."

The bullets narrowly missed Chase. "We need cover!"

Wen searched for anywhere they could avoid being slaughtered.

"In here!" Chase yelled.

Wen looked up at the Smithsonian's National Air and Space Museum and almost smiled. It was ready-made for a shootout. With endless places to hide and lots of fortified warplanes, it was just the kind of setting she needed to take out one or two dozen soldiers of fortune.

"I think you're getting good at this," Wen said.

Suddenly, the huge, windowed entrance walls exploded, shattered shards of glass raining all around them.

"I think our friends back there just paid the entrance fee for us," Chase yelled as he dove into the building, Wen close behind.

"Yeah, with RPGs," Wen said, stunned that their attackers would use rocket propelled grenades in the

Nation's capital in *broad daylight*. "That'll get someone's attention."

"It got mine!"

Chase and Wen were nearly stampeded by the terrified, screaming crowds running for the exits.

Inside, it was as if they had entered another world. The vast space was filled with full-sized planes suspended from the ceiling, protruding from walls, and parked on the floor. Silver, gleaming, colorful flyers of yesteryear, all gathered for history and posterity. One could easily imagine the beautiful, winged machines having personalities all their own, as if they could tell stories of great adventures, of flights they'd flown.

However, there was no time to talk of aviation splendor. Chase and Wen had just stumbled into more of a disaster movie than a history class. The museum had an instant feel of plane crashes, death, and destruction as the armed men machine-gunned through the crowd with a complete disregard for innocent life.

Chapter Forty-Seven

NEW YORK CITY

Jie Shi took a sip of water and brushed her long, silky black hair from her eyes, looking even prettier in the backdrop of the five-star hotel suite. The room, a perk available when vacant and at no charge to her important lover, had been arranged by a simple phone call.

The congressman smiled, glancing over at the tussled and unmade bed as if he might want to return for a second round.

Jie Shi allowed the sparkle in her eye to leave it up to him. He checked his watch, a disappointed look on his face.

"Tomorrow," he said.

"I hope so," the-twenty-six year old whispered, as if there was nothing she would like more. However, nothing could be further from the truth. Happy he preferred room service, and young Asian women, Jie Shi considered herself lucky. The congressman could have been an overweight, bald, sixty-something pig. And although more than twenty years her senior, he was actually fit and handsome. She marveled that a man so close to fifty could be nearly insatiable in bed.

"I was wondering if you could do me a favor," she asked in her sweetest voice.

"Name it," the congressman replied, sounding as if he were a generous person, which he was. Happy and content after their encounter, and now finishing a fine lunch, he was ready to give his "little China doll" anything she desired.

"You are familiar with the company Denny Tech?"

He raised an eyebrow and set his glass of wine down. "I am."

"Then you know that the FBI is investigating them?"

He looked at her carefully, his facial expression going from confusion to approaching anger.

"Don't get so upset. You are chairman of the Intelligence committee. I know you have oversight and connections with the Bureau. All I'm asking is that they don't raid the offices this week."

"How are you involved with Denny Tech?"

"I'm friends with one of the junior executives. It's really not that big a deal, I don't really care what happens to them. But I have all my savings tied up in their stock. He gave me a tip, and so I bought in. I just need to sell it, but there is a funding thing. It means I can't sell it until the end of this week."

"So you bought stock with an insider-trading tip. That isn't good." He almost asked her if she was wearing a wire, trying to set him up. However, she had almost no clothes on, and *he* had chosen the hotel and booked the room, so it had to be safe.

"It's hardly insider-trading. It's not a lot of money, it's just everything *I* have. My same friend told me they knew they were being investigated, and that there was some big scandal. I don't even know what it's all about, but they said they were expecting to be raided any day. I just need a few days to get out."

The Congressman frowned. "I can't do it."

"You *can* do it. I know you have the authority and the contacts to get the delay."

"Well . . . you're right about that. I probably could."

"You're so important and good at negotiations." She touched his leg gently. "People do what you ask because you're so smart."

He thought for a few moments longer, then shook his head. "I'm not going to do it," he said at last. "I'm sorry you're going to lose your savings, but I refuse to jeopardize my career."

She looked hurt.

He stared at her for a moment, considering whether he should offer her some money, but that was another complicated mess. He wasn't exactly the wealthiest member of Congress—not yet, anyway. And getting funds out past his wife, or even his small team, from his campaign war chest for the next election, always brought up challenges. There was nothing he could really do to help her financially, so he just made another apology.

"I've never asked you for a favor before," she tried again. "This isn't that big a deal."

"You're asking me to interfere with a *federal* investigation."

"I don't want you to make it *stop*. It's not really interfering. What's a few days? They aren't going anywhere. The timing doesn't matter to anybody except me."

"I can't."

She looked down. "You don't really care about me."

"I do."

"No. All you care about is your career and your family."

As skilled a politician as he was, the congressman didn't know how to agree with her and deny it at the same time, at least not without consulting focus groups, polls, talking to a speechwriter . . . and of course none of *that* was going to happen. "I'm sorry," he said again.

"So am I," she said, looking back up, steel in her eyes. "It would be a shame if your wife found out about us. And I guess the voters wouldn't like it much either."

Chapter Forty-Eight

WASHINGTON, DC

April 3rd - 10:54 am

As bullets ricocheted inside the Air and Space Museum, Chase and Wen found cover around the many large exhibits.

"They may not be shadow people," Chase yelled, "but they seem just as intent on killing us!"

Wen, climbing on top of a giant gray bomber, didn't answer. Instead, she returned fire to the gunmen below.

Chase moved behind the polished silver antique Boeing and quickly found a staircase leading into the old craft. Inside, he found three kids who couldn't have been more than ten or twelve years old. Seeing the two boys and a girl huddled against the plane's inner wall, Chase quickly abandoned his idea of making a stand there. "Stay down," he whispered. "Don't go out there."

One of the boys gave him a crazy look, as if they had any intention of leaving.

Chase jumped from the top of the staircase and got

lucky, catching one of the black ops unaware, killing him with one shot.

Three more fell to the ground not far from him. Wen's handiwork gave him hope they just might survive this. Then he saw that the main concentration of their enemy was now under the gray bomber. Somehow, Wen had moved, and was now high in the air on a red, blue, and silver vintage Eastern Air Lines Douglas DC-3 that looked as if it had just rolled off the assembly line.

"Talk about the high ground," Chase muttered to himself while running to another staircase. Soon he was on a now-deserted elevated walkway heading toward the nose of a giant 747 that hung from the wall like some kind of avionics hunting trophy. From that vantage point, he spotted another group of armed men circling under a gorgeous TWA plane that must have been seventy years old, but still looked sleek and modern.

Wen wing-walked to the end of the Eastern turbo prop and made a death-defying leap to an ancient American Airlines mail plane that looked like it needed the cables holding it to the glass ceiling in order to fly.

From the top of the 747, Chase picked off two men running on the walkway, trying to stop Wen. A second later, she dropped from the plane and caught the railing, somehow dodging bullets and signaling Chase.

By the time he caught up to her, they were in the main hall heading away from the plane party.

"What are we doing?" he asked.

"They're chasing us," she said. "We can use that to our advantage."

"Ambush?" he asked, knowing her tactics.

"Exactly."

"Do we really have time?" He knew the police would be

there any second, and they might be taken into custody along with the mercenaries. "Getting arrested isn't going to help us figure out the weapon or target. The clock is ticking."

"We'll just have to make time."

"If it's that easy."

They entered another cavernous section of the building, this one filled with spacecraft. "A little more room to navigate," she said.

"Look at that," Chase said, pointing to the moon lander. "And those are *real* rockets! Do you see how *big* they are?"

"Another time."

"Yeah, we've got to bring Tu here. He'll love this stuff."

"Find cover."

"I wonder if The Astronaut has ever been here?"

But Wen was already gone. He couldn't believe how quickly she'd gotten on top of the Apollo-Soyuz capsules.

Chase dashed behind the Apollo 11 moon lander and tried not to look at all the supersonic jets filling the ceiling. Reality came roaring back as ten men entered the mammoth space.

Four of them were dead before Chase could line up a shot, but then it was his turn. The survivors were so distracted by Wen's surgical assaults that Chase was able to cut down two of them with ease.

Wen, now concealed on the wide wing of a blue angel, higher than before, sprayed the scattering men and got two more.

"Two left," Chase whispered to himself, guessing where Wen would go next. If he got it right, they could trap the last two between them. He moved around a rocket and spotted her across the opening. Seconds later, two more men went down, and their ambush was complete.

"Are there any left?" Chase asked.

"Maybe somewhere else in the building, but we don't have time."

"Oh, *now* we don't have time!"

She pointed to the large doors as if to make him hear the sirens.

"Oh . . . That's a lot of police."

"Remember where we are."

They slipped out a fire escape, concealing their guns.

Anatoly, still inside the museum, found himself engaged in a gunfight with police officers. A gunfight he would win.

"They weren't shadow people," Wen said again while they snuck through a bit of landscaping and found their way onto Maryland Avenue.

"Then why were they so intent on killing us?"

"Because they know we're the only ones who can stop this thing."

"Blackout?"

"Yeah."

"I'll call Tess. She might be able to get somewhere if they can identify some of those bodies back there, find out who they belong to."

"Some were Russian," Wen said. "And I heard a German. Strange . . . "

"World War III," Chase said.

"Worse," she said. "At least in World War III there's a chance to fight back."

Chapter Forty-Nine

WASHINGTON, DC

April 3rd - 11:03 am
17 hours 41 minutes until 4:44AM on 4/4

Anatoly did not like to waste time talking to superiors. "The job does not always go smoothly, but it gets done."

"You started a war in one of America's favorite museums, in the middle of monuments to their democracy, and you failed to kill the targets."

He laughed. "So?"

"*Twelve* cops dead. Six more in the hospital."

Anatoly laughed again, as if this was amusing. "*So?* I will have Chase and Wen in the next hour."

"How many people did you lose?"

He fiddled with the space on his left hand. A ring finger was missing from long-ago, when he wound up on the wrong end of a torture session. "It does not matter. This will happen."

Tolstoy took a deep breath. Soon enough, she would see

to it that Anatoly wound up dead. "Try not to wreck another landmark in the process."

"What do *you* care about American history?"

"I care that we do not lose sight of our objective. *More* attention is not something we need. Understand?"

"I killed The Astronaut. We took care of Skyenor. Hell is with me. These two will join them soon."

"Make sure it is *very* soon."

Tolstoy ended the call and took another. Two more dead scientists. *They are certainly easier to kill than this former MSS agent*, she thought as she checked the time. *Maybe making noise in Washington isn't such a bad idea. Distractions, distractions. Keep them busy.*

Vienna, Virginia
April 3rd - 11:19 am

Coco Jordon was the now-acting head of DARPA. The African American engineer had a deep background in both AI and lasers, specifically for military applications. Tess had met her several times and liked her, although she was concerned with Coco's jumping back and forth between the government and private-sector positions.

"So tragic about Jay," Tess said as soon as Coco came on the line.

"I know you were old friends," Coco said. She had not been a big fan of Skyenor, believing he had been too conservative in dealing with the white-hot tech competition.

"Yes. And this is an initiation by fire for you. Have you reviewed the files I sent over?"

"How reliable is the data?" Coco asked, implying she was familiar with the situation.

"Very. We're going to lose an American city in seventeen hours."

"And you think it's the Russians?"

"There seems little doubt."

"Then they bought themselves some serious tech. And they did it in the dark."

"Doesn't that make sense? If they want to circumvent the 1967 space treaty to avoid the militarization of space, they need to keep it secret."

"They would need 500 kilowatt High Energy Lasers to do something like this, and a lot more systems beyond that HEL. However, last I checked, they were barely getting 100KW."

Linda interrupted, "Hyland is on from Moscow."

Tess muted Coco. "Tell him I'll call back in five minutes." She unmuted. "Where's DARPA? Skyenor told me there was a lot going on with Laser Weapon Systems and Direct Energy Weapons."

"It's not LaWS, DEW, or even HEL you should be worrying about. It's the Photon momentum Chemical lasers such as COIL, and Nuclear-Induced Plasmas of Gas Mixtures and Nuclear-Pumped Lasers, or NPL. Plus Space Based Lasers, or SBLs, Air Based Lasers, or ABLs, which are capable of delivering deadly payloads."

"That's a lot of alphabets and acronyms," Tess said. "Even for Washington. I don't see how shooting satellites down with lasers, or even hitting targets on the ground, is tied into destroying an American city."

"They aren't trying to shoot satellites out of the sky," Coco said in an icy tone. "They are using the satellites for *guidance*. If the intel bears out, then I believe our adversaries are preparing to push a nuclear payload through precision stacking into a mid-sized city."

"Lasers by nuke?" Tess said.

"Afraid so."

"You're telling me that's really possible?"

"The technology exists. Who has it other than us, that's hard to say."

"Terrifying."

"You have no idea. Incredibly far beyond Hiroshima and Nagasaki, and without the fallout."

"What evil have we brought," Tess said. "This arms race, tech run . . . "

"Our job is to stay one step ahead, to always have the best weapons."

"We develop these things and our enemies steal them. When will it end?"

"Maybe sooner than we'd like."

Chapter Fifty

WASHINGTON, DC

April 3rd - 11:54 am

Chase and Wen walked briskly down Independence Avenue, planning to cut across the Mall just before the Washington Monument on 14th Street.

"It's The Astronaut," Wen said as she answered her phone.

"There's a list of scientists, high classified projects, DARPA, HITE, NSA data seeks, and others on Hayward's watch," Nash said in his all-business tone.

"What's HITE doing involved in this?" Chase asked, having only slight knowledge of the agency almost no one had ever heard of, and a few in the know weren't sure *really* existed.

"I've been tracking down the scientists," The Astronaut said, not bothering to respond to Chase's question. "Quite a few of them have died in the past twenty-four hours."

"Because they know something," Wen said. "If they don't know the target, they must know the weapon, and if they know the weapon, that might tell us how and where and even who . . . where are these scientists?"

"Scattered all over the country. I'm trying to find them, get them on the phone. I just spoke to one in DC. She knows what's going on. She's scared."

"Will she talk?" Chase asked.

"Not over the phone. But I got her to agree to meet you."

"Where?"

"I hope you're still near the Mall. She doesn't work too far from there. I told her Jefferson Memorial."

"Why?" Chase asked, not wanting to mention the Lincoln Memorial.

"She wanted somewhere public, but out-of-the-way. She'll be there in fifteen minutes."

"Okay. How do we recognize her?"

"I just sent you her photo. I got it from a government website."

"We'll be there, " Chase said. "Thanks."

After the call, they decided there wasn't time to retrieve their car. "It's about a ten minute walk. We can get a cab after we meet with the scientist," Wen said.

"Why didn't you tell The Astronaut what happened at the Air and Space Museum?"

"Just trying to keep him stable. He's got enough to worry about without thinking we might die any minute."

A man heading toward them caught Wen's attention. By the look of him, and the way he carried himself, she could tell he'd been trained. *But by who?*

"Potential shadow," she whispered only loud enough for

Chase to hear. She moved her hand into the duffel that concealed her submachine gun. "Coming up twelve o'clock."

Chase knew to remain casual. He glanced up and agreed with her assessment, having seen so many shadow people. Chase gripped the pistol under his parka, and immediately looked for others. There were always more.

When the man was about ten feet away, he looked up and met Wen's eyes. To her surprise, he spoke.

"Don't shoot."

She barely heard him, and registered his words as an odd statement under the circumstances, which instinctively made Wen *want* to shoot him.

"Watch him," Wen said quietly to Chase as she swiveled continuing to look for additional threats, only taking her eyes off the man long enough to do the most cursory survey. "Who are you?" she asked.

"I believe you call us the 'shadow people'."

Wen raised her duffel, her hand already poised on the trigger of her MP7, and pointed it at him.

"Don't shoot," he repeated.

"Why not?" she asked, her eyes darting in every direction, finger ready.

"Grimes sent me."

"Now *I am* going to shoot you," Chase said as they all stopped a few feet from each other.

"The Caymans wasn't his fault," the man said.

"This way," Wen instructed, moving toward something with better cover in a cluster of trees bordering a Rugby field across from the Bureau of Printing and Engraving.

"Don't worry. I'm alone," the man said, complying with Wen's corralling. "And I've got a message."

"I bet you do," Chase said.

"Let's hear it," Wen snapped, backing him up against a large tree.

"Belfort, the guy who hires us, found out that Grimes was meeting you. He keeps pretty close tabs on all of us, but especially Grimes and Shelby. He's been suspicious. Anyway, somehow he found out." The man stared past them into the trees, a worried expression on his face, then looked back to Wen. "They were waiting for Grimes and Shelby. Would have killed them both."

"But Grimes never came," Chase said.

"Grimes has a few friends . . . and many contacts."

"Someone told him?" Wen asked, still holding her gun against the man.

"Yeah."

"Then why in the hell didn't he get word to us *before* we walked into that ambush?" Chase demanded.

"He tried. Obviously it wasn't successful."

Chase scoffed. "*Obviously.*"

"Why should we believe any of this?" Wen asked.

"Because the same people are after Grimes and Shelby now."

"*What* people?"

Chapter Fifty-One

NEW YORK CITY

April 3rd - 12:19 pm

Jie Shi was furious with the congressman, but there was still time. She placed a call. "Liquidate my position," she said to the man on the other end.

Someone listening in might have believed she was speaking of stocks. They would be wrong.

Jie Shi checked her hard drive back up. She had enough dirt on six powerful US politicians to make things go her way on any number of projects her superiors were involved with, but her future depended on just one.

Mister congressman, she thought, looking at his photos and the details of his life she had amassed, *why do you believe you are safe?*

Chasing Time

Vienna, Virginia

Tess sat in Mission Control surrounded by her top analysts. "We have to figure this out."

"Five-Fours?" a man said.

"Yes, we need to know the meaning of five fours. Why did they choose that date and time?"

"We've run it a million different ways," the analyst replied. " We looked at it as fifty-four, as five plus four being nine, and a number of other variations."

"And?"

"It appears that five fours is twenty. Twenty being the number for teamwork and diplomacy."

Tess stared back at him for a moment. "Are you serious?"

"There could be five teams of four," another analyst suggested. "Maybe five strike points, not a single one."

"You're telling me nothing," Tess said, annoyed. "In fact, you're telling me we know *nothing*. How can we have the code name of this operation, the date and time it's going to happen, and yet we have no way to attach any *meaning* to it?"

He tilted his head. "It could simply be that was the time it all comes together."

"It is not random. Five fours *means* something." She sighed, rubbing a hand over her face. "Maybe it does mean twenty. That seems logical, but what does twenty *mean*?"

The two men shared embarrassed, blank looks.

"Linda, find me The Astronaut!" Tess shouted. "And not the dead one."

"You mean Nash Graham?" Linda asked.

"Yes," Tess said impatiently, even though it was a fair

question. CISS had, over the years, employed the services of eight different Astronauts, including the one killed on the mall. But Nash was her favorite. Nash was the best. And Nash was being hunted now, so he would not be easy to reach.

"I've got it," an analyst said, getting to his feet. "To the Chinese, the number four is considered bad fortune. Similar, but worse to how the number thirteen is seen in the western world."

"Why?"

"Because 'four' is pronounced 'Si' in the Chinese language, the same as 死 death."

Washington, DC
April 3rd - 12:22 pm

Popov stared at the two agents. The two men were her performers. "You take care of this, and then get out of Washington by midnight, understand?"

"Yes." The tall one glanced at the file. "Jie Shi is an important MSS asset. Do we really have the okay to eliminate her?"

Her stern stare gave him the answer, *Either way, don't ask.*

"What about the congressman?" the other asked.

Popov shook her head. "He'll be dead tomorrow."

They nodded. "We'll let you know when it's done."

The Russian agent was managing far more than her fair share. Blackout had changed her life. *There is so much to do,* she thought. *And almost no time remaining.*

Washington, DC
April 3rd - 12:31 pm

The man stood nervously against the tree, knowing Wen could kill him in an instant, but he thought she was beginning to believe him. However, it was Belfort and the Circuit that worried him more than the woman in front of him—submachine gun or not.

"What people?" Wen repeated. His time to answer had expired.

He looked at her as if this were a silly question. "Shadow people," the man said. "But that's only what *you* call them. They're all really just mercenaries for the Circuit."

"I know that much. Who are they? Who is the Circuit?"

The man looked back out to the street.

"*Who are they?*" she demanded, all patience lost.

"I wish I knew."

"Then why are you here?" Wen asked, keeping her concealed gun trained on him. "Why are you and Grimes putting your life at risk to allegedly help us?"

He looked back to the street. "There's enough people in Washington gunning for you. Belfort has a private army in the city, seventy or eighty people all looking for the kill. First one who brings in your heads earns a ten million dollar bonus."

"Why?"

"I don't know. They just want you dead. Apparently you ticked off the wrong somebody."

"Now the Circuit finds out you talked to us . . . "

He glanced back into the trees. "They'll put me on the same list with you and Grimes."

"Are you expecting someone?"

He stared into Wen's eyes. "Haven't you learned anything? They know *everything*. When the Circuit is after you, you *always* have to be expecting someone. They keep coming."

Chapter Fifty-Two

WASHINGTON, DC

April 3rd - 12:34 pm

Chase looked around at the trees, at the steady traffic and the Bureau of Printing and Engraving across the street. It didn't feel right. "Something's off," he said. "I don't believe him. I think it's another trap."

The man didn't take his eyes off Wen. "You know I'm telling you the truth. Wen Sung, former MSS agent trained under Rong Lo, parents deceased. Sister terminated by MSS. You both regularly work with the secret CIA division known as CISS." He quickly rattled off additional facts about her—preferred weapons, language skills, martial arts proficiencies, number of suspected kills, affiliations—and then started on Chase before Wen cut him off.

"How do you know all this?"

"I told you, they know everything."

Chase tapped her. "We have to go, remember?"

"What's the message?" Wen growled.

"Grimes is on your side."

Chase laughed. "So Grimes wanted you to tell us he's our friend now? Why? Just so we wouldn't think he's a jerk? Because it's too late for that. You don't get to try to kill us for years and then say, *Time out, let's be friends.*"

"Grimes is crazy," the man said. "And angry—"

"Bad mix," Wen said.

"Maybe, but in his case, it works in his favor. He is also patient, and should not be underestimated." The man stopped talking for a few moments, as if listening for something, then continued. "He wants to take down the Circuit. And he needs your help to do it."

"Why would we do that?" Chase asked.

"Because you also want to take down the Circuit. And you need *his* help to do it."

"Keep talking," Wen said.

"You want the shadow people gone from your life. So does Grimes. In spite of his history with you, he's a good man."

"Really?" Chase scoffed.

"Grimes simply took the wrong assignment. He had no idea in the beginning. It was supposed to just be a big payday. But you can trust him."

"And I'm supposed to take your word for it?"

"Yeah."

"Why?" Chase asked.

"Because you could kill me, and maybe I could've killed you. We're both just standing here because Wen has already decided that I'm telling the truth."

"How do you know that?" Chase asked.

"She hasn't killed me yet."

"Seems a big risk to just tell us Grimes is a nice guy," Chase said.

"It's not just about you anymore. You have to think

about the little boy, Tu. It's not just the MSS after him. Belfort has made deals . . . there's a lot of big stuff going on. The Circuit is out of control. Grimes can help you get to them."

"And what about you?"

"I'm hoping they won't find me out. Grimes couldn't find another way to get word to you. It had to be in person. He asked me to do it. I owe my life to Grimes, so . . ."

"And if they come for you?" Wen asked.

"I'll go underground."

"Not a fun life," Chase said. "We've been on the run a few years. You won't like it."

"That's because you've been doing it wrong. You keep getting mixed up in trouble. I'm going to just disappear. There are any number of tropical paradises scattered around the globe for a guy like me. I've got a little cash stashed. I'll just blend in and have a little too much tequila every now and then. I've seen enough action in my life, I don't mind sleeping the rest of it away."

Chase nodded, thinking, *I know exactly what he means.*

"I assume Grimes wants to try again? Set another meeting?"

"Yeah, but first there's one more thing, the most important part of the message—"

Wen saw the red laser dot on the man's forehead an instant before his head exploded.

Wen crawled to the man's body. She knew he was dead, but had to see if he had a wallet or phone. "Nothing." She wasn't surprised. His car must be nearby, but there would be no way to find it, even if they had time.

She and Chase moved through the trees until they reached Maine Avenue. They dashed across, dodging an ice cream truck and a tour bus. Safely in the grassy median, they stopped behind a lone tree surrounded by shrubs. "See anything?" Chase asked.

"I saw the laser sight on him, but my brain couldn't send the words of warning out to him or get my nerves in action before it was too late."

"I mean the sniper, the shadow people, anyone still on us?"

"They're going to have to find us again," Wen said. "Later." She pointed to three Metropolitan Police cruisers racing up Wallenberg Place.

"That was fast," Chase said, surprised they had anyone to spare after the war at Air and Space.

Chase and Wen fled across the other lanes of traffic, through more trees, and were suddenly jogging along the Tidal Basin, a hundred and seven acre body of ten-foot deep water created to harness the tides of the Potomac River to clear silt and sediment from the Washington channel. The two mile trail was flanked by Cherry blossoms. The floral scent would have calmed most people—or at least those who weren't running for their lives.

Chapter Fifty-Three

VIENNA, VIRGINIA

April 3rd - 12:40 pm
16 hours 4 minutes until 4:44AM on 4/4

Tess looked at the large screen inside Mission Control. "Zoom that one," she said. The satellite image showing real-time footage of Washington grew larger. She studied the rutted face of the man.

"Who is he?" Tess asked, feeling fortunate to have a lead on the space weapons fiasco.

"Spinx is the only name we have," an analyst replied. "Obviously Caucasian, no data base match."

"Nothing?"

"No. We picked him up on footage outside Columbia, and he matched footage from Cornell yesterday."

"Show me," she said, having already reviewed data from the deaths other prominent scientists at the top universities.

They replayed the footage for her. At the same time, IT-Squad operatives reported in from the field.

"Eyes on," one of the operatives reported.

"At 4th and C Street, have visual on him," another announced.

"Where'd we get the name?" Tess asked.

"We had brief audio when he made a call," the analyst explained. "Identified himself to the person on the other end as 'Spinx.'"

"Who was on the other end?"

"We're working on it. Archive feed review at NSA found where Spinx is staying. A team is there now." Another screen showed the crew inside his hotel room.

"Shootout at the Smithsonian," another analyst reported.

"Which one?" Tess asked.

"Air and Space. Spinx was involved."

Tess watched the footage obtained minutes before as Anatoly and three others left the museum. "Why there?"

"There's nothing in here," the lead operative on site at the hotel reported. "He seems to have scrubbed or taken anything from the bathroom that might've given us DNA samples."

Then Tess saw earlier frames from Air and Space. "Chase and Wen," she whispered, astounded, but not surprised.

"We have a name on who Spinx called," an analyst said. "Tolstoy."

"Confirmation on what we already suspected," Tess said. "Tolstoy is having the scientists killed. Who the hell *is* Tolstoy?"

"Should we grab him?" the IT-Squad leader asked.

Spinx worried Tess. He was too careful, too mysterious. "Not yet."

"Reports of several Metropolitan Police and Park

Service Police killed at Air and Space," the man said. "Let's get the bastard."

Tess shook her head. As much as she wanted to arrest and interrogate Anatoly, she needed to know where he was going.

"Why not?" the man asked, frustrated.

"Torture takes too long. What he's done is of no consequence compared to what's going to happen in sixteen hours."

She called Chase. No answer. "Find Chase Malone," she said. "He was at Air and Space. He and Wen left there alive. Most likely they're the reason Anatoly was there. Tell me where they are this moment."

Tess again stared at the footage of Hayward Hughes' murder. "It's Spinx," she said, seeing Anatoly fire the fatal shot at Hayward and then check The Astronaut's body. She questioned her decision not to grab him.

As if reading her mind, Linda asked, "Why is he going to all that trouble to hide his identity?"

"Spinx isn't the mastermind. He's not even the trader of information and secrets. He's simply a killer."

"You think he'll lead us to Tolstoy?"

"Eventually."

Linda looked at the clock. "We don't have eventually."

"The more dots we connect and the more people within his orbit we identify, the closer we get to solving this."

"The audio came in from Air and Space," an analyst said. "Spinx is speaking Russian. The others are, too. Someone called him Anatoly."

"Feed that in," Tess said. "Tell me who he is."

"Already on it."

"It's all about his trail and his network, that's what we need from him."

"It just seems we could learn a lot more by questioning him directly," Linda said.

"A guy like this, someone who cleans up their DNA, the only kind of question he's going to answer is via enhanced interrogation techniques," Tess said, utilizing the preferred euphemism for torture.

Linda raised her eyebrows as if to say maybe that's what was needed.

"We'll see," Tess said. "Right now he's more important to me out in the world making and answering calls."

"Are we doing the plant?" one of the Squad members in the hotel room asked for confirmation. Tess considered the options. A man who knew enough to scrub his DNA would be able to locate listening devices inside the room. "Negative," she said. "Do joiners and surrounds instead." It was a much more complex process, particularly for a room the man could vacate at any time, but it was the prudent approach. "I just don't want to do anything to spook this guy, especially when we don't know what city they're targeting."

Joiners and surrounds required the installation of high-powered listening devices in the adjoining rooms, including the ones above and below. Video would also be acquired in the same level insertions. Quality wasn't quite as good as doing in-room surveillance, but it was almost impossible for a target to detect them.

"How much time do we have?" the man asked. His workload had just tripled. One benefit of joiners and surrounds meant getting caught during installation would be far less likely.

"Looks like he's getting on the subway," another agent reported.

"That's odd," Tess commented. "Why? I thought they had vehicles. Why is he on the subway?"

"Maybe he's meeting somebody," Linda said.

"Stay alert everyone!"

Chapter Fifty-Four

WASHINGTON, DC

April 3rd - 12:47 pm

After a sprint, Chase and Wen made it to the Jefferson Memorial, only two minutes late. The imposing monument, rising up out of granite and marble steps, forced an onlooker to pause.

The circular, open-air structure, constructed of white Imperial Danby marble, featured a shallow dome supported by a circular colonnade composed of twenty-six Ionic columns. "Kind of invokes the Parthenon," Chase said breathlessly. Even with the danger they had just escaped, the picturesque monument was especially beautiful now, with the cherry trees ringing the Tidal Basin in bloom. The Memorial and trees all reflected in the water like a painting, or at least a postcard.

"That's her," Wen said, seeing a nervous lady standing at the base of the bronze Thomas Jefferson statue towering twenty-five feet above her.

After quick introductions, the three of them walked out,

descending the steps. They found a private sitting area by the trees. The no-nonsense professor, Joan Osborne, pulled out a tablet and began her lessons.

"Here's what they're doing," Professor Osborne said. "It's both brilliant and frightening, and it changes the world forever." She drew a black line on the screen. "This is a city —doesn't matter which one, doesn't even matter how big. Now, this appears as a satellite. Once the satellite is in position, it shoots a laser straight down to the center of the city."

"But you said there can't be enough power on a satellite to do any real damage," Chase argued.

"That is correct. With currently known technologies, no significant damage can be done to a large earth-based target by a space-based weapon. *Significant* being the key word. Keep in mind there can be surgical strikes, certain assets that could be affected by something from space. That capability already exists. For instance, if you wanted to damage an aircraft carrier, or a specific building on a military base, even a vehicle driving on the road, that is all possible. But what I'm talking about is large-scale damage."

"Killing a million people, taking out a city," Wen said.

"Exactly," Osborne agreed, this time making a red line on the image. She drew it coming up from the ground at an angle. "That single laser from the satellite in space is not meant to be the entire weapon. It is more akin to the laser sights that the military uses on munitions. But it's a little more complex than that."

Wen involuntarily thought of the laser dot that appeared on the shadow person only minutes earlier.

Osborne drew three more red lines radiating up from different points around the city to form a pyramid, the black line from space now piercing the top center of the apex.

"These four beams come from power plants located outside of the target city. The closer the better, but ultimately distance is not a major factor. They are carrying the load. If they have the right facility, the beams form the pyramid. They are filled with intense energy. With the right power and settings, the city underneath will get so hot . . . it literally melts the city and everyone in it."

"That's frightening," Chase said, looking up and reading the inscription below the dome, *I have sworn upon the altar of God eternal hostility against every form of tyranny over the mind of man.*

"Would Russia really do this?" Wen asked.

"Do you know it's the Russians?" Osborne asked in reply.

"They're the ones running around killing everyone."

"It's their chance to finally win the cold war," Chase said.

"I thought the cold war was long over," Osborne said.

"Tell that to the Russians," Chase replied. "Can you imagine that kind of destruction? What happens if we lose a city and a million people in an instant?"

"Ask Japan," the professor said.

"Right, but this is so much worse."

"You want to talk about worse?" Osborne continued. "The power demands for a weapon such as this are so great, that it would effectively drain the power grid to the point of total collapse."

"Meaning?" Wen asked.

"We are talking about *complete* failure. No power on the entire East Coast. I'm no expert on the grid, but I would imagine we would lose most of the Midwest, and possibly Texas as well, if it was an East Coast city. If they hit somewhere in the middle of the country, we could lose it all. The West Coast, same scenario as the East."

"That will cause a whole other disaster," Chase said. "More deaths and massive economic destruction, especially depending on how long it takes to get the grid back up."

She looked at him as if his assessment was too simplistic. "The grid within a five hundred mile radius of impact might require massive repairs, or even need to be completely rebuilt."

Chapter Fifty-Five

WASHINGTON, DC

Osborne told Chase and Wen she was leaving town. "Washington is not the likely target, but I am a target now because of my knowledge." She closed her eyes, as if absorbing the dire news again for the first time. "An old friend of mine has a place in Luray, Virginia. I'll be safe there until this blows over."

They escorted the professor to her car, then hailed a cab back to their own. After the short taxi ride, Wen called The Astronaut.

"There is another scientist in Washington," Nash told them. "He is one of the world's experts on lasers."

"Will he meet with us?"

"I haven't been able to reach him, he didn't show up for work today. One of the government's secret labs. But I have a home address."

"He could already be dead," Wen said.

"Or in hiding," Chase said, thinking of Osborne.

The Astronaut gave them the address. Chase plugged it

into the navigation system. "Not far," he said. "Let's hope we're in time."

Vienna, Virginia

Tess watched a series of screens in CISS Mission Control as facial recognition programs sorted and identified everyone in the subway station.

"Look who we have here," an analyst said, reading from his monitor as a match came in from the man Spinx was speaking with. "Eddie Lukeman."

"Who's Eddie Lukeman?" Tess asked, sure she'd never heard of him before.

"He works for Belfort."

"*Shadow people* Belfort?" Tess asked. CISS had been trying to crack the mystery of Chase and Wen's secretive pursuers for nearly two years.

"The same. He was also a large donor to a certain congressman."

"Which one?" Tess asked, already dreading the answer.

"Jie Shi's boyfriend."

"Incredible," Tess said. "So the Russians must be very worried about Chase and Wen. Jie Shi is deep in the MSS, who have an execution-order on Chase and Wen, and now the shadow people who've been attempting to assassinate them forever."

Another IT-Squad was tracking Jie Shi. Tess hardly had time to check in on what yesterday had been her number one priority, but Blackout had suddenly made Jie Shi a distant number two. Yet anything having to do with China always easily stole her attention since she considered them the greatest threat.

"Where is Jie Shi?" Tess asked. "And Chase and Wen?"

"Jie Shi was in New York with the congressman this morning," the analyst said.

"Is she in DC now?"

"Checking."

"Maybe Spinx is also having an affair with Jie Shi," another analyst joked.

Tess shuddered.

Tess took a call from Gatewood in Secure. "Power isn't necessarily the problem for these weapons," the HITE director told her. "We've been working on other energy sources for lasers."

"Enough to let them destroy a city from space?" she asked, always frustrated by Gatewood's refusal to ever share all the details.

"It would be an amplification of where we are, but it is possible."

"How would someone have obtained that technology from HITE?" she asked, knowing of what Gatewood referred to as the agencies "death-sentence-secrecy."

"They did not obtain it from HITE. If someone has the ability to transform these substances to mass-power, they did so before we got there."

"What are we talking about here?"

"Minerals. Extremely rare minerals that can add to the power source."

"If I can do anything about this, I need you to elaborate."

He scoffed. "Tess, you can't do anything to stop the source. I just needed you to be aware that if you're counting on cutting this thing off by narrowing the possible power plants or denying the destructive capabilities of what Blackout could unleash . . . *don't*."

"Are you telling me Russia has access to these minerals in sufficient enough quantities to power a laser weapon capable of taking out a city?"

"I don't know. Intelligence is your business, mine is technology. It's there. They could have it, or someone else could." Gatewood thought of the only person in the world that he feared, a man who used to have his job, the only living former head of HITE, Kalor Locke, and worried that he might somehow be involved. But he did not express his suspicions to Tess.

"Thanks for nothing helpful, Holt. If you decide to give me some information I can *use*, you have my number."

"I'm just saying, don't count on the power supply to lead you to the perpetrators. And it may not be Russia." He thought again of Kalor Locke. "It could be anyone."

Chapter Fifty-Six

WASHINGTON, DC

Reviewing the latest information from Osborne and the new data The Astronaut had recovered from the assets Chase and Wen had collected, the three spoke for more than twenty minutes trying to find a breakthrough. Finally, without much progress, Nash gave them some good news.

"Certain interesting information from the flash drive you found at Hayward's place," The Astronaut said. "There is a man named Rod Irwin, who was convicted of espionage. Turns out he never gave up one of his co-conspirators."

"And?"

"They were trading all kinds of high-tech secrets. Advanced weapons systems, aerospace, all kinds of classified and restricted technologies. Hayward had traced some of the transactions to a foreign operative known as Tolstoy, and noted many of Irwin's schemes were connected to Blackout."

"Can he tell us anything?"

"Prosecutors believed that the co-conspirator was a US

agent—CIA or FBI. I think if we can find that agent, we can unravel Blackout."

"Where is Irwin now?"

"As luck would have it, he's serving his sentence at the federal prison in Petersburg, Virginia."

"We just caught our first break then."

"Only problem is, he's in the high security section of the facility."

"I'll call Tess," Wen said. "She can get him moved to the minimum security section where Mars is."

"And I'll get a hold of Mars," Chase said.

Petersburg, Virginia

Mars, a forty-five-year-old convict at Petersburg, was Chase's oldest friend. Years earlier, Mars had worked for Chase's mother's auto repair business, and been like an older brother to the up and coming billionaire, who was fifteen years younger.

He still had seven years remaining behind bars, two from his original sentence, and an additional five from a new charge after he'd escaped to save Chase's life. The billionaire had vowed to either get the conviction overturned, or break Mars out.

This might finally be the chance to get him out. If Mars helped stop Blackout, a presidential pardon would be a reasonable reward.

Mars scratched his chin. His weeks' worth of stubble was only slightly shorter than his close-cropped hair. The 6'4" convict looked out at the trees that separated the minimum security portion of the prison from a river, and freedom. Only a low, chain link fence prevented him from running. Mars had spoken to Chase minutes earlier, and now had a mission.

Save the world.

"Again?" Mars responded.

Mars thrived in prison by running multiple underground businesses while incarcerated. He'd also developed a method to help keep Chase's whereabouts unknown by utilizing "decoying." The plan flooded intel agencies, law enforcement, and other surveillance organizations with false reports and sightings of Chase and Wen, occurring at random intervals around the globe. The many people looking for them would get a constant stream of bad information. Through credit card use, surveillance cameras linked to facial recognition data bases, and a number of other related methods, the sightings would pour in at critical times and overwhelm those seeking Chase.

Being behind bars normally meant all communications were monitored and there was zero access to cell phones. However, Mars had several guards on his "payroll." He couldn't always get a phone, but he'd arranged many advantages that could be bought in any corrupt prison system; including the world's largest—the American system, which held more than 2.3 million people, giving it the highest incarceration rate of any country. The message had come in from his case worker, a career Bureau of Prisons employee who was building his retirement on what Mars, and a few other incarcerated high rollers, "tipped" him.

Mars spotted Irwin and started casually walking in his direction. Passing on the way to the weight pile, Mars nodded, a kind of not-too-friendly greeting one inmate gives to another when there was some familiarity between them.

Irwin nodded back. "You used to be inside," he said, his short white beard perfectly matching his white hair. Although Irwin was at least five inches shorter than Mars, he appeared big enough to handle himself in any routine barroom brawl. Prison fights, though, were a different thing. Size wasn't always the deciding factor. Experience and anger were generally more important, as well as alliances. Maybe that was why Irwin had initiated a conversation with Mars after recognizing him from the inside.

"Yeah, that's right," Mars said. "Got transferred over here about six months ago."

Irwin nodded, but said nothing.

Asking details was generally frowned upon between inmates, but in this case, Mars volunteered the information. "I was originally finishing up a dime at Lompoc, but I escaped."

Irwin's eyes widened, and he looked out toward the fenceless perimeter of the minimum-security prison as if wondering why Mars hadn't bolted again. "Really? You escaped?"

"Yeah." Mars allowed his gaze to wander to the perimeter as well.

"How much time did you have left on that dime?"

"Two years."

"Man, you were there and you ran? Why would you blow that for a new charge?"

"Friend was in trouble. Thought I could help."

"Must be some friend."

"Like a brother."

"I got a couple brothers I don't give a damn about."

"Not that kind of brother," Mars said. "The good kind."

Irwin nodded. "I guess so." He looked out to the old

soybean fields for a moment. "Still . . . that's a crazy thing to do. You end up helping him?"

"Yeah."

"Five years' worth of help?"

"I think so."

"Wish I had a friend like you."

Chapter Fifty-Seven

GEORGETOWN, WASHINGTON, DC

April 3rd - 1:34 pm

Chase knocked on the polished wood door of the stately row house. Wen scanned the area. The end unit allowed her to see around to the side street. Any number of suspicious vehicles concerned her, but when the tall, bespectacled scientist answered the door, very much alive, she relaxed a bit.

"Doctor Forbes?"

"That's right," the man replied somewhat cautiously, a mess of thick black hair betraying his calm demeanor.

"We're friends of Hayward Hughes. We really need to talk to you."

"About what?"

"I think you know," Chase said. "Laser weapons."

Forbes went still. "I don't know what you're talking about."

Chase spotted two suitcases in the hall behind him.

"That's not true. You were working with Hayward, helping with the DARPA project."

"Why isn't Hayward here?"

"I think you know the answer to that, too."

"He's dead?"

Chase nodded. "Afraid so."

"Did you kill him?" Forbes asked shakily. "Are you here to kill me?"

"Quite the contrary, Doctor Forbes. We're here to help you."

He started to close the door. "I don't need any help."

"You're scared."

"Damn right, I am. Four of my colleagues are dead, the DARPA director, and now Hayward. Scientists are becoming an endangered species."

"We can get you to a safe place," Wen said.

"I don't even know who you are."

"Listen, please, if we were here to cause you harm, we could have killed you already. We need to know what you know about laser weapons."

"It's classified."

"We're way beyond that," Chase said. "Somebody is using technology you helped to develop. They're planning to destroy an American city. They're going to do it tonight."

Forbes leaned heavily against the door. "Oh my god . . . I warned them this could happen."

"Who?"

"Skyenor, and the others on the team." He looked back inside, as if deciding how to escape.

"We need your help to stop it," Wen told him.

"Don't you want to know if such a thing is even possible?"

"We know it's possible," Chase said. "We want to know

what city, and who's doing it. In order to find that out, we need to learn how it works."

Doctor Forbes stared at them. "I'll give you five minutes." He stood aside and let them in. "I've been telling them for years that this could be misused. My research has always been in the area of lasers and energy development, but just like nuclear energy can be turned into a weapons program, so can lasers. That's what DARPA wanted . . . an insurmountable weapon."

"How is it insurmountable?" Wen asked, knowing they would have to find a way to stop it.

"There are two things you need to know about lasers," he said. "They are incredibly accurate and highly controllable as far as damage setting. Those are sought-after attributes for military applications. Although, that wasn't my initial area of research."

"You made that clear," Chase said. "But now a million people are going to die. Weren't there safeguards?"

"A laser is, of course, a beam of light, meaning it travels at the *speed* of light. That's 186,000 miles per second. Nothing goes faster. As a weapon, that is a devastating advantage." He paused and met Chase's eyes. "The only warning you get from an incoming laser is when it hits you."

"What's the second thing?" Wen asked, hoping there was a way to deactivate the weapon if they could find it.

"Lasers require a vast amount of power."

"And where would they get this power?"

"There are brokers in these things. The Russians are—"

"You think it's the Russians?"

Forbes nodded. "DARPA and the top brass at the Pentagon are concerned about the Kremlin's Peresvet, an ultra-secret and extremely complex laser weapon, but it's only part of Russia's high energy laser directed energy weapon system."

"You didn't answer my question," Chase said. "Could it be the Russians who are about to pull the trigger on this thing?"

"The Russians are all in, and have been pursuing lasers as long as we have. They could have the capability, but would they dare? I don't know the answer to that. I'm a simple scientist, not a geopolitical analyst."

"How can we find out their target? How can we stop it?"

He looked at his suitcases, and then at the closed door as if trapped, and sighed. "There could be dozens of potential strike points, depending on how they have configured the weapon, but—"

"A pyramid configuration," Chase said.

The doctor's face went ashen. "Then my guess is it will be one of two places." He took a deep breath and rubbed the back of his neck. "Power is the key. It's—"

Doctor Forbes collapsed to the floor at the same time the window shattered.

Chapter Fifty-Eight

PETERSBURG, VIRGINIA

April 3rd - 1:40 pm
15 hours 4 minutes until 4:44AM on 4/4

Mars and Irwin went silent as a couple of guards passed by.

"Why did you get put out here?" Mars asked, looking at the double high fences capped with razor wire. The gun towers could see and control the minimum security side where they were now, but they were only there for the "inside" convicts. Being moved from the locked-down higher security section to the "camp" was a world of difference.

"I'm not entirely sure." Irwin appeared suddenly nervous, as though a sniper might be waiting to take a shot at him. "My attorney thinks it's because some Fed wants to question me, and they'd rather do it out here than inside."

"Then it may just be temporary."

Irwin looked around. "I hope not."

"It can make you go crazy doing time out here," Mars

said. "This close to freedom, as if you could just walk over and touch it."

"Or just leave." Irwin smiled for the first time.

"Yeah, well, that didn't work out too good for me."

"You touched it and got burned."

"Yeah," Mars said, sighing. He watched a couple of hulking convicts bench pressing a scary amount of weight.

"How long were you out?" Irwin asked, clearly wanting to continue the conversation. "Before they got you, I mean."

"Few days."

"Five years for a few days . . . crazy." Irwin shook his head. "Did you at least get a decent meal with your woman?"

Mars looked out to the gun towers. "I did have the best pizza in New York."

"Must have been Lucali's."

"It was!" Mars said, laughing.

"That's not just the best pizza in New York, it's the best pizza in America. How they roll out the dough with empty wine bottles, that wood-fired oven . . . "

"And that tomato sauce. So perfect, I could eat it with a spoon." Mars licked his lips. "To have a Lucali's pizza right now, mmm, that alone was worth a few months onto my sentence."

Irwin smiled. "For one of their large basil and cheese, maybe just a few pepperonis, I might do an extra month, especially if it was out here." He lit up a cigarette, held out the pack towards Mars.

Mars shook his head. "No thanks. Never got the habit."

"Good thing. It's a nasty one. I was going to quit, but then there was the investigation, the depositions, the trial, all that stress. But I decided to quit again . . . then prison . . . and I finally thought, if there's ever a time in a man's life to smoke cigarettes, it's when he's doing twenty-five years in federal prison."

Mars whistled. "Twenty-five years, who'd you kill?"

Irwin laughed, an angry, bitter laugh. "Hell, if I'd killed someone, I probably would've gotten half the sentence. It was actually a big misunderstanding between me and the government."

Mars smiled. "Isn't it always?"

"Yeah, well, in this case I worked for the government, and they didn't appreciate the kind of friends I kept."

"It seems friends is a theme with you," Mars said, as if trying to make sense of what Irwin had just told him.

"Huh?"

"No, I mean, I'm guessing you either stole government property, did some sort of bid-rigging, or maybe a tax thing, but none of those would give you twenty-five years. Unless you had a real jerk for an attorney?"

"Aren't all attorneys jerks?" Irwin said.

"I was a lawyer once." Mars made a comical expression. "And I have to agree with you."

Now it was Irwin's turn to laugh. "I've observed there is a disproportionate number of attorneys in prison compared to other professions."

"So it was a bad lawyer? You can appeal."

"Nah. I was selling classified information."

Mars raised his eyebrows. "The feds frown on that kind of thing."

"I'll say."

They were silent again. A group of three inmates went by and eyed the new guy suspiciously. Finally, when they were out of earshot, Mars turned to face Irwin.

"I can get you out," Mars said.

Irwin's humor vanished. "What are you talking about?

Talking about getting an inmate out early is either a crime, or a cruel joke." His eyes narrowed further as he grew angrier. "And there is a third option. You're a snitch!"

"No. I may be many things, but a snitch is not one of them. The friend I told you about is a rich and powerful man."

"He's got enough juice to get me out of prison? That's mighty powerful."

"Yeah."

Irwin continued to stare at Mars. "This release you're talking about, it comes with a pardon?"

"No, not *that* kind of power."

"So I'd still be wanted." Irwin laughed, then let out a few expletives. "Why would I want to do something like that?"

"Because you like money."

"Now you're trying to get me onto a new charge. You really think anybody's interested in tacking on another nickel or dime to their sentence?"

"How much money do you need?"

"For what?"

"To disappear and start a new life."

"Are you serious?"

Mars nodded. "I'll get you enough money, and a new identity, if you tell me what I need to know."

"Hell, see? You are a snitch."

"Not a snitch. I'm also not a charity. I'm a businessman."

"You got this kind of friend, what are *you* still doing inside?"

"I've got a lot less time than you. I'm just trying to finish."

Irwin studied Mars. "Uh-huh . . . and just what do you want to know?"

"Everything you know about a certain FBI Special Agent."

"I don't know what you're talking about."

"Yes, you do."

Chapter Fifty-Nine

WASHINGTON, DC

April 3rd - 1:43 pm

Tu had asked his two favorite technologists from the think tank to join him. They plugged in every scenario of how a city could be destroyed.

"Are we sure the terrorists plan to level the city, or are they just going to wipe out the residents?" one of them asked at the start of their session. "Because if they're using chemical or biological weapons, they could kill a million people and leave the buildings standing."

Tu looked at her and blinked, his mind processing the question and all its potential answers and ramifications in an instant. "I think this is about power. They will take it all."

She nodded, as if his vetting of the possibilities was enough.

With the available information, it didn't take them long to narrow the applications and origination points. "We are limited by our knowledge of classified military weapon systems," the other said.

"But we are not limited by our imaginations," Tu said. "Think like a child. Imagine what they could use to do the worst."

"I'll try," he said.

Tu looked at him and smiled. "Yoda says, 'Do. Or do not. There is no try.'"

"Yoda is right," the man said.

The advanced computer systems employed by the think tank projected and illustrated an endless stream of doomsday scenarios. Tu watched, riveted, as the simulations of killer satellites attacked, but none came anywhere close to destroying a building, let alone a city.

"We're missing something," the woman said.

"Someone must have developed a laser amplification system, or a photon delivery for nuclear," the man said. "Or it's not space-based. Maybe they're using Amtrak to deliver a train full of nukes to New York."

Tu continued watching the space simulations. He zoomed in and increased the number of monitors displaying the action until, finally, he paused.

The two technologists stopped what they were working on and looked at the largest screen. "Why did you stop?" the woman asked, staring at an image showing a distant view of the moon. "Do you think they have a lunar base?"

"That's no moon," Tu responded absently.

They both recognized the famous Star Wars quote spoken by Obi-Wan Kenobi when the Death Star was spotted for the first time.

"They're getting the power for the weapon from the sun!" Tu said. "I have to call The Astronaut."

Undisclosed location

The gray-haired man and the diplomat in the red tie had reconvened in the big room. They sat alone at the large table, framed by an eight-foot wide bronze sculpted hammer and sickle mounted on a slab of wood painted deep red.

"We are now only hours from Five-Fours," the gray-haired man said, fiddling with a computer tablet that controlled various screens displaying live feeds from Washington and several other points of interest.

Tolstoy's voice came through a speaker. "Am I connected?"

"Yes," the diplomat replied.

"Is the US president going to have ashes for breakfast?" the gray-haired man asked.

"It appears he will be in Philadelphia," Tolstoy said.

"That's not what I mean," he snapped back.

"We are on schedule. The Astronaut definitely caused some issues."

"But he's dead."

"Yes. However, he sent warnings before our people removed him. The CIA is leading an investigation, unprecedented in size and scope, to uncover the details of Blackout."

"Could they find the source before Five-Fours?"

"Highly unlikely."

The two men exchanged a glance. *'Highly unlikely'* was not the answer they required.

"Perhaps we should abort," the diplomat said.

"No," Tolstoy said, a little too quickly. "We will prevail. I can deliver this."

"What about the billionaire boy wonder and his spy girlfriend?" The gray-haired man's bitter tone reflected his loathing of Chase and Wen.

"They will be dead soon. Spinx, and a number of our agents, are closing in on them. There is also a large presence of other operatives in DC tasked with eliminating them for other reasons."

"The Circuit?"

"Yes."

The gray-haired man pursed his lips. "The Circuit is our next problem." Although at the moment their objectives aligned, the shadow people worried him.

"Even they will be weakened after Five-Fours," Tolstoy reasoned.

"They may prove more resilient than the young democracy."

"Either way, everything is different in the morning."

"It better be," the gray-haired man said, thinking of death.

Chapter Sixty

GEORGETOWN, WASHINGTON, DC

April 3rd - 1:45

Chase hit the floor and reached over to check the doctor.

"Sniper!" Wen yelled, crawling toward the window.

"He's dead," Chase yelled back.

Wen fired one shot out the window. "Get out! Get out!" she shouted as she dove toward the door. Chase, just behind her, had only crossed the threshold as the entire first floor exploded in a fireball.

By the time they recovered and the smoke cleared, there was no one left to shoot at. "Who was the target?" Chase asked. "Us, or Forbes?"

"All of us," Wen said as they got into their car.

"Then why didn't they finish us off?"

"Maybe they thought they did," she said, pulling out her phone. "They blew up the whole building!"

"Who are we calling?"

"Astronaut. We need to know where to go next, and I want to give him the new information on Russia."

Before Wen could say anything, Nash started talking. "I just sent a breakdown to your device," The Astronaut said. "It turns out the strike could be anywhere. At least, when you initially sift the data. Exterminating a million people in the United States via a space weapon, there are almost . . . well, hundreds of possibilities, more than a thousand if you consider overlapping parameters."

"I'm hoping the news gets better," Chase said.

"'Gets better' is a relative term. We are talking about a million deaths and the related obliteration of a major metropolitan area in the United States."

Chase gave Wen a glance, as if to say, *I walked into that one, didn't I?*

"However," The Astronaut continued, "when one factors in population overlays, sorted in conjunction with nearby power plants, it starts to narrow."

"Right," Chase said. "They can't power it from space. Have you approximated the requirements for this kind of weapon?"

"*Approximate* is a good word, since we don't know exactly what the weapon is."

"Professor Osborne believes it has to be an advanced laser delivery system, siphoning power from nearby utility plants," Wen said. "Doctor Forbes said power was the key to the location of the strike."

"The information I obtained on Heaven is part of the DARPA cache, and other classified Defense Department data, but everything is incomplete."

Wen told him about the attack on Forbes and also about the pyramid model from Osborne.

"That may not be the exact process, but I think we're in the neighborhood—some sort of reasonable framework for what they would have to use."

"But that's the weakness," Chase added, looking over his shoulder to change into another lane. The car behind honked. It startled Chase as, weirdly, he had not seen the vehicle. "They have to have a certain amount of power close to a target of that size. How many could there be?"

"Again, that isn't as exacting as you might think," The Astronaut said. "Assuming my numbers are right, there are sixty-one possible targets. It could even be more."

"Still, it must give us *something*."

"The East Coast is the most likely choice. Obviously, there's a high concentration of population, as well as a surprising number of power plants that correlates to that population. We can't rule out the West Coast, however, it is less likely."

"Where?" Chase tried again. He kept his eyes on the rearview mirror on that honking car. Something about it made him uneasy.

"We're looking at cities in Florida, Maryland, Pennsylvania, New York, New Jersey, Ohio, Indiana, Texas, Virginia, Washington DC, and North Carolina as the most likely areas.

"That's eleven places," Wen said. "We can never cover that much ground." She looked at Chase and silently asked, *What?*

"That's the same as not knowing anything," Chase added, shaking his head at Wen, meaning *it's nothing*, yet he continued to check the car behind them, especially after a cop pulled out from a side street just then and fell in line behind the suspicious car. Chase gripped the steering wheel tighter. Wen, of course, noticed all this and took the back seat, ready.

"I know. And we got there by factoring in nearby nuclear power plants. There are around one hundred active nuclear power reactors operating in the US right now. Most of them are located near cities with populations of one million or more."

"Can't you narrow that with other factors?" Chase asked.

"Yes. I've been working the data. We come up with a list of twelve cities within those ten states: Indianapolis, Atlanta, Miami, Jacksonville, Charlotte, Columbus, Baltimore, Philadelphia, Houston, New York City, and Norfolk. But as I went further, it narrows again: Jacksonville Florida, Baltimore Maryland, Philadelphia, and the Tidewater Virginia region, which includes Norfolk."

"So we're narrowed down to four, potentially?" Wen asked. "Forbes said it had to be one of two places."

"Too bad he didn't finish that statement," Chase said.

"With each narrowing, I am less confident with those conclusions," The Astronaut continued. "However, Jacksonville is perhaps the least interesting of those four cities. Baltimore, being a port city, I'd rate at number three. Philadelphia, as the birthplace of American democracy, would be two. Virginia's Tidewater region, which is home to one of the largest concentrations of military bases in the world, has to be number one. A strike in that region would cripple the United States military and limit any response."

Chase looked at Wen. "Then those are the top three? Norfolk, Philadelphia, Baltimore. We should tell Tess."

"You think they will evacuate those three areas?" Wen asked.

"In whatever hours we have left, that cannot even begin to do anything except make it worse by causing panic," Chase said. "Of course, that's ultimately the decision of the president."

"Based on what we have," Nash began, "they should be evacuating at least twelve cities right now."

"That alone would do great damage."

"Perhaps that is what the Russians want," Wen said.

"There is another option," Nash said. "We could suggest taking all US power plants off-line."

"Imagine *that* catastrophe," Chase muttered.

"But it would be in the middle of the night," The Astronaut said.

"Thus the name," Wen said. "Operation Blackout."

"I can make that suggestion," Chase said, relieved as the suspicious car finally took a right into a mini-mart, "but I don't think they'll go for it. How long do you keep it shut down?" Unfortunately, the cop car was behind them now. Chase and Wen eyed each other.

"It is possible," Nash began. "We could do an unauthorized shutdown . . . without their permission."

"We have that capability?" Chase asked. Wen motioned for him to get off the road and pull into an upcoming gas station.

"I don't know for sure, but we can try."

Chapter Sixty-One

PETERSBURG, VIRGINIA

April 3rd - 1:52 pm

Irwin looked off into the distance for a minute. "It's a long story, man."

"Not much time?" Mars laughed. "We've got nothing *but* time."

"Yeah? Well, time is a funny thing."

"True."

"I got that line from a book. *The Last Librarian.* Ever read it?"

"As a matter of fact, I did. Read the whole series. *The Lost TreeRunner* had quite an influence on me."

"*The List Keepers* blew my mind," Irwin said. "I read a lot in here."

"Reading transports you to another world."

"'*In the meanwhile I obtained the horror of the dungeons, after the discovery of the plot to break prison. And never, during those eternal hours of waiting, was it absent from my consciousness that I should follow these other convicts out, endure the hell of inquisition they endured, and be brought back, a wreck and flung on the stone floor of my stone-walled, iron-doored dungeon.*'"

"*The Star Rover*, by Jack London."

A genuine smile appeared on Irwin's face. "You know it?"

"It's helped me through prison more than any other book."

"Me, too, but so few have read it. One of London's most obscure works."

"Yeah. Quite a journey though."

"I don't want to come back. If I do this, and I get out . . . I *can't* come back. You know what I mean?"

Mars nodded. Irwin's eyes revealed the desperation and loss that had infiltrated him. Mars recognized it as one does their own fear and weakness in the mirror, at least when they look with an honest gaze. "Give me a number. My friend needs this information. I'll have the money and the identity sent in the care of your attorney, Stuart Hampton, within the hour."

Irwin's eyes widened at the mention of his attorney's name. "You may not be a snitch, but you're good. How do you know who my attorney is?"

"Talk to my friends," Mars said, ignoring his question.

"What if I said I want two hundred million dollars?"

"My friend is rich, but not *that* rich."

"Then save me the trouble, what's the upper limit?"

"You want me to give you a number?"

"I'm not buying a used car here."

"Fair enough." Mars didn't like to spend Chase's money, but had a feeling most of it was going to be reimbursed from a CISS slush fund. "Ten million. A new iron clad identity and the best part of all . . . " Mars met Irwin's eyes, "you'll be out of prison."

"It's a big risk. I spill on something like this, I may not wake up one day, know what I mean?"

"Yeah."

"You sure you can't do better than ten?"

"What good is the information to you in prison? This FBI guy has done you no favors. I'm talking to you. You know they've already got him. How long do you think until your valuable information becomes useless, and your FBI buddy joins you in here? It's just a matter of time."

"Yeah . . . and time's a funny thing, right?"

"It's working in your favor for another sixty minutes or so. After that, you're looking at twenty-some-odd years back on the inside. Take the deal, man. Go live out your days on a beach. Don't be a Star Rover, breathe it."

"I need to think about it."

Mars nodded. "Then go back and check with your attorney. The ten million good faith money and the identity will be there. But you don't get out until you give me all the information."

"Yeah, well, no offense, but I don't really know you. And you're in prison, so that makes you only somewhat honest." He paused and smiled.

"I'm not really guilty," Mars said, holding his hands up beside his chest in a gesture of innocence. "It was all a big misunderstanding."

"I've heard that before. But I'm serious, ten million under my mattress doesn't do any good if someone offs me."

"You'll be gone. New identity."

"What if I tell your friends everything I know and then I don't get out?"

"With ten million in your control, I think you can find

someone to kill me. Maybe not today, maybe not next week, but you have time, and I'm easy to find."

"Yeah."

"Ask around about me. I will *not* screw you. We *need* this information."

They stared at each other silently for at least fifteen seconds.

"I'll get back to you," Irwin said at last.

Mars couldn't push any further, but felt confident Irwin would take the money. He just hoped it was in time.

Chapter Sixty-Two

VIENNA, VIRGINIA

April 3rd - 1:54 pm

Mission Control descended into momentary chaos when the feeds from the subway station went black.

"What the hell is going on down there?" Tess yelled. "Get me a picture!"

Amid a rush of terrified commuters fighting to escape up the long escalators, the IT-Squad Commander ordered four more operatives down into the Metro underground. A few minutes later, their images began to appear on the feed.

The news was not good. Two IT-Squad agents and Belfort's employee were dead. Spinx, aka Anatoly, had disappeared.

"Get me Hyland!" Tess snapped at Linda. "It's time to tell Russia we're onto their game, and they're playing with war."

As Tess watched the unsuccessful hunt for Anatoly, her frustration grew. For the first time in her career, she believed they might not be able to avert a nuclear war.

Russia has to back down . . .

Linda ran breathlessly back into Mission Control. "Hyland is dead."

Tess closed her eyes. "Then get me the president."

"He's on the way to Philadelphia."

"Not the president of the United States, I want the president of Russia."

Petersburg, Virginia
April 3rd - 1:56 pm

Irwin found Mars at the softball field.

"What the hell, I'm a gambling man," Irwin said. "I don't want to go back inside."

"You won't have to."

Mars and Irwin sat on the top bleachers, their backs against a chain-link fence. Ostensibly, the two cons were watching the game. Quite a few of Mars's friends were playing. It wasn't like the relaxing athletics on the outside, as prison softball was almost a full-contact sport. Broken bones occurred in most games, while bruises and blood were part of every outing. The inmates and guards enjoyed watching the gladiators. Lots of money was wagered, won, and lost by both.

However, on that day, Mars and Irwin weren't paying much attention to the competition. They stayed in the 'cheap seats', far enough away from anyone not to be overheard. No one paid them any mind during the raucous scene.

"I checked it out," Irwin said. "You're a man of your word."

"Ten million safely transferred," Mars said.

"Yeah. My attorney tells me the new identity papers are perfect and complete. Even have three credit cards. Nice touch."

"Happy?"

"You're like a fairy godfather. You might really be able to get me out."

"Paperwork is already being processed. You'll hear from your caseworker after the four o'clock count."

"Everything is cool if I don't take a bullet." He looked out to the field, as if a gunman might emerge any second and kill him.

"And your end?"

"All right. The agent is a guy named Gary Bollinger. Works out of DC, lives in McLean, Virginia on Seacliff Road." He handed him a slip of paper. "Here's the location of a storage bin."

"What's in it?"

"All kinds of incriminating information on Bollinger. Stuff he's been involved in, information on an international terror group. They're connected with some kind of black market tech deals, and they pay him big money to slow or stop investigations. Your friends will like it."

Mars smiled. He would've been happy with just the name, but the extra information might make Chase and Wen's job easier.

Mars decided to push now that the deal was done. "Where did you work?"

Irwin looked at him carefully. "DARPA."

Shouts grabbed their attention as a fight broke out on the field. Bats were used as weapons, broken noses, blood. A surge of guards worked to regain control.

"I need to get this information out," Mars said. "I'll see you at dinner. Your last one in prison."

"I'll buy you dinner."

Mars laughed.

A guard found Irwin as Mars was leaving. "Your case worker wants to see you after count."

Irwin looked over at Mars, climbing off the other end of the bleachers, still unsure if it was a trap. He *wanted* to believe it was real though, and smiled.

Mars waved back. It was bittersweet for Mars that he had to stay and Irwin got to go.

There was no time for a call. Instead, Mars sent a text with the information, hoping Chase was still alive to receive it.

Washington, DC
April 3rd - 2:00 pm

Anatoly smiled as he took the call giving him the update on Chase and Wen's location.

"They are still alive? That is lovely for me." He hadn't wanted someone else to have the fun of killing the two nuisances.

"I thought they had you in the metro station."

"They are incompetent. I know their surveillance protocols, I can identify their agents, I spot the weak ones, and I can change my appearance. How could they ever catch the Spinx?"

"Good work. I was worried you might be dead. I still need you. Finish Chase Malone and Wen Sung."

"On my way," he said, as if going to a concert or some other enjoyable event. "And do not worry. Most people live their lives from the confines of fear. Not me. I am not afraid. And that makes all the difference between success and failure, living and dying."

Chapter Sixty-Three

VIENNA, VIRGINIA

April 3rd - 2:12 pm

After Tess's call with the Russian president, Linda could tell her boss was distressed.

"Didn't go well?" she asked, rolling a green apple over the desk toward her boss.

"He claims they aren't behind it." Tess took a bite out of it hungrily.

"But isn't that what you would expect him to say?"

"Yes, but I've known him for years. We've had a mutual respect since his days in the FSB."

"Are you saying you believe him?"

She shook her head, took a few more bites, then set the apple down. "There's one sure way to tell when the Russian president is lying."

"How?" Linda asked.

"His lips are moving."

She let out a nervous chuckle. "So the Russians *are* behind it?"

"I don't know. Get me the president."

"Ours?"

"Of course, ours."

Tess took the video call in Secure. The president had already cancelled his trip to Philadelphia and was in the situation room, consulting with the Secretary of Defense, Secretary of State, Chairman of the Joint Chiefs, the Director of National Intelligence, the CIA director, and the National Security Advisor.

"We've been waiting for your update, Tess," he said.

The 5,525-square-foot Situation Room, officially known as the John F. Kennedy Conference Room, located under the West Wing of the White House, always appeared cramped to Tess, and she was glad not to be there.

CISS had been sending constant updates to the president, but he always wanted her personal take.

"Russia denies it."

"I know," the president said. "He called me after your conversation."

"Do you believe him?" she asked.

"*Nyet*," he replied.

"Then you should move to PEOC," she said, referring to the Presidential Emergency Operations Center. The bunker-like facility buried under the White House East Wing was a secure shelter and communications center for the president. Built to withstand a direct nuclear hit, its entrance was located behind multiple vault-type doors with biometric access control systems.

"Are you saying Washington is the target?" the president asked, alarmed.

"We still don't know, but based on the Russian activity in the city today, and the fact that it could be anywhere, I think PEOC is a prudent choice."

"Tess, if it's Washington, we have to consider a first strike against Russian targets."

"I know."

"Are you still confident of the timetable?"

"We have no indication it has changed."

The president looked around at the solemn faces of his top foreign policy advisors. Each one of them knew the possibility that if the United States was about to launch a preemptive strike and ignite a nuclear exchange, it meant World War III. "We can't wait until 4:44."

"I know. We still have at least fourteen hours."

"Not that many," he said. "Instead of moving to PEOC, I think we might be spending the night on the E-4." The president was alluding to the Doomsday Plane, officially known as the Boeing E-4 Advanced Airborne Command Post, a highly modified Boeing 747-200B. Designed to be "the most secure plane on earth," it was a fully functional war room.

"Understood," she said.

"Damn it, how can we *not* know the target yet?" the president said. He pointed at the top intelligence people in the room, and then at the screen displaying Tess. "Get the answers!"

New York City
April 3rd - 2:15 pm

Belfort unleashed the full force of the Circuit's technological might. "If we can't kill these ghosts," he said of Chase, Wen, Grimes, and Shelby, "then we'll break them."

"Yes, sir," a nerdy looking woman said.

"Strip them of their wealth, take away their identities, erase their existence."

"Yes, sir," she repeated. "It will take some time."

"No. No more time. This needs to happen *now*. Find out who's helped them hide their wealth, find the assets, and destroy them. Do you understand? Spare no expense, but make it happen!"

"Yes, sir."

Washington, DC
April 3rd - 2:17 pm

The Astronaut watched as the screen displaying Skyenor's DARPA phone scrambled into an unrecognizable matrix of characters. "I've lost it," he said. For hours he'd been nursing it along, trying to prevent the self-destruct app that held control over the data contents he so desperately needed to access. "Whoever set this up was better than me," he whispered to the phone, which began to emit a thread of white electronic smoke. "I'd like to meet you." And he suspected he already had.

Still, he had seen enough. After speaking with Tu about his theory and piecing together what he had taken from the phone, the watch, and the flash drive, he had a clear view of the weapon that Tu called the "Death Star Death Ray." The Astronaut had never seen Star Wars, so he did not understand the reference, but Tu had explained the concept well enough, and with the rest of the data and what he could extrapolate, he'd proven the mechanics of it.

He called Chase and Wen.

"They are going to melt a city . . . and everyone in it."

Chapter Sixty-Four

GEORGETOWN, WASHINGTON DC

April 3rd - 2:21 pm

After the call with The Astronaut, in which they learned of the death ray, Chase and Wen felt more urgency than ever. "We gotta find the facility!" Chase said as they moved through the crowded streets of the Georgetown shopping district.

"We have to find out *which* city first," Wen said, checking the time. "We have just over fourteen hours left."

"It's Norfolk, it has to be. Even The Astronaut thinks it's the most likely target." Chase thought about how many incredible minds had already died. "There has to be a way to stop it. They wouldn't kill all those scientists unless they were hiding something."

"You remember what Osborne and Forbes told us," Wen said. "The weapon that's being targeted against America was mostly developed here by DARPA and others. Stolen secrets."

"That doesn't matter now," Chase said as they turned

their car up the street. "I've got a helicopter on standby. Let's fly to Norfolk."

"And just try to spot the facility from the air?"

"It has to be big, and we have to be there. Remember what The Astronaut said, once the countdown has begun, the weapon cannot be canceled. They designed it that way. So we need to be where it's happening. There won't be an option of extra time."

"We don't know where '*there*' is."

"Our answer is in the power," Chase said, stopping. "The weapon requires enormous amounts of energy, meaning there must be a way to deny it that power."

"But The Astronaut just told us the weapon is controlled by artificial intelligence. The documents from the DARPA phone showed they had tested a similar weapon, and when they shut down the power source, the AI figured out a workaround."

"I know, but that doesn't mean there isn't another way to beat it," he said.

Wen grabbed his arm. "See that silver SUV?" She glanced at a vehicle pulling up to the curb on the other side of the street. "I think those are shadow people."

"They never stop!"

Wen pivoted, scanning the street, crowded with pedestrians. "Traffic's too heavy. Let's stay away from the car. Easier to escape on foot."

As they moved up the street, away from the SUV, they saw four more shadow people running on the sidewalk toward them. "This is Grand Cayman all over again," Chase said.

"And there," Wen said, turning. "Six more."

"Let's never go to a place named Georgetown again,"

Chase griped as they crossed the street and ran away from the SUV.

"Cayman's George Town is two words, named after King George. This one is one word and named for the two George's who founded the city."

"Either way you spell it, that's a lot of George's, and let's just hope our luck holds out."

"In here," she said, dashing into a store.

"You think it has a backdoor?"

"With city fire codes, there's probably a good chance, but it doesn't really matter."

Inside the designer clothing store, Wen surveyed the space quickly. They each got behind solid brick columns.

"Can I help you find anything?" a slightly suspicious female clerk asked Wen.

"No, I just saw my ex-boyfriend on the street and he's very abusive. I'm hoping he won't see me."

"Oh. Should I call the police or anything?"

"Only if you see him come in."

"What does he look like?"

The bell hanging over the door jangled. Three men came in.

"I think that might be him," the clerk said, suddenly nervous. "He doesn't look friendly, and he has a couple of friends with him."

"I think they have guns," Wen said, pulling out her own MP7 Submachine gun. "Get down!"

She killed two of them, but the third one disappeared behind a rack of fancy leather jackets on clearance and returned fire from behind another brick column. Chase slid under a display table filled with expensive tee-shirts and got two shots off. One found the man's head.

"Let's go!" Chase yelled.

The clerk was screaming.

"If you have a back door," Wen said, "we'll leave before anymore come."

"Yes, yes," she said through tears. "But it will trigger the fire alarm if you open it."

"We'll risk it," Chase said. "Where does it go?"

"Into the alley. Now can I call the police?"

"Sure," Chase said. "Sorry about the mess."

Chapter Sixty-Five

GEORGETOWN, WASHINGTON DC

April 3rd - 2:24 pm

Wen peeked out the backdoor, looking up the alley and out toward Wisconsin Avenue. She saw three more men. They saw her, too, and raised their weapons.

"Come on!" Wen said, running in the opposite direction.

Across the street, a Mercedes SUV side-swiped her. Chase barely dodged it. Wen ran up on the hood and onto the roof, thinking this really was like Grand Cayman all over again. She leaped onto the top of another car and kept running, using the cars as stepping stones while bullets began ricocheting all around. She leaped off the last roof, spun in the air, and based on the trajectory of the bullets, shot toward where she believed the shadow people were.

Wen managed to kill one as she skipped onto the now deserted sidewalk. Shoppers and pedestrians had all fled in panic and were taking cover behind cars, kiosks, vending machines, or wherever they could find it. She swiveled her head, spotted Chase, decided his route looked good, and quickly caught up with him.

Chase and Wen jogged up the streets. This was not an early morning hotel on the edge of a business district, this was Georgetown, an affluent commercial center of the capital founded in 1751, home to Georgetown University and many other landmarks and embassies. It was also filled with high-end shops, bars, and restaurants full of tourists, workers, shoppers, and residents. The police wouldn't have to come there, they were already present. However, they had no idea what they were up against that day.

Two officers went down almost immediately while trying to engage the shadow people. They did not understand that these soldiers-for-hire did not see the police as an authority, merely another obstacle to overcome; more expendable human life between them, their target, and a big payday. Several innocent bystanders also died in the malaise.

Unfortunately, Chase and Wen, now running with their guns in the open, crashed into a couple of officers. Wen kicked one in his knees, knocking him down. The other one, much more experienced than Chase with firearms, separated himself.

"Don't move," he said, pointing his pistol at Chase.

Wen spun around and held her Glock against the downed officer's head. "You're not going to believe this, but we're the good guys."

"It doesn't look like it!"

"CIA officers pursuing Russian operatives intent on carrying out a massive terrorist event. And if you don't lower your weapon, I'm going to have to blow your partner's brains all over the sidewalk, and I don't have much time to think about it."

"It doesn't *sound* like you're one of the good guys either!"

"Weapon down!" she repeated.

"I don't think—"

Two shots rang out so fast that Chase didn't even try to move. He thought he might be dead until he saw that the cop had dropped to his knees, joining his partner on the sidewalk.

Chase kicked the man's gun away.

"I'm truly sorry," Wen said, grabbing his radio, "but I was telling the truth. If I wasn't, I would've killed you."

"Screw you," the cop grunted, clutching at the two bullet wounds in his thigh.

Wen looked at Chase. "You're bleeding. Were you hit?"

Chapter Sixty-Six

WASHINGTON, DC

A guard gave the news to Mars. He wasn't surprised, but he was a little sad. He'd given his word, and he'd meant it. But now Irwin was dead.

"Hung himself in his cell," the guard said.

"Couldn't they come up with something more original?" Mars asked rhetorically.

"Apparently not."

Mars got to one of his hidden phones and tried to call Chase, but there was no answer. He texted him instead. "Irwin dead. Obviously he knew too much. Hope you got to Bollinger."

After he sent the message, he worried that this time it was bigger than Chase, bigger than all of them. Mars looked at the phone once more, wanting to call Chase again, suddenly afraid he might have been killed. *Who else can I call?* he thought. The well connected inmate felt the familiar dark feelings return—of being trapped and isolated. He put the phone away and went to a secret computer, one that he used to implement decoying. "It's the one thing I can do to help," he muttered. And he set in motion more than forty false sightings of Chase and Wen around the globe. "God speed, my friend."

It would be a long time before he discovered who had actually killed Irwin. Normally, it wouldn't have mattered that much, but in this case, with the stakes being so high, world peace, a million lives, and the very real possibility . . . they could easily be coming for him next. It did matter.

Washington, DC
April 3rd - 2:35 pm

Tu looked at Nash over the video call and wished he could be there in person. Yet, the excitement of his discovery kept him rambling. "It's only been in the last hundred years that humans have had any clue as to how seemingly limitless energy is created by stars, including our own sun," Tu said. "An English astrophysicist, published an essay, 'The Internal Constitution of the Stars,' theorizing that sub-atomic energy must be the source."

"He was correct," The Astronaut said.

"Yes, and ever since then, people have tried to duplicate that unlimited, carbon-free power."

"I'm aware."

"Hundreds of reactors have been built, scientists have slammed hydrogen atoms together . . . the elusive dream has never quite been fulfilled."

"There's a joke about fusion energy that it's thirty years away and always will be."

"That's funny," Tu said giggling. "And it's been more

than three decades since engineers started designing the International Thermonuclear Experimental Reactor."

"Ah, yes ITER. Excess of $25 billion spent. Constructed of ten million parts. I've been there." The Astronaut smiled at the memory. "It's in France, surrounded by vineyards. The main machine is twenty-five thousand tons."

"Wow!" Tu said. "I would like to see it."

"I'll take you someday, but tell me, what does ITER have to do with lasers destroying a US city?"

"I think they've built one here. They aren't getting the energy from power plants. It's coming from fusion. It provides the power to destroy a city . . . maybe many cities," he said sadly. "Fusion energy will be ten times hotter than the sun."

The Astronaut was silent for a few moments. "But the ITER campus is four hundred-forty-five acres, it consists of dozens of buildings. Where would they hide such a facility?"

"America is a big country, with lots of land. Four or five hundred acres is not so much, it could be disguised as anything." Tu grew angry. *The military industrial complex weaponizes everything,* he thought. *Fusion energy could save the environment, but now . . .*

The Astronaut did a quick online search—Defense contractor Lockheed Martin was building a nuclear fusion reactor. The Massachusetts Institute of Technology was developing a compact Fusion reactor that would "fuse together under high pressure and temperatures of tens of millions of degrees." He scanned the article and saw that the entire donut-shaped reactor could be "about the size of a tennis court," and would produce about ten times more energy than is required to ignite and maintain the fusion reaction. China successfully powered up its "artificial sun" nuclear fusion reactor. Russia developing a hybrid fusion-fission reactor. The US military, DARPA, Germany, the UK . . . It was moving too fast. "Someone has done it," he whispered. "Unlimited energy, and they're using it to power a laser weapon."

"A death ray," Tu said.

Chapter Sixty-Seven

WASHINGTON, DC

Chase looked down at his blood soaked pants, surprised by the wound. "I don't think I got hit."

Wen checked the street and saw they were still clear, then quickly examined his leg. "It's not a bullet wound. Must be a ricochet, maybe a chunk of the sidewalk, I don't know."

"I'll live."

"Famous last words," one of the cops sneered, flipping him off.

Wen blew the officer a kiss.

Chase and Wen stayed low behind vehicles. More men appeared at the other end of the street.

"There!" someone shouted. Bullets started hitting all around them.

Chase grabbed Wen. "Bus."

The Metro bus rolled up, giving them temporary shelter. Traffic came to a standstill after a motorist was killed at the intersection.

"This way," Chase said, leading her up the street still

shielded by the big vehicle. They cut through an alley and managed to get to the other side of the block, where they spotted more shadow people.

"This is like a military invasion," Wen said.

Still more shadow people streamed in from both directions.

"Belfort must be desperate," Wen said.

"What if they're connected to Blackout?" Chase asked the question that almost always came up when they were involved in an operation and shadow people kept appearing.

"I think whoever is behind the shadow people have something much, much bigger going on."

"Bigger than laser nuking a million people!"

"Wait a minute," Wen said. "What if it's not one city?"

"What are you talking about?"

"It could be 100,000 people in ten cities or, 50,000 people in twenty cities or any combination like that."

"Then we can't save them," Chase said, as they jogged past a normally busy outdoor cafe.

Police helicopters were now overhead and given the proximity to the capital and the White House, Wen knew the National Guard and even special ops were soon going to be on the ground.

"We're going to get some help," she said, looking up at the sky. "The feds are going to be killing shadow people."

"As long as we don't get caught," Chase said. "We. Can't. Get. Caught." They both understood that they had the information and best chance to stop the attack, but even that might not really matter, they were running out of time. "I can feel the seconds ripping away."

Three men armed with submachine guns jumped out of a doorway. Only one fired before Wen kicked him, slid into his body, threw an elbow to his face, grabbed his gun, spun, and killed the numbers two and three. She slung the gun over her back as Chase got the other two machines guns off the dead men. He handed one to her as they dashed away amidst sirens and screams.

"Through here!" she said, rounding the corner.

They were suddenly staring up the steepest steps they'd ever seen.

"We're trapped!" Chase said, as they looked over their shoulders and saw shadow people closing in from both directions. "I don't think we can get to the top before they catch us, or at least their bullets catch us."

"Won't matter," she said, panting as they started up the steps. "We'll have the high ground."

"About a third of the way up, the first group came around the corner, Chase and Wen stopped and fired. "Three down," Chase said. "A thousand more to go."

Two more shadow people peered around the opposite corners. She waited for them to come into full view, before firing. With those dead, they continued to back their way up the endless steps. "Wen," he yelled, gesturing to the top.

She saw at least six shadow people up there.

Wen moved to the wall and sprayed bullets above them. In the pause that followed, Chase laughed.

"What could possibly be funny about being surrounded on dungeon steps?" Wen asked, between firing bursts down and up.

"A few weeks ago, Bull showed me a picture of herself standing on these steps, you know she loves horror flicks," Chase said. " These are the Exorcist steps! I remember she told me they date to 1895, but it was the 1973 movie scene where the priest falls down them and dies, that made them a historic landmark, she'll be excited we were here."

"Not if we die on them."

"Good point."

Wen fired up to the top again, knowing she wouldn't hit anything, but needing to keep them from descending. She looked down. An unknown number were still at the bottom, too many. The police might be there soon, but would it be soon enough, and would the police get past the private army arrayed against them. All this flashed through her mind in an instant. There was no time. She pressed closer against the wall of the old building that framed the wide steps. A flat section gave her a bit more concealment, but she believed this time they might actually be doomed. They didn't have enough ammunition and they were trapped. The walls on either side of the steps were too high and too far apart to scale.

She looked at Chase. He saw it in her eyes. He looked up and down the steps, crowded with killers, and then back at her questioningly. "Really?"

"They have the high ground." She motioned up as the men were slowly moving down. "We go back down. I can clear the way with this Uzi," Wen said firmly. "If we make it, you go the other way."

"No," he yelled. "They'll kill you."

"They'll kill us both if we don't."

Chapter Sixty-Eight

WASHINGTON, DC

Wen started down the steps but the barrage from below was too much. She looked back up and fired long enough to get the ones above to retreat. "There's a window in the middle of the high wall on the right side," she said. "Can you tell if there are bars on it?"

"No, and it's high enough they might not have installed any. Maybe if we can get there, we'd have a chance." But as he said it, he knew he could only climb that wall, if she stayed below and fought off their adversaries.

Shadow people began advancing from above and below. For the first time in Wen's life, she could see no way out. *There's always a way,* she thought, but knew she'd eventually run out of bullets. *Outnumbered, outgunned, and trapped in some horror movie tomb.*

Wen was about to fire another burst when suddenly two of the shadow people fell. She knew it hadn't been from her bullets. "Was that you?"

"No," Chase said, surprise in his response.

She looked up to the top of the steps to see if they had

somehow shot their own men in crossfire, and watched as bullets ripped into the heads of three more who tumbled down the steep steps.

"Where's it coming from?" Chase asked.

Wen followed the trajectory of the shots and craned her neck across to the top of the other wall, covered in ivy. "There's a sniper up there."

"Helping us?"

"So far."

"But who? Why? What's going on?" Chase hissed, as two more fell below, and another up top. The shadow people retreated again behind the corners.

"Someone's up there," Wen repeated. "Someone on our side."

"Someone who's a damn good shot," Chase said.

They heard continued gunshots as the sniper cleaned out the area. Then a solitary figure appeared at the top of the steps.

"Chase, Wen, this way!" A male voice shouted down. They exchanged a quick glance unable to tell who the person was, but they had been dead for sure before he arrived on the scene. "The sniper could have easily killed us already," Wen said.

"Let's go!" Chase said.

They worked their way up the steep stone steps, staying close to the wall, and keeping their guns pointed both ways. Finally reaching the top, they discovered the man was gone. All that remained were eleven dead shadow people.

"We should check them, Wen said breathlessly.

"No time," Chase said, trying to catch his breath. Police cars were roaring down the street. "Now we have a new problem. We can't get arrested."

Wen took a few quick high-res photos, before bolting

across the street, where they climbed the side of an old 19th century house. Once up on the metal roof, they watched as the police cruisers stopped below and began checking the bodies.

"Washington is seeing a little more crime than usual today," Chase said, as they dropped to another level and sprinted along the roofs of several connected houses, before dropping down and off the other side.

"I think we're only about three blocks from where we started," Wen said, as she looked for the next ambush.

"Hey, look that's our car," Chase said a short time later.

Wen smiled. "You don't think that's a coincidence do you?"

Chase knew better, realizing that when Wen was on the roof she had surveyed the area, her knack for memorizing maps once again coming in quite handy. He'd learned long ago never to question her directions.

"Who was it?" Chase asked, as they got in the car, finally feeling safe enough to think.

"There were at least two of them," Wen said.

"Maybe it was someone Tess sent."

"It wasn't Tess. If it had been, it would have been a full IT-Squad, and they would have waited for us at the top."

"Then who?"

"Grimes and Shelby?"

"What?" Chase was astonished at the thought. "After what they did to us at the other Georgetown."

"The Caymans wasn't them," she said, as they navigated through heavy traffic.

"Maybe not, but Grimes sent us there, into an ambush, an army waiting to kill us."

Chase and Wen concealed their guns on their laps under light jackets as Chase drove out of Georgetown.

"Mars came through," Wen said, reading a text from The Astronaut. "We've got a meeting with the dirty FBI agent."

"Great, I hope he can tell us where the weapon is."

She nodded as she texted The Astronaut back, then gave Chase the location of the meeting.

"Anything else?" Chase asked, as he also noticed a text from Mars.

"I gave Nash the information on where we were, the Exorcist steps."

"You want him to check surveillance cameras and see who helped us?"

"Yes, I want him to confirm what I know."

"Why would Grimes and Shelby save us after years of trying to kill us?"

"I think what the man on the Mall told us was true, Belfort found out that Grimes and Shelby were going to meet us," Wen said.

"Or Grimes told Belfort and he sent that full force."

"That's possible."

"But you really don't think it happened that way?"

"No."

"So your theory is that Grimes felt bad about sending us into the lion's den, so he tracked us down here, and came just in the nick of time to save us?" Chase asked skeptically.

"Maybe he was going to try to talk to us again, and . . . think about it, if Belfort did find out about the meeting, then it would be just like that man told us, Grimes and Shelby are now being hunted like us."

"Best we stick together," Chase said sarcastically.

"Yeah."

"So why just appear and disappear? Why not let us know it was them?"

"Maybe they will, but that was hardly the place and

time with the police showing up and ten or twenty shadow people who might be able to identify Shelby and Grimes."

"I guess."

"Who knows how many more shadow people Belfort sent."

"They saved us and left."

"We were dead back there, Chase."

"Yeah." He couldn't argue that point. Someone had saved their lives.

"Whether it was Shelby and Grimes or someone else, we owe somebody . . . and we owe them big."

Chapter Sixty-Nine

WASHINGTON, DC

April 3rd - 3:17 pm

Chase believed this was too important to let go, as if the identity of the people who saved them could lead directly to the answer of where the Russians were going to strike.

"Could've been Astaria," Chase suggested, recalling the former Mossad agent who often collaborated with Wen and had saved them before.

"Maybe," she said. "I hadn't thought of that. But it was a man at the top who called our names, and it just doesn't feel like Astaria."

Chase thought back to the time Astaria had helped them escape when they were surrounded behind a strip mall in Des Moines. "Feels a lot like Des Moines to me."

"The Astronaut will find out soon enough," she said. "Although he's pretty busy erasing us from as much of the surveillance feeds as possible, reviewing the plans from Forbes and trying to figure out the target city . . . looking for our mysterious guardian angels isn't high on his list."

"He shouldn't have to erase us," Chase said. "I'm confident our vIDs were working. We had just sprayed it on before we went to meet Forbes."

"The less sightings of us the better. It's likely Belfort is using surveillance networks to help find us."

"Speaking of finding us, I guess we better check-in with Tess."

Wen's phone buzzed.

"Is that Tess?" Chase asked, not surprised, since she often called when they were talking about her.

"No, it's The Astronaut," Wen said, tapping the speaker button, maybe he found our mystery people.

"I'd rather he found our target city."

"Can you talk?" The Astronaut asked.

"Yes, go ahead."

"I think the data we recovered from the Hayward's flash drive, tells how to disarm the weapon."

"So you know what the weapon is?"

"I'm afraid I do."

"Is it bad?" Wen asked.

"Bad? Depends on if you considered Hiroshima and Nagasaki bad?"

"Oh no," Wen said. "They can do it?"

"I believe they have a weapon that is capable of killing a million or more people in a single strike."

"So it is nuclear?"

"I don't know the answer to that yet, it can be nuclear based, but not deliver nukes. It is certainly a laser and will inflict mass destruction. Tu was correct, it is a kind of death ray, properly referred to as a directed-energy weapon, and likely fueled by nuclear fusion power."

"My god," Chase said. "Please tell me we can use the plans to disable it?"

"Apparently they constructed a grid so that it is magnified in its destructive force by a factor of seventy."

"But you said there's a way to stop it."

"I'm not sure that can be accomplished in our time frame and the parameters with which we are working, particularly since there's so much we still don't know. However, if you can get to the source, we now have a blueprint to disarm it."

"That's why they killed Hayward and all the scientists," Wen said. "So we would not find the way."

"Yes, I believe that's why they killed Hayward because he discovered the flaw." The Astronaut's voice shook a little.

Wen trying to keep him on track and spare him anymore emotional trauma, pushed on. "How does it work?"

"It's not easy, but there is a process, where an insertion can interrupt the sequence, the item is used to control systems for industrial lasers, and an Actuating Leading Edge Sight Stimulated Emission Nanometer."

"That's a mouthful."

"It's called 'ALESSEN' for short and it's not readily available."

"Where do we get it?"

"Maybe DARPA, even then, it may need some modifications . . . if we can't obtain the correct one . . . I'll send you the steps for the insertion."

"We still have to find the origination point, where the weapon is based. What if we're wrong and it's not Norfolk?"

"Then let's hope it's Philadelphia or Baltimore."

"That's a lot to hope for," Chase said.

"There are also coded sequences of randomly generated

numbers that change every three minutes. A kind of failsafe."

"Every three minutes?" Chase asked.

"I'm working on a program that can duplicate and substitute the generating algorithm."

"How are you going to do that?" Wen asked.

"It works from numerical patterns in sixteen, twenty-four and eight digit combinations. I'm good at patterns."

"Okay, get the ALESSEN, find the location, figure out the pattern, do the insertion . . . " Chase said. "What about Skyenor's phone."

"That is taking a little longer than I anticipated, the data on the phone self-destructed, but I am still working on the back up. I've been spending most of the time on Hayward's assets. The watch yielded the names."

Once again Wen heard the strain in his voice. "On an entirely different subject, any progress on the shadow people photos we sent you?"

"I let the system hunt detailed queries, and checked it just before I called you. We got a few more hits with Finale," he said, referring to a group of mercenaries that had supplied many shadow people to the Circuit. "But nothing earth shattering."

"What about Belfort?"

"Nothing by the name, but the programs did come up with some suspected affiliations. Addresses in New York City, London, and one in Panama."

"Affiliated how?"

"Financial affiliations, again no connection to the names, these are just deep patterned pickups by the algorithms. So it may be nothing. I'm having it focus more on those addresses and re-crosschecking the connection. It will take time until we know more."

Chase sighed. "We're always chasing time."

Chapter Seventy

WASHINGTON, DC

April 3rd - 3:40 pm

Wen scoured the area, always worried it might be a trap, but in this case, it was more likely they were doing the trapping. *How many covert deals have gone down in a small DC park like this one?* she wondered.

She studied special agent Gary Bollinger, he looked like a classic G-man; short hair, pressed white shirt, dark suit, shades. He appeared to be in his early to mid 40s, but she knew from the file The Astronaut had provided that he was fifty-one, and had twenty-four years with the Bureau. Wen suspected he wasn't that good with a gun.

Bollinger was connected and had been involved in many of the FBI's most important cases for the previous fifteen years, including Americans accused of espionage, as well as illegal activities by foreign corporations.

At first glance, and knowing his history, one would never have guessed Bollinger was a corrupt agent. However, Wen could see it in his eyes, a dissatisfaction, a rules don't apply to me, I'm better than you, kind of look. She'd been trained to identify candidates that could be turned. Wen had been good at working double agents for the MSS, but she never liked that aspect of her job. It was the gritty sleazy side, never able to trust anybody, danger and double dealings lurking around all the corners.

Bollinger too was wary and observant since he had also been trained to read people, he studied them, looking for the details that might reveal a secret, their body language that could provide an answer, detect a lie. He had already checked the area, and chosen the location.

"This way," he said, walking around to an area he'd obviously used before. A place where they could be out of view of cameras, and anybody who might want to watch. The overhanging trees made aerial surveillance nearly impossible.

"Nice office," Chase said.

"Just need to check you for any listening devices," he said, holding up an electronic wand.

Chase looked at Wen. She nodded.

Wen raised her hand slightly as he traced the outline of her body, she turned and allowed him to do the front and back. He ignored her Glock. Weapons weren't what he was looking for.

"I appreciate that," Bollinger said, as it showed clear, then repeated the operation on Chase. "Thank you for not wearing any wires."

"We're not here to trick or trap you, Agent Bollinger," Wen said.

"Right," Bollinger said. "We have a mutual friend who thought we might be able to do a little business."

Although Wen was used to using weapons or muscle to obtain information from subjects, sometimes even torture if the situation was desperate, and Blackout was certainly the most desperate situation she'd ever been involved with, those methods were not always preferable, and unlikely to work in this case. *This is about money,* she thought, *it is all Bollinger cares about. And Chase has the ability to make it happen.*

"So then what assets are you looking to acquire," Bollinger asked.

"We aren't really—"

"Something in Federal Bankruptcy Court? Register country? Venture capital?"

"We actually aren't looking to acquire any assets," Chase said.

"No?" He eyed them suspiciously."

"We actually want some information."

"Yeah, I don't give information. That's not my department. Want information call 411." He turned to go.

"Wait," Chase said. "We'll pay for this information, the same as the other services, and it's a lot less work for you. No investigation, no time. We just need a few names and addresses."

"Names and addresses. What agency are you with?"

"Let's just say we have a competitor who we need to know more about."

"A little corporate espionage." He almost smiled. "I don't want my reputation damaged. My clients . . . "

Chase narrowed his eyes, suddenly annoyed by the "bad cop," as the pressure of what they had to do against the ticking clock felt heavier than ever. "Wait a minute, you're an FBI agent, telling secrets, looking the other way, exactly what reputation you talking about?"

Bollinger looked at Chase like he wanted to hit him, but then sloughed it off with a quick laugh. "Like hell," he said. "You may think you're smart, but I'm providing a service.

No one's getting hurt. I'm a businessman, and I do have a reputation with my clients."

Chase thought of the million people about to die.

"Were looking for a sizable facility, owned or operated by a foreign entity, something that might be a big research complex in excess of a hundred acres. Something that you might've helped get the approval for."

Wen watched a shadow through the foliage.

Chapter Seventy-One

WASHINGTON, DC

April 3rd - 3:44 pm

Bollinger stopped and stared at Wen. "Something worrying you?" he asked, seeing she was obviously distracted.

"Always," she said, deciding the shadow may have been just a shadow. He couldn't know how they haunted her.

He nodded, almost amused. "Anyway, I don't really get the approvals, that's the committee's job, but I do the investigations to make sure, it's not violating acts or codes, that it complies with foreign ownership rules. I don't actually go look at these places."

"However, you do read the reports? This would be a pretty large facility."

"What country is the parent for whoever bought it?"

Chase shook his head. "Don't know. We need you to tell us. More than likely Russia, could be China or North Korea, but aren't there ways of cloaking that?"

"Yeah, there's a lot of ways, that's why I asked who originally funded the venture capitalist okay. That money can be based anywhere, I get a lot of companies from Panama, various European nations, that I doubt have anything to do with the transaction. But that's where the corporate parent is allegedly based."

"I don't understand how it gets the approval of the office without somebody in Congress."

Bollinger looked at Chase as if he might be a gullible child. "Because most of the politicians who run things are corrupt or soft corrupt."

"Soft corrupt?"

"They aren't selling national secrets or anything, yet they can make things happen. For the right donations."

"Which ones?"

"Which ones what?"

"Which ones are corrupt or soft corrupt?"

"You want a list?"

"That would be great," Chase said.

He rattled off nine names.

"Are those the corrupt or the soft corrupt?" Chase asked.

"Those aren't the corrupt ones," he said with a laugh. "Those are the only ones who *aren't* corrupt."

"You're telling me that out of the five hundred thirty-five members of Congress, only nine are completely honest?"

"Yep, corrupt or soft corrupt, a few haven't been tested I guess."

"Okay, back to the facility," Chase said pulling a slip of paper out of his pocket, struggling for a minute to read his own writing from the notes he had taken during an earlier call with The Astronaut. "These are some pretty specific parameters; minimum number of square-feet, it also would have to have let's call it, an internal deep well . . . " he read the rest. "Surely, you can remember some of these characteristics."

A painful look crossed Bollinger's face, as he nodded slightly. "I may recall that one."

"Talk to us," Chase said. "We need to know where it is. And if you know about a person called Tolstoy . . . Laser technology . . . and an operation called Blackout."

"I think we need to transfer some funds first."

Chase and Wen waited impatiently as a series of glitches took almost twenty-five precious minutes to get the money into Bollinger's account.

"Mechanicsville, Virginia," he told them and then provided the specific address.

Wen pulled it up on her phone. "Just outside Richmond."

"It is," Bollinger said. "Now, that concludes our business, so if there isn't anything else."

"Do you have blueprints? Plans, Plats, Schematics, engineering . . . "

"I can get them to you." He took out his phone. "I won't even charge you extra," he said smiling, as if he'd just thrown in a set of floor mats for a used car.

A few minutes later, all the data arrived, and Wen switched it to her tablet. "Got it."

"A pleasure doing business with you," he said to the now very distracted Chase and Wen, who were studying the specifics on her tablet.

They all left at the same time, but Bollinger exited the park from a different direction.

While Chase drove, Wen continued to study the materials. "We have thirteen hours," she said. "Assuming the countdown has already begun we're inside the ponor window."

"Ponor?"

"Point-of-no-return."

"Which means there may be no way to stop it."

"But if we insert the ALESSEN," Chase said, referring to the Actuating Leading Edge Sight Stimulated Emission Nanometer that was now waiting in their helicopter. "There might be a chance to stop it."

"How close are we to a landing spot?"

"Call Walt and have him meet us at this high school," Chase said pointing to a map in the dash. "I think it's the closest spot for an easy landing."

Wen called and arranged for their pilot to rendezvous with them at the school football field.

"We'll be there in five minutes."

Wen checked the time. "Walt said it's about a thirty minute flight to Mechanicsville."

"Let's get the location and all this information to Tess," Wen said.

"Tell her to bring in the Calvary."

"She'll probably beat us there."

"Fine with me," Wen said. "I suspect the place is well fortified."

"I can't believe the Russians built this monster facility right under the nose of the Americans."

"It's a pretty large industrial park. Apparently lots of front companies. They've obviously been working on it for years. It has prefab house manufacturers and other phony businesses that wouldn't raise any suspicions when truckloads of materials are brought in."

"Smarter people than me planned it well," Chase said.

"I didn't think there was anyone smarter than you." Wen winked.

"Laser weapons from space . . . Nuclear fusion energy . . . Creating artificial suns . . . there might be a few."

"Don't worry, at least you're cute." Wen's smile turned quickly back to concern. "Tess's phone is coming up out of range."

"That's strange," Chase said. "She would take our call. She must be in a secure meeting."

"Probably with the president."

"I hope so." He pulled into the high school. "Call The Astronaut. Send him everything. He can track her down and or get the location and weapon specs straight to CISS."

Chapter Seventy-Two

WASHINGTON, DC

April 3rd - 3:50 pm

Chase grabbed the duffel full of weapons from the trunk of the car. As they jogged to the chopper, Wen sent the data to The Astronaut. Just before the helicopter lifted, she called him. "We can't reach Tess. I sent you everything we have. Can you make sure CISS gets all this and meets us there?"

"Of course," The Astronaut replied.

"Have you figured out the target city?"

"The radius projections say it has to be Norfolk, Tidewater, Virginia. They're going to take out as much of our military as they can. So we don't have a chance to retaliate." He paused. "But there is a secondary option. There is a chance it might be Washington."

"I thought DC was not one of the possibilities?"

"The latest data changed that."

The pilot signaled they were going up.

"You have to get Tu and my grandmother out of the city, now."

"I will," The Astronaut said. "I won't let you down."

"And get to Tess. Hopefully, she'll get half the military to meet us there."

"I'll make sure."

Washington, DC
April 3rd - 3:52 pm

As Nash ended the call, he quickly skimmed through the data for a minute so he would be able to relay specifics to Tess or one of her assistants. But knowing every second counted, even before finishing his review he pushed the button to connect with Tess.

He looked at the out of range signal as if it was mocking him, then scrolled his contacts to get Tess's deputy, Linda's direct line.

With a sudden flash and bang, the door to his office blew in. Eight black clad gun wielding special ops agents filled the space. Someone grabbed him. The phone flew from his hand.

Before he could even process what was happening, Nash was face down on the floor with what felt like one hundred rough hands grabbing, patting, and holding him down.

"Stop this! Stop now, please stop!" He moaned, as panic and confusion locked his brain. "No, no, no!" he screamed "I do not like this, I do not like this."

He continued rambling repetitive phrases, which became more and more nonsensical while they dragged him from the premises. Several armed men shoved him into a black van. Others stayed behind to ransack his space.

The next thing he knew, The Astronaut found himself

cuffed to a chair in a tiny room with hard floors and plain walls. Everything looked foreign to him. The table seemed to take up the entire room, as if any movement from him and the woodgrain laminate top might cut him in half.

Inside the two-way mirror, his reflection stared back, but the image of himself was a stranger, a scared and hollow man who looked weak, yet somehow dangerous, only to him. He knew someone else was behind the mirrored glass watching, but it was impossible to focus on that, only the strangeness of it all kept him conscious as, strangely, Einstein's theories filled his mind.

The longer he sat in that silent room, the louder the sounds inside his head screeched, creating an agonizing chorus of terror. The torment continued to increase, and he was unable to hold a solid thought with any continuity.

It never occurred to him that he had not gotten word to Tess, or Tu, because all he could think about was the horror of being touched and trapped. He wondered when the execution would come and hoped it would be very soon.

Undisclosed Location
April 3rd - 3:55 pm

The Gray-haired man read the report. "The Americans are close to figuring it out, they may be able to stop it . . . Soon they could know it is us."

"Oh no," the diplomat said, he had been concerned from the beginning that this would happen, that they would be caught.

The gray-haired man looked at the diplomat. "Do you know what this means?"

"We must stop it," the diplomat replied.

"No! Don't be foolish. We must move it up." He typed a message into a computer tablet.

"What have you done?"

"Washington DC is now going to be removed from the world in exactly forty-nine minutes," he said. "At 4:44 *pm* local time."

"But what if they figure it out?"

"There is no time. Even if they do, all the theories and evidence will be obliterated in forty-nine minutes and forty-seven seconds, forty-six, forty-five, forty-four . . . "

Chapter Seventy-Three

MECHANICSVILLE, VIRGINIA

April 3rd - 4:04 pm

After what seemed to Chase and Wen like an eternity in the air, but was actually closer to forty minutes, the helicopter circled above a massive campus of nearly forty buildings surrounded by dense woods on all sides.

"Perfect place to hide a death ray factory," Chase said.

The area did look like an industrial park, complete with signage and an assortment of 'commercial vehicles, including semis all lettered with various phony front companies.

"We've got more than twelve hours," Wen said, having no idea that time had been sped up.

"Should be plenty of time," Chase said.

"Depending on how many Russian Spetsnaz are waiting for us?" She said referring to Russia's Military's elite special forces units.

Chase double checked to see that he had the tablet with

the facility's plans and the ALESSEN to be inserted, which would change the control unit, then he took a deep breath.

"Ready to go into battle?" Chase asked. "This took years to plan, and I assume they've thought of everything."

"I doubt they thought of me."

The pilot landed the chopper on the roof of what appeared to be the main building, about the size of a super-Walmart, but nine stories high. "This is the one with the underground silo," Chase said, double checking the plans.

"Stay here," Wen said to the pilot.

"What if someone starts shooting?"

"Hover at a safe distance, but you're our ride out of here, so stay close."

"Roger that."

Chase and Wen jumped out.

"Cameras," Wen said, pointing to numerous surveillance arrays, as soon as they hit the roof's rubberized asphalt surface. "Expect company," she shouted above the still spinning rotors.

Each armed with MP7s, they ran toward a railed opening that was supposed to lead to the sub levels. Chase had once detested guns, and still preferred not to need them, but he'd grown comfortable with the lightweight and compact Heckler & Koch submachine gun, and efficiently helped Wen mow down the four security personnel that challenged them.

"We're in trouble!" Wen shouted. "Those men were MSS."

Chase hadn't noticed, he'd just been trying to stay alive. "How? Where are the Russians?"

"In Russia," she said, suddenly realizing the play. "Classic MSS misdirection."

"What?" Chase said, as they descended narrow metal steps.

Wen was too busy shooting more agents to immediately respond, but Chase felt as if he was droning in the shock of what the Chinese had pulled off—their brazen deployment of a new super weapon was made even more horrible by their ploy to frame the Russians as the aggressors. *The MSS has just initiated war between its two biggest rivals,* he thought. *A war that only China will win.*

After the initial skirmish, two MSS agents survived unseen on the roof.

"Should we go after them?" one of them asked the other, as they surveyed the bodies of their fallen comrades.

"Not yet, they have no idea what is waiting for them inside. They will be dead soon."

"Yeah, but just in case, we must be sure they have no means of escape." He pointed to the chopper. "The pilot has not seen us yet. He pulled out two electronic containment grenades. The ECGs had been developed by the MSS, and featured programmable blast radius and concussion force.

Quickly initiating the digital firing pins, he tossed two ECGs into the helicopter, then ran back a safe distance. As the chopper exploded and the fuel line caught, propelling a third fiery blast, the agent smiled. "They will not leave here alive."

"Now, we go kill them?"

"Yes," he said, photographing the burning wreckage.

"What's the picture for?"

"For our superiors. We are going to be decorated after this night is done."

"Where the hell is Tess?" Chase yelled, as they came to an open level, which seemed to be a large indoor firing rage with them as the targets.

"Hopefully they aren't going to send a Reaper predator drone to unload its payload of hellfire missiles into this place."

Chase shuddered. "That's what they're going to do!" He looked around as if wanting to find an easy way out, but he knew they couldn't leave until the laser weapon was disarmed.

Wen stripped three agents of their ECGs and quickly cleared the floor. "Where are we going?" she asked Chase.

"Four more floors down."

She shook her head. "Call Tess."

He took out his phone as they continued down the metal steps. "Can't get a signal."

She checked hers. "Damn, I should have thought of that, it's a secure facility. All signals blocked."

"Maybe we can find a land line."

"They'll likely have biosensors."

"Don't worry, The Astronaut has already alerted Tess." Then he thought of the hellfire missiles and wondered if the predator drone was already overhead.

Washington DC
April 3rd - 4:09 pm

Tess and Gatewood, along with the new DARPA head, Coco, sat in the Presidential Emergency Operations Center, under the White House, with other top officials. As a precaution, the president was in the doomsday plane, ready to launch nuclear strikes on Russia. The three of them reviewed the DARPA simulations and other reports on the pyramid laser attack.

"Where did this come from," Tess asked. "Even we don't have this kind of technology, yet."

"Yes we do." Coco said.

Tess looked at Gatewood.

He nodded.

"A pyramid from space," she said.

"Quite elaborate," Coco said. "But without the target city, we can't stop it, and even then, we don't know where the other legs of the pyramid are, or which of the thousands of satellites up there is the one acting as the key sight."

"So now another arms race, this one secret, silent, and science based, has brought us to the brink," Tess said.

"The Russians brought us here," Coco said. "Proving we are right to be developing these weapons. They got there first, barely, and this time, apparently they don't want to be in second place for fifty years."

Chapter Seventy-Four

MECHANICSVILLE, VIRGINIA

April 3rd - 4:11 pm

Chase and Wen burst into a large control room filled with machines and equipment and thousands of pipes and conduits.

Thirty-two Chinese scientists and engineers turned toward them startled.

"It looks like a space aged boiler room, the underbelly of some steam powered rocket ship," Chase said under his breath to Wen. "Where are the lasers?"

"Who's in charge?" she yelled in Mandarin, raising her gun.

One older man stepped forward. "Is it just you?" he asked in perfect English.

"What do you mean?" Wen replied.

"The MSS will kill you in a minute," he said. "Aren't there more Americans?"

"Where is the ALESSEN?" Chase asked, ignoring his question.

"What is that timer?" Wen asked, looking in horror at a red digital countdown clock, it's two-foot high numerals showing thirty-two minutes and twenty-one seconds remaining."

"That's how long until detonation."

"No," Chase said, checking his watch. "We have nine and a half hours left."

"They moved it up," the man said sadly. "Washington will be destroyed in thirty-two minutes."

Chase and Wen looked at each other, desperate and sad, hoping Tu, Zu Mu, and The Astronaut were already out of the city.

"How can we stop it?"

He looked at them confused. "It can't be stopped."

"There must be a way," Chase said, looking around the room.

The man quickly explained that most of the scientists and engineers were essentially held prisoner. "They said they would kill our families," he said looking at Wen. "I have a big family. At first we didn't know what they were going to do. We can't stop it, but we may be able to send it to another location."

"Like the ocean?" Chase asked. "If we insert another ALESSEN?"

"You have one?" He asked impressed.

"Yes."

"We can try, maybe conclude with a self-destruct sequence."

Wen looked at the ticking clock. "Where do we go?"

"To the silo," the man said.

"What about them?" Chase said, motioning to the thirty-one other scientists. "Can they be trusted? I mean should we just leave them here?"

"They will not stop us," the man said.

Chase looked at Wen and shrugged.

"Is there anywhere we can lock them?"

"It's not necessary," he said.

"I'd feel better," Wen said. "We can't have them running around talking to the MSS."

The scientist was going to argue, but decided against it. "In there." He showed them a second room that contained computer servers. "It has a secure lock."

They quickly marched the thirty-one scientists in and locked the door.

"We've got to get this done and then back to the chopper," Chase said. "This isn't done until we find Tolstoy," Wen said firmly.

As they walked, the older Chinese man explained, the basics of Fusion. "It's a nuclear reaction. Understand that multiple atomic nuclei combine to form different atomic nuclei, or often subatomic particles. That's how they do this. The light elements release energy, and the two opposing forces dance, you see."

Wen wasn't listening as she was in full assault mode.

"Yeah," Chase said, also looking for more MSS.

"So the nuclear force holding protons and neutrons together in the nucleus," the scientist continued, sounding as if he were a baker describing the perfect cake. "It's the Coulomb force that creates the magic. It causes positively charged protons to repel each other."

"How much further?" Wen asked, starting to jog.

"Not much, the process—"

"I meant until we get to the lower control room."

"Oh, two more floors." He looked around as if missing more students. "The nuclear binding forces are much more persuasive, shall we say, than the forces holding electrons in orbit around a nucleus. That's the reason fusion fuels offer infinitely higher energy density, fusion is a million times denser than fossil fuels."

"But they're making lasers hotter than the sun," Chase said, trying to sound interested.

"Yes, well. Proton-proton fusion powers stars like our sun. However, that process would take nearly one billion years."

"Not very practical."

Wen opened fire. Chase pulled the old scientist down. "How many?" Chase yelled.

"Too many!"

The firefight lasted six long minutes. In the end, Wen had a stab wound above her hip and the scientist had been shot in the leg.

Chase helped him limp along, while Wen refused any attempt to assist her or check the injury.

"You were saying," Chase prompted the old man, hoping to take his mind off his bleeding leg. "Powering the sun?"

Yes, well," he began, his voice now somewhat hoarse and a little shaky. "Deuterium-tritium reaction is best for fusion energy because it overcomes Coulomb repulsion better. It also produces an extraordinarily energetic neutron. That in turn, produces more tritium."

Chase tried his phone again. Nothing.

"That won't work here," the scientist said. "Full lockdown. Can't even get on the internet without credentials."

Do you have credentials?"

"No. Only MSS commanders."

"Speaking of . . . " Wen began as another dozen MSS stormed in from two adjoining corridors. "Get down!" She lobbed an ECG at one group and fired countless rounds into the other, charging through the smoke and debris like an immortal warrior fighting mythical monsters.

Then she went down, disappearing with a scream into some hidden cavity in the floor.

Chapter Seventy-Five

MECHANICSVILLE, VIRGINIA

April 3rd - 4:13 pm

Chase charged ahead, knowing Wen had been so reckless because she was trying to save Tu.

Now he took up the cause, firing into the blind, until his magazine was empty. Like a seasoned soldier, he replaced it in a seamless motion, and continued his rampage. Convinced everyone was dead, he called for Wen. It took a couple of frantic minutes to discover she had dropped down into another level and could not get back up.

"Are you okay?" he yelled down to her.

"Yes, get the scientist and come down. We're at the silo."

Chase went back for the scientist and found him on the floor, dead. Several MSS bullets had hit him during the barrage.

Chase realized he had also sustained a wound on his shoulder. There wasn't much blood and he didn't think it was serious. He was more concerned with the ALESSEN. He checked it before he dropped down to join Wen. *It's fine.*

After some fast wandering, Chase and Wen located the control room and quickly went to work. Chase strained to reach behind the inverted column. His fingers barely reached, but it still wasn't enough. He could not hold on to the ALESSEN and insert it at the same time.

Looking into the narrow silo, he guessed it had to be fifty feet down, all concrete, and heated coils, it would be certain death. Chase would've been willing to sacrifice his life to save the city, and especially Tu, but there was no guarantee he could make the insertion before he fell, and even then, he had the best chance to understand the command panels and to navigate the coded sequence. *There must be another way.*

"The time," Wen yelled.

"I know, I can't get it in." The heat from the silo was making him sweat. His hand slipping. Chase knew he had to go back.

"Why did they design it this way?" she asked.

"It's an override, not meant to be done on a regular basis . . . if ever." That's when it hit him. They were in a multi-billion-dollar facility, engineers would have designed a way. He looked up the silo. Twenty feet above he saw it. "There's a maintenance vehicle."

"Where?"

"Two floors up."

Wen thought of the security force they had just come through. "That's not going to be easy."

Chase nodded, although she could not see him. He

looked down and back up the silo again, tried one more time to reach the insertion point, but whatever acrobatics he employed, he was still inches short of the proper angle. "It's the only chance."

"Then let's go, the clock is ticking."

With the sequence underway in the count down, relentlessly evaporating their remaining time, Wen took one last glance around the control room painfully reluctant to open the vault door. She looked out the thick glass window between the impact circles from where the MSS agents had tried to shoot their way through. The view was limited, but she did see one shadow. "Unfortunately, this is not a silent opening door." She motioned to Chase. He cranked the dial handle all the way counterclockwise until they heard the click. As he pushed it out, she used the massive door as a shield.

The shadow turned out to be three men from the security force. Wen killed them all. They would have to kill everyone they saw, to prevent anyone else from going into the control room. She knew from the schematics and digital blueprints of the facility, that the stairwell which wrapped around the silo was going to be the second door from theirs.

They jogged along the corridor, its walls and ceilings completely covered in pipes and large conduits holding fiberoptic, laser tracers, other cables, and cooling lines. They had not covered this end of the facility before. She had no idea what to expect, and the danger of the unknown kept her on high alert. Wen looked down through the metal grid floor, and recalled the earlier attack where an MSS agent lurking in the dark underbelly came within a centimeter of killing her.

This time it wasn't below that she had to worry about. As the corridor curved, it opened into a vast hanger-like room, that was a maze of catwalks, pipes, conduit, and machinery and high above on reinforced platform four agents, and five security forces were waiting, ready, aiming. In a split second she knew the only choice was to throw the containment grenade. The risk was that it would damage some piece of equipment or rupture a vital conduit that would make shutting down the lasers impossible. *If they kill us, we can't stop it either.* "Get down!" she yelled to Chase, as she tossed the ECG.

The flash cleared and she confirmed nine down.

"Are they dead?" Chase asked, getting up.

"If they aren't, they are wishing they were."

The noise brought two more rushing in, but they were careless and died quickly.

"There's the door!" Chase yelled. Having enough tactical experience now, he opened it slowly allowing Wen to lead with her MP7.

"Clear," she announced.

She escorted him to the top where the vehicle was, kissed him, fearing she might never see him again, then made her way back down the steps. They both knew his attempts to insert the override module would be futile if they lost the control room.

Chapter Seventy-Six

MECHANICSVILLE, VIRGINIA

April 3rd - 4:19 pm

Chase looked down what was now seventy-feet to the depths of the silo. The heat threatened to overpower him. In a sudden flash, he imagined cooking to death in the seemingly bottomless shaft. *What an awful way to die.*

He pulled on the harness, since the vehicle would not move until it was locked around him. Engaging the tiny motor that he was depending on, the cage jolted, crawling lower. He felt like a hot dog being broiled. Chase studied the shaft, there would be no way to climb up or down if the vehicle stopped, the walls were just too hot.

"Hey, come on, come on," he muttered impatiently, not because the unbearable heat penetrated to his core, but he couldn't stop thinking of Tu and that each second was precious.

Finally, the vehicle jerked as it hit the programmed stop. Sweat dripping down his face, Chase pushed the button to release his harness.

He wanted to yell to Wen, wondering if she'd made it back yet, but didn't dare risk it. If someone else was in the control room, they could kill him easily. However, it would require great effort to see him if they didn't know he was there. *I'll find her after.*

The insertion would be simple now with full access from the silo. The ALESSEN almost slipped from his sweaty hands. *Deep breath. Relax. Relax.*

He carefully pressed the ALESSEN in place, heard the click and then rotated it clockwise forty-five degrees. A tone rang out indicating a successful process. Chase exhaled. *Time to go back up.*

He pressed the keys on the control and waited for the vehicle to engage. *I'm not sure I can survive the sixty seconds or so it's going to take to reach the platform.*

Then he thought about navigating his way back down to the control room without Wen. "I'd like to talk to the idiot engineer who designed this system," he muttered. "But then they probably weren't expecting to have to do this process."

Every inch seemed like a strain for the vehicle. His mind returned to the idea of cooking to death. Finally, as the vehicle got within a few feet of the top he felt momentarily safe, since he thought he could climb to the platform if he had to, but that turned out not to be necessary as the machine did what it was designed to do, and he silently thanked the engineers he had cursed moments earlier.

Getting to the room, he was relieved to find it still empty. Back out in the corridor, he quickly retraced the route they had taken and saw several extra bodies on the floor. Evidence Wen had come this way.

A few minutes later he found her waiting behind the vault door with a Chinese man wearing a white coat. The flash of elation on Wen's face upon seeing Chase, told him that she'd been extra worried this time. He figured she had returned to the control room slower than she should have, to make sure the way would be clear for him.

"Who is this?" Chase asked, as the three of them rushed into the control room and locked the vault door.

"He was being escorted by three MSS agents, so I knew he was important and took him."

Chase didn't need to ask what happened to the three agents. "Where were they taking him."

"Detainment," Wen replied. "Apparently, he's one of the top engineers here. He told me that his superiors are crazy, that they are trying to destroy Washington, but he thinks they will end up destroying the world. He believes Beijing doesn't understand the forces they are unleashing."

"I can't argue with him there." Chase looked at the time. "Does he know the protocols and sequence?"

She asked him in Mandarin.

The man answered in Mandarin.

"He says he does."

"Tell him that we've inserted a new ALESSEN."

She told him. The man looked confused.

Chase led him over to the instrument column, then described how he inserted the ALESSEN, pointing to the various parts of the column, even demonstrating with his arms how he rode the cage down.

"You cannot do that," he said in broken English. His face contorted from confusion to terror.

"Why not?"

"No good."

Wen asked him in Mandarin what the problem was.

She translated his answer. "He says, that within thirty minutes of a full initiation, any attempt to override . . . you cannot do."

The man's eyes teared.

"Why?" Chase asked again. "What's going to happen?"

"This stops energy," he said. "It is pyramid."

"Yes, pyramid."

"Now all force, the power . . . " he said, then switched back to speaking Mandarin.

"He says all the energy stays here," Wen said.

"Good that's what we want to save Washington," Chase said. "Save all the people."

"Yes, but . . . make full-load meltdown."

"Oh my god!" Chase looked at the engineer, and could see he was now crying. "You mean?"

"We all die."

"How can we stop it?"

"No stop."

Chase looked at the clock, and thought of the helicopter. "We have thirteen minutes. We can still escape."

"Not enough time."

Chapter Seventy-Seven

WASHINGTON, DC

April 3rd - 4:20 pm

Tu looked at the research again. It confirmed what he already thought. "The Russians don't have the technology to build the Death Star," he muttered, while pulling up another screen. "Only one country could make a weapon such as this. China."

He called The Astronaut. There was no answer. He tried Chase and Wen. Nothing.

He sent an urgent message to one of his colleagues in the think tank asking them to find out if the Russian and Chinese ambassadors were in Washington. Then he went on to research the Mechanicsville facility.

Ever since he'd been copied in on Wen's text to The Astronaut he had been scouring the internet, government data bases and the dark net for any information on the mysterious industrial park. All the waivers for construction, component histories, material deliveries, recorded manifests, and personnel records pointed to the Chinese not the Russians.

"Come on Astronaut," he said, as the phone went to voicemail again. "We need satellite imaging. We need to know what's going on there right now."

He kept digging, hoping to find what kind of deliveries were made, any incriminating images, official records . . . a smoking gun. "I need more time!"

He received a text back from his colleague. "Both the Russian ambassador and the Chinese ambassador are out of the country. And oddly, many key personnel from both nation's diplomatic corps are also absent."

That information didn't necessarily point to China exclusively, however it made him more convinced that this was a Chinese operation. It made sense China would want their key people out of the country when they destroyed a city.

Desperate, Tu circumvented the think tank's firewall, and routed to an outside server through a series of global hops. He was risking detection by using the techniques The Astronaut had taught him. He recalled his mentor's warning, "Never access Ghost Dragon or Heaven from where you live."

The ultra-classified intelligence networks run by the Chinese and US, respectively, were dangerous and convoluted. "A world where one can enter and never come out," The Astronaut had cautioned, attempting to impress on Tu that the ramifications of treading in those realms could be brutal and far reaching. "World ending."

Getting in and navigating Ghost Dragon was much more complicated and time consuming than he thought, but eventually he found his way deep into the forbidden secret network. Using the facility's address and entering key components related to the laser weapon, he was able to gather additional circumstantial evidence and inconclusive proof connecting Chinese firms. *Now I am positive.*

He tried The Astronaut again. Still no answer. Both Chase and Wen's phones came up out-of-range. Trying not to worry about the three of them, he called the only other person he could think of. Tess Federgreen.

It took him a while to get through to her and while waiting, he calmed himself and rehearsed his delivery. *Grown-ups don't normally believe children, on things like this, especially when they are hysterical."*

Tess finally came on the line.

"My name is Tu. I belong with Chase and Wen and . . . "

"I know who you are, Tu," Tess said, trying to sound pleasant. "It's a very busy time, do you have some information about Chase and Wen?"

"Operation Blackout, is not from the Russians. It is China, they are framing Russia. It is China behind destroying the city, I am certain of it."

Tess knew of Tu's genetically modified super-intelligence, and that he was a star participant at the leading think tank on Asian affairs. She also understood Chase, Wen, and The Astronaut kept him involved in their activities. Still, with everything on the line, a million lives, the future . . . she couldn't just take his word for it. "What proof do you have?"

He rattled off a list of reasons and ended with a plea. "It is China, it is always China. They have gone too far this time. I know it."

"I'll see what I can do," she said, then ended the call. Tess knew the President was minutes away from launching a preemptive strike against Russia. Tess closed her eyes. She believed Tu. All along it hadn't felt right to her that Russia would make this kind of move.

Tess called the president and told him she had new intelligence that it was actually China behind Blackout. She didn't dare tell him it was from a "kid."

The president was relieved to pause. "A preemptive strike against Russia is about the most dangerous thing a president can do."

"You can always launch," Tess said. "We may still find a way to stop this thing.

"But I can't un-launch," he said.

Tess knew the extra breathing room from the president didn't stop the clock, but Tu had given her an address and now there was at least some hope.

Washington, DC
April 3rd - 4:28 pm

The Astronaut muttered a continuous loop of everyone he knew who was involved in the unfolding catastrophe. "Wen, Chase, Tu, Zu mu . . . every few minutes or so . . . he repeated the names in a hypnotic mantra. After almost forty minutes of that repetition, he added the name Tess Federgreen and ten minutes later he came out of it. "I need to call Tess Federgreen!"

Fortunately for him, he was being held by DARPA. The agency's secret black ops division had traced Skyenor's phone and taken The Astronaut as an accessory to the director's murder, among other pending charges.

The woman behind the glass was Coco's deputy and

knew her boss was with Tess at that very moment inside PEOC.

DARPA had had a day. In addition to picking up the Astronaut, the agency's operatives had been scrubbing data from the dead scientists' secure network positions, tracking satellites capable of Blackout participation, and upon orders from Coco, they staged the prison suicide of a former DARPA employee, Rod Irwin. "We can't have that snake slithering around out in the world," Coco had said upon learning of the deal to spring him.

However Coco's deputy believed the Astronaut was different, and she got in touch with her boss at PEOC, who in turn informed Tess that they had Nash in custody.

Tess took the call.

"It's Norfolk," The Astronaut yelled. "The facility is outside Richmond."

"Are you sure it's Norfolk?" Tess asked.

Analysts listening in on the call checked their calculations.

"Yes, yes. Chase and Wen are there now. They need to send IT-Squads, the army, air force, everyone!"

"They've been on stand-by. I'm sending them now."

"There is still time."

"Yes." Tess simultaneously gave the orders to take the facility and then told DARPA to release Nash. "Wait, I'm being told it's more likely Washington," she said.

"It could be . . . " The Astronaut said, thinking through the coordinates and radius overlays. Then he remembered Tu. "I have to save Tu!"

Chapter Seventy-Eight

MECHANICSVILLE, VIRGINIA

April 3rd - 4:30 pm

"I cannot stop the energy, it is too far into process," the engineer said, as if ashamed. "This safety feature. It cannot shut down. Energy must go somewhere. It will go here."

"I understand," Chase said. "But—"

"We will be dead in twelve minutes twenty-two seconds." He looked at Chase and Wen, his frightened expressions that of a condemned man.

"But we saved the city," Wen said. "The laser pyramid . . . it will not launch against Washington?"

"City safe."

"We have a helicopter on the roof."

The engineer shook his head. "Look." He pointed to a bank of monitors showing security zones. Chase quickly found the one displaying the still smoldering tangled black carcass of their helicopter.

"Cars?" Wen asked.

"Too far, take us fifteen minutes just to get to them. Another ten to drive far enough away from the blast."

"There must be a way," Wen said.

Chase fiddled with his multi-tool, wondering what wiring he could cut, what screw he could turn, to stop the fury about to consume them.

"Not worry," the engineer said. "It is instant death. We will not feel. It happens so fast, so powerful."

"Screw that," Chase said. "Let's go!"

Washington, DC
April 3rd - 4:33 pm

Tu looked at his calculations again, and held back tears. "Zu mu," he called out. "Zu mu!"

"What's wrong?"

"The Death Star . . . Washington is Alderaan," he said, referring the mystical Star Wars planet destroyed by Darth Vader.

"What?"

"The laser pyramid, that Chase and Wen and The Astronaut have been looking for . . . It's going to destroy Washington, tonight! We're going to die!"

"No, sweet boy, do not worry. Chase and Wen will save us."

Mechanicsville, Virginia
April 3rd – 4:34 pm

A loud warning buzzer wailed as Wen, Chase and the engineer ran toward the closest exit. "It's futile!" the engineer yelled above the insentient electronic caterwaul.

Neither Chase nor Wen responded. They'd had the debate, there was nothing left to do but try. Every fifty feet a red flashing light warned of the impending end of the world. They had encountered two other groups of civilian employees fleeing, but otherwise they were rushing through an industrial ghost town. They navigated the endless catwalks, conduits, pipes, and multiple-layers across levels of machinery that only the engineer understood.

"It's a damned maze," Chase said following the engineer, but looking at the facility's plans on his tablet.

"Wen Sung! Chase Malone!"

Hearing their names shouted, and echoing amongst the laser factory, like an avant-garde fusion forge seemed suddenly even more eerie, a scientific tomb. It also stopped them cold.

"IT-Squad?" Chase said. "They made it!"

Wen wanted to believe that but the use of their last names and the fact she could not see who had called them, made her think otherwise. "Identify yourselves!" she yelled, while moving to cover. "Get down!" she hissed to Chase and the engineer.

"There's no time to get down," the engineer said, an instant before the bullet penetrated his skull.

"They call me Spinx," Anatoly yelled. "And I'm tired of chasing you all over the damned city, and now I had to come all the way down to this god-forsaken part of the Confederacy just to kill you."

Chase looked at Wen as if to say, they were going to die anyway.

"Why do you want to kill us?" She asked, still not sure where he was.

He laughed. "It's my job."

"You're Russian."

"Yes, sorry about my accent."

"But this is a Chinese facility."

"So they own everything, but they pay well."

"This guy obviously doesn't know the place is about to blow up," Chase whispered.

Then Wen got a visual. "You killed Skyenor."

"Yes, you admire my work? Or are you just upset you couldn't stop me?"

"Behind us," Wen whispered to Chase. "He's stalling so his guys can get behind us."

Chase turned to cover the rear.

"You're just a hired gun," Wen yelled, inching forward. "You're nothing special. "Did you hunt down an unarmed, defenseless man in the dark two nights ago?"

"Maybe. I might have been taking in the sights. The Lincoln Memorial is pretty at night."

"You're a coward."

"Yeah, well, you're a—"

Wen's bullets cut through his legs and brought him screaming to his knees. "What am I?" she asked, suddenly standing above him.

He looked up, reaching for his gun. "You're a b—"

Wen shot him in the face. "That's for Hayward."

She ran to join Chase and arrived just in time to help him kill the six men Anatoly had brought with him.

Chase looked at his watch, then to Wen.

"How long?" she asked, as the flashing red light kept time with the buzzer, as if counting down the final breaths until death.

"Six minutes," he lied. It was closer to four.

Washington DC - PEOC
April 3rd - 4:43 pm

"Get me eyes on the facility," Tess said.

The screens filled with satellite images of the entire campus. "Zoom on the big building, what is that?"

"Looks like a smoldering helicopter."

"Put the IT-Squad there."

Twenty seconds later, the first team dropped down on the roof. Tess looked at the clock. "We've got nine hours to secure this facility and shut down the fusion ray," Tess said, having no idea the Chinese had moved up the launch.

"Another team is five minutes out," Linda said, speaking from an open line to Mission Control.

"ETA on full military presence?"

"Eighteen minutes."

"Hold on, Chase," Tess whispered. "The Calvary is on the way."

The screens suddenly erupted with fire and smoke.

"What just happened?" Tess yelled.

Only silence answered as everyone watched, speechless. The satellite images showing a massive world-ending explosion worse than any images they'd seen of nuclear detonation.

The IT-Squad had been incinerated instantly. "Anyone

left anywhere near that place is gone," Linda said, not wanting to say Chase and Wen, but knowing if they hadn't gotten out at least twenty minutes ago. They were fried.

Chapter Seventy-Nine

WASHINGTON DC - PEOC

April 3rd - 5:12 pm

Tess only turned away from the live feeds of the disaster area because Linda had called from CISS Mission Control. "I have Nash Graham on the line," Linda said. "Can I patch him through?"

"It's unlikely he's going to provide any additional information, at least not now."

"I know, but . . . "

"I guess in a way I owe it to Chase and Wen," she said, "Okay." It took a few seconds until she heard the click indicating The Astronaut was now on. "Hello Nash."

"Did you get them out?"

"No," she said in her gentlest voice. "I'm sorry."

"Sorry, no!" A few moments of silence followed before he began again. "They must have escaped. Wen and Chase always escape."

"We were trying, we just didn't know exactly where they were in time. But I've watched the satellite feeds. We scrolled back in time, saw them arrive. I'm sure they were expecting to exit on their helicopter. Did you know it was destroyed?"

"No," he said in a whimpering voice.

"Apparently neither did they, and when they found out, there wasn't enough time left to get out another way. I'm sorry, the facility locked down."

"But now you have people there trying to rescue, and looking for survivors?"

Tess stared at the monitors displaying images from the satellite live feed and another showing the footage being aired on the cable news networks. She knew The Astronaut was seeing the same, it had to be obvious to him that there were no survivors. However, she understood that during emotional trauma people, particularly those on the spectrum, could have a difficult time keeping a grip on logical reality. "I'm sorry," she said again. "No one could live through that blast. More than half a mile wide radius was leveled. Even if the facility had not been locked down, even if they had access to another vehicle, they didn't have time, there was no way to escape. It's tragic, Nash . . . Chase and Wen died in the blast."

"I don't want that."

"The state police, local governments, and FEMA are estimating that more than 12,000 people may have died. You're not alone in your grief."

"You should've rescued them," he said bitterly, "You should have gotten them out. I need them."

"We all needed them," Tess said. "But whatever they did, whatever happened at the factory. Chase and Wen saved a million lives, they saved Washington DC, they saved America."

"They saved Tu and me."

"Yes. Imagine the world if this had gone another way. If they had not succeeded and the horrible people had actually melted Washington. What would've come next?"

"I don't know." The Astronaut was closing down.

"That kind of power . . . once unleashed . . . allowed to run unchecked . . . Chase and Wen didn't just give their lives for Washington DC, they saved the world." She was going to add that she thought that was worth dying for, and that obviously Chase and Wen thought it was as well, instead she simply said, "They died to save us all."

The Astronaut did not respond. Tess wasn't sure what to do. People were waiting to speak with her, there were many decisions to make, actions to take, retaliations being weighed, counterattacks, all kinds of urgent deliberations, operations to plan, espionage to conduct, and Tess was one of the few in charge of most of it, yet she didn't feel right about abandoning Nash, so she sat there watching the horrific images and listening to his labored and distressed breathing, knowing his world had been shattered. In the last forty-eight hours he had lost three of the people closest to him.

Linda buzzed in on the line. Tess had to get off.

"You are still alive," Tess finally said. "They would want you to live, to continue their work. You need to get Wen's grandmother and the boy, Tu. Take them to Dez and Bull, the five of you need to comfort each other, you've all lost so much, not just in his last few days but these last few years." Tess thought of Wen's grandmother losing all the people she knew and her homeland. Tu missed the children he'd been raised with. Bull and Dez had lost the use of their legs. Nash had not recovered from Hayward's death. "You still have each other. Chase and Wen would want you to be together. I can send an IT-Squad to protect you and Tu. We can put you in a safe house . . . if you want you can come here. Whatever you need, just let me know."

"I want Chase and Wen," he whispered.

"I know."

After another few silent moments, The Astronaut cleared his throat. "Thank you, Tess. I never liked you very much. Really not at all . . . "

"I know," she said. "That's okay."

"I think I was wrong."

Epilogue

VIENNA, VIRGINIA

April 5th - 10:29 am

Tess stood in Mission Control, staring at dozens of monitors all filled with images relating to the worst situation she had ever faced. One of the screens was a live feed of an overhead view of the Washington historic district—the Jefferson and Lincoln Memorials, the Washington Monument, White House, Capitol building were all visible.

"I like to see them still standing," she said to Linda.

"And that," Linda said pointing to another screen showing Tolstoy being interrogated.

"Yes, that pleases me, too. I spoke to her myself, yesterday."

"She's still not cooperating?"

"No, but she will," Tess said, a determined tone that Linda knew not to question.

"What a plan, she masterminded," Linda said.

"Remember we don't yet know how high it went . . . But

our sources believe China's president was not involved, that it was a member of the Central Committee."

"That's more than two hundred people."

"We have it narrowed down to six," Tess said. "Three of them have completely disappeared."

"The Party cleaning house, removing the evidence?"

"Looks that way. Apparently, Blackout had been designed to make the destruction of Washington look to the world like a mistake made by the US, as if we were creating a super weapon and lost control of it."

"It might have worked."

"For a while, but the Chinese knew we would figure it out, so they had a backup ploy."

"Make Russia the fall guy."

"Yes, China left a big trail leading right to Russia."

"And with most of our intelligence community and military command destroyed, we wouldn't be able to mount a real investigation into the events, all evidence would point to Russia. And it would be so easy to believe."

"Incredible, how close they were to getting away with it."

"We almost sent a preemptive strike to Moscow," Linda said. "Imagine . . . "

"I'd rather not." Tess stared at Tolstoy again. "The Chinese used Russian code names. We almost missed Tolstoy's true identity, because we were looking for a Russian. Incredible that it turned out Tolstoy was Jie Shi."

"She'd been paving the way for this for years, greasing the right people to make sure the facility got built, operational, and went undetected."

Tess had no idea that the Chinese diplomat had already been executed, and that the gray-haired man, code named, Yuri, had been arrested and sent to China's largest and most secret prison camp—the brutal Lingchi Prison. Those who knew about it said, "If you go in, you never come out." The name, roughly translated, means a slow, lingering death, or death by one thousand cuts. The isolated labor camp, located in the far western region of the country, had been operated by the MSS for more than two decades—although the government steadfastly denied its existence. Lingchi was as close to a cold, bitter hell as there was on earth.

"At least it's over," Linda said.

Tess shook her head and looked at another screen showing Popov leaving her coffee shop, but the image was old, the Russian agent had disappeared. An IT-Squad had detained one of her associates who had told them that Popov had stumbled upon Blackout, and informed her superiors in Moscow. "True the Russians were not involved, but they knew it was coming and said nothing . . . the blood of the twelve thousand dead Americans is on their hands, too." Tess thought about how close the world had come to nuclear war.

"Would we have told them? Linda asked.

Tess shook her head. "I don't know. If your neighbor is planning to blow up your house and another neighbor finds out about it, and they don't tell you . . . "

"But it's over," Linda repeated.

"No it's only beginning. Now that the Chinese and the Russians . . . even us, know how easy it is to destroy cities with lasers and fusion energy weapons, no place on earth, or for that matter, in space, will ever be safe again."

Washington, DC
April 6th - 4:11 pm

The Astronaut and Tu had just finished saying their goodbyes to their colleagues at the think tank and were about to get Zu mu and head to the Joint Base Andrews, where Tess had arranged a flight for them, when unexpectedly, Tess found them.

"What are you doing here?" The Astronaut asked, concerned.

"I have news," she said. "Our top engineers were reviewing all the plans, and data on the facility, trying to learn as much as they could about the operation. One of them saw a rod cavity at the bottom of the silo and realized it could have been used as a kind of bunker. I figured it was worth a try . . . "

The Astronaut's eyes widened.

"The space extended almost twenty stories underground. It took several days, working and digging around the clock . . . Due to the reinforced construction in the lower chamber, large sections of the subterranean areas held solid, making it easier to clear. And . . . we found them."

"Alive?" The Astronaut's voice made the word sound less like a question and more like a prayer.

"Yes."

Tu threw himself into The Astronaut's arms. "Chase and Wen! I knew it! I knew it! Chase and Wen are alive!"

Tess couldn't help but smile, and quickly wiped what may have been a stray tear. "Turns out Chase had the plans to the facility and saw what our engineers discovered. He and Wen were able to get down there in the final seconds."

"But they're okay?" The Astronaut asked, still hardly believing it.

"They were in rough shape. Dehydrated, hungry, battered, both with serious injuries, but . . . alive."

"Where are they now?"

"We have them at Walter Reed," she said, speaking of the National Military Hospital Center, in Bethesda, Maryland. "No one knows they're alive. We're making sure the MSS is able to 'steal' the satellite images of Chase and Wen entering the facility and not coming out."

The Astronaut paused, while he digested her meaning. "So they are finally free?"

"Well, partially. The MSS thinks they're dead, but there is still the matter of the shadow people . . . "

"Can we see them?" Tu asked.

"I'll take you there now."

Undisclosed location
April 26th

Wen and Chase walked the deserted beach, both still stiff and sore from their injuries. "We shouldn't be here," Chase said.

"It's totally safe," Wen said. "You know it's been checked and cleared multiple times."

"That's not what I mean. We should have died back there, buried in that concrete tomb."

"We didn't though."

"Maybe a little," Chase said, recalling the second day underground when they had decided no one could reach them in time, even if anyone guessed they might still be under there. "I don't know if I'll ever be able to go in a tunnel again . . . We were dead."

"Look around, feel that humid ocean air . . . We're alive." She kissed him.

"It may have been worth it," he said. "The MSS

believes we're dead. And Tess says she's covertly spread the word widely enough that the shadow people will think we died that day, too."

She stopped and savored the feel of the soft, warm sand on her bare feet.

"Being buried alive under an exploding sun is a high price," Chase said. "But I'm sure looking forward to life without the shadow people chasing us."

Wen glanced at him, a determined look on her face. "Yes, this time we'll be chasing them."

They gazed down the beach and saw the people who had saved them at the Exorcist Steps coming toward them. Shelby and Grimes waved. "The Circuit is about to find out that power goes both ways."

Next in the Chase Malone Thriller series

vinci-books.com/chasing-lies

Trust nothing. Believe no one. Lies are the only way out.

Fugitive billionaire Chase Malone and ex-spy Wen Zhou find themselves ensnared in a labyrinth of deceit, where every truth is masked by layers of manipulation.

Turn the page for a free preview…

Chasing Lies: Chapter One

On a cold November day, at a busy truck stop along Interstate 35, outside of Ames, Iowa, a dead man dropped down from the cab of a Peterbilt tractor-trailer and walked around inspecting the first of the eighteen wheels. He recalled learning that the word "dead" from the Middle English 'ded,' originally simply meant "having ceased to live."

Light snow flurries blew haphazardly as the dead man walked the perimeter of the truck. In his jeans and flannel shirt, a John Deere cap, and cowboy boots, no one gave him a second glance. They would never imagine he was the brilliant tech billionaire, Chase Malone, because he had died more than six months earlier.

Or had he simply ceased to live? Chase didn't particularly *feel* as if he'd stopped living, but as far as his enemies were concerned—the Chinese MSS, various multinational corporations, and a secretive group known as *the shadow people*, Chase Malone was no longer alive.

Yet for Chase, being dead actually left him feeling more alive than ever.

As a semi pulling a load of live hogs rolled by, Chase made a quick check of the remaining tires, although he knew they were fine. He'd actually gone out there to have a look around the area. Scanning past a pair of Kenworths, one a tanker loaded with milk, the other hauling Amazon—the pale blue arrow seeming to be smiling at him—the coast appeared clear. There was no sign of the two killers they were expecting.

There were cameras mounted on all sides of the big rig, so his "tire-check" was not only risky, but completely unnecessary. But he liked to be sure, liked to see it with his own eyes.

He climbed back inside the cab. Wen, processing security issues through the sophisticated computers onboard, had watched Chase's excursion, making sure he encountered no problems. He went through the well-camouflaged door connecting the cab's sleeping area to the fifty-three-foot trailer. The trailer, more like a command center, was outfitted with every bit of technologically advanced surveillance equipment available. It was from there they monitored not just their immediate surroundings, but the world.

The first six weeks after they'd died, they'd stayed on a remote island in the South Pacific, healing as much as hiding. However, they both knew there was work to do. "We can't pretend the world doesn't exist forever," Wen had said. Chase hadn't argued. Part of him would've been content to live on that island for at least another ten years, to be sure the shadow people had forgotten about them, to avoid the bullets, bombs, and chaos that had been their lives for so long. But he would've missed Tu, the little boy they had rescued from China, who had become like a son to them.

Wen said they might have brought him to the island, but Chase didn't believe that would be safe. So in the end, he'd agreed, and they'd built the truck.

Then they got ready to go to war.

Several monitors showed their expected "guests" approaching. Chase checked the date time stamp on the feed and whispered, "November seventeenth, the day the shadow war officially begins."

Cranson looked like a schoolteacher, not a killer, but that only made him better at his job. He was a hunter; a *bounty* hunter, but he never brought anyone back alive. It wasn't his objective, ever.

He waited for Belfort on the veranda of the fully restored antebellum mansion a few hours outside of Atlanta, and wondered again what Belfort's first name was. He didn't *need* to know it, but Cranson was a curious guy. He didn't like mysteries, and Belfort was a big one.

I'm not even sure if Belfort is his last name… might be his first, probably isn't real anyway. What the eff is his real name? Cranson cared because Belfort could easily screw something up and get him killed, or if Cranson screwed something up, Belfort might *have* him killed. *I'd sleep easier if I knew this slug's name…*

Cranson didn't much care for Georgia—*too effin' humid*—but in the middle of November, it was almost bearable. He didn't much care for Belfort either, but the money . . . oh the money was *so- way- too- good* that he would put up with about anything.

"Cranson, you look a bit watered down," Belfort said as

he came through the two huge oak doors and crossed the brick floor. "Want a lemonade?"

Cranson looked at the African American butler trailing Belfort. The man was dressed all in white, appearing as a slave might have two hundred years earlier. Cranson thought Belfort might like it that way. The butler extended a silver tray with two glasses of freshly made lemonade balanced upon it. Cranson took one and thanked the man.

"What's going on with the team hunting Chase and Wen?" Belfort asked. It was always his first question. Cranson didn't get the obsession. Those two were dead. Bigtime dead and buried deep—*really* deep—under a zillion tons of rubble.

Besides, there are bigger fish to fry.

"Nothing new," Cranson said. "Chase and Wen are dead."

"Are they?" Belfort asked. "I see no bodies."

"No one could have survived that blast. They were there, *inside*, we know they were. They *are* dead. *Very* dead."

"I don't think they can be killed."

Cranson laughed.

Belfort's face went from serious to annoyed. "Did I say something funny?"

"You've seen the footage, the reports . . . Inside that facility, it was equivalent to a nuclear blast."

Belfort's expression remained skeptical.

"More than six months, and not a trace of them," Cranson tried again. "Someone would have seen them by now. They're dead. It's *over*."

"*I* decide when it's over."

Cranson suppressed a sigh. "I'll keep at it."

"Yes, you will."

Chasing Lies: Chapter Two

Even though Chase and Wen both recognized their visitors, they waited until the AI system made a positive ID before they opened the door to the trailer command center.

Grimes always seemed to appear as if he'd just walked off a beach, and that was often the case. His sandy, perpetually messy hair, stubble, and tan gave him that beer commercial look.

"Brought a box of chocolates," Grimes said, handing a multipack of Reese's Peanut Butter Cups to Chase. "And a long-stemmed rose." He handed the single flower to Wen.

"Thank you," she said, thinking the gifts a little odd. They hadn't seen Grimes and Shelby for months, but they'd stayed in regular contact.

"Peace offering," Shelby said.

"Peanut butter cups are always welcome," Chase said, unwrapping one and slipping it in his mouth. "Mmm. Nothing like it."

"So why are we risking this face-to-face?" Grimes asked.

"It's time to start the war," Chase replied.

"Excellent." Grimes reached for a peanut butter cup. "But if we start this, we're on a one-way track . . . there'll be no turning back."

"This war has been in the planning stages ever since the day we died," Chase said.

"Last chance to walk away," Wen added, looking at Chase. Their deaths had given them a kind of freedom they hadn't known since they'd begun fighting those who used technology to harm and control. Shadow people had, for unknown reasons, been pursuing them for years.

"We sure aren't going to just ride off into the sunset," Chase said. They'd had this conversation many times, they didn't need to have it again. They both knew the answer. Even if they weren't determined to right the wrongs, there was no denying that the world would eventually catch up to them. "The only way to make them stop is to face our demons," Chase said bitterly. "To find the shadow people and destroy them."

"Same," Shelby said. "Ending Belfort and his people is also our only hope at a normal life."

Chase studied her. Shelby, still attractive, looked older. Grimes, as always, unless he was on a beach somewhere, looked tense, ready for a fight. "You two look terrible," he said, smiling, but also concerned. "Been tough?"

"Yeah, well..." Grimes began. "The difference is they *think* you're dead, but they *want* us dead."

Chase nodded.

"They know we're alive," Shelby added. "And it's driving Belfort crazy!"

Belfort was the mysterious man behind the shadow people. He had hired Shelby, Grimes, and a whole lot of others to kill Chase and Wen, but instead, through an odd series of events along the way, they had saved each other's lives. Now the four of them shared a common enemy . . . the Circuit.

Belfort snapped his fingers twice, summoning the butler. "Is that sandwich ready yet?"

"Sir?"

"I'm hungry. Where's my sandwich?"

"I didn't know you wanted—"

"No excuses, boy! Bring me my damned sandwich."

"Yes, sir." The butler placed the silver tray on a wicker end table and quickly retreated into the massive home.

"Grimes and Shelby are still eluding us," Cranson said, preemptively bringing up another unpleasant topic. *At least they're alive and can be found and killed.*

"Yes. Impressive they've avoided us, but they're probably hiding under a rock in the Middle East somewhere. Eventually, they'll come out." He downed his lemonade. "But I didn't ask you here to talk about those two traitors."

Cranson was relieved. "A new assignment?"

Belfort nodded. "There are six key people in US intelligence that we don't own, that won't play ball . . . "

The butler appeared with the sandwich. Cranson guessed it might have been egg salad. Belfort snatched it from the silver tray with one hand, then waved the butler off with his other.

"This one is first," Belfort said, his mouth full. "Tess Federgreen."

"She knew Chase and Wen," Cranson said, recalling Tess's name from Chase and Wen's files.

"Quite well."

"Is that why she's on the list?"

Belfort scoffed. "I must admit, it gives me extra pleasure to kill a friend of Chase Malone. However, she's on the kill list for a more important reason."

ANC - Always News Channel - Top Story

"Stu Lemon reporting. Our top story at this hour: Researchers at the University of Maryland have discovered a new and dangerous computer virus dubbed NoLiv, that they say could not just harm your computer, but is capable of causing catastrophic damage to the economy. We have Bill Doorset, who made his fortune in the computer industry before turning to philanthropy, here to explain."

"Thanks, Stu. This really is the perfect storm. For anyone who remembers Mydoom, which was the world's fastest spreading computer worm, or viruses like Sobig, or the ILOVEYOU worm, this is something far more lethal."

"'Lethal' seems an unusual term to use for a computer virus."

"This is a very unusual virus. It can literally kill your computer, and NoLiv has all the necessary components to be able to self-replicate at speeds we've never had to deal with."

"Sounds terrifying."

"It is."

"Can we stop it?"

"We don't know yet. Finding solutions for something this sophisticated takes time. Fortunately, the government, universities, and numerous tech companies have been preparing for something like this, running simulations, looking for ways—"

"When do you think a patch will be available?"

"This is way beyond a patch. I'm optimistic that eventually we'll find something to stop NoLiv, but your viewers need to be prepared. This is going to get a lot worse before it gets better."

Chasing Lies: Chapter Three

The *Destino* creaked in the wind. The name they'd given the truck—Spanish for destiny—had been inspired by the inevitable showdown with Belfort and his shadow people. "Our life comes to this," Wen had said. "It begins or ends with the final breath of the last shadow person."

Yet they both understood that it also went beyond the shadow people. Their true enemies were the people who *paid* the killers.

The small sounds and movements outside, brought on by the weather as a front moved across the flatlands, made Wen nervous. She checked the cameras while Chase, Grimes, and Shelby continued talking.

"For better or worse, the four of us are uniquely qualified to go after the shadow people," Shelby said.

"We're doing more than going after them," Chase replied. "We're going to find out who the Circuit is."

Shelby and Grimes exchanged a glance. "Nice little truck you got here," Shelby said, changing the subject. "Does NASA know you stole it?"

Chase laughed. "NASA doesn't have anything *this* sophisticated." Then he explained the name, the reason behind it, and vowed again that they would never stop.

Grimes studied a section of controls closely.

"Hey, don't touch that," Chase admonished him.

Grimes pretended to push a button. "Why? If I do, will a satellite fall out of the sky?"

"Maybe," Chase said impatiently. "Let's get to it."

"We've got some interesting information to share," Shelby said. For the past six months, she and Grimes had been methodically pulling leads together. "But it hasn't been easy navigating all this. Getting help from past associates when there's a price on our heads has been exceedingly difficult."

"Welcome to our world," Chase muttered.

Grimes squinted, as if this didn't amuse him. "We've been working hard to convert a few more to our side."

"Shadow people?" Wen asked.

"Well, we don't really call ourselves that, but yeah, contractors. The ones we know who don't like Belfort, who might have the guts to cross a line. Know what I mean?"

"I think so," Chase said. "How's it been going?"

"We've lined up a few," Shelby said, rubbing at her forehead. "It's slow work."

"There are others who we're close to turning," Grimes added. "But we have to be extremely cautious or Belfort will get wind."

Chase started adjusting settings on a large control board.

"So what's all this stuff *do*?" Grimes asked, pretending as if he might start pushing buttons again.

Chase looked up from the keyboard. "Give me something to go on," he said. "That's why we're here, right? You finally have something? A breakthrough?"

"Yeah, we do, but first, how are we doing with following the money?"

Chase and Wen had been tracking the funds around the shadow people and the mysterious group funding them known as *the Circuit*. "We're into financial transactions amounting to hundreds of billions of dollars. There's nearly a million separate transactions—we call them *MEs*, for monetary events. Our programs can uncover the faintest trails, but the walls are high, and every time we think we've reached an endpoint which might result in an identifying feature, the walls close in on us."

"Try this," Shelby said, giving him a name. "We've been running down Belfort's complex web of hitmen, fixers, and others who have operated within the influence of the Circuit."

Chase fed the name into SEER, or the Search Entire Existence Result program. Chase had developed SEER in strict secrecy, and was not about to share its details with Shelby and Grimes beyond that he was using a machine learning program to assist in finding the Circuit and their assets.

However, SEER was way beyond simple machine learning. It employed advanced photonic quantum information processors and utilized deep learning, AI, quantum algorithms, and virtually every data point in digital existence to predict the future with stunning accuracy. It was their best weapon against the Circuit. As Chase told Wen, "It's how we're going to bury the Circuit."

"Who's that?" Chase asked as SEER began processing the name.

"We were hoping you could tell us," Shelby responded.

"Is there a physical location?" Chase asked hopefully. "Something I can pair with the photo?"

"There's a web address." Shelby spouted a string of numbers from memory.

"That should help." Chase typed it in. "Here you go," he said a couple of seconds later. A photo of a man filled one of the screens.

"That's him," Shelby confirmed. "He's as close to Belfort as we've been able to get."

Chase spoke several voice commands to the computer.

Wen continued monitoring the Destino's cameras. She felt exposed, vulnerable, with the truck just sitting out in the open. *Not many places to hide in Iowa . . .*

Twenty seconds later, when results began filtering through, Chase said, "It's not his real name."

"We know *that*," Shelby said. "That's where we got stopped, but you're the computer genius."

Chase flashed her a smile and began instructing the computer again. The AI took over.

"What's happening?" Grimes asked. "Are you developing some sort of profile on him?"

Chase shook his head. "It's building a net."

"Meaning?" Shelby asked.

"'Net' is a simple term for what the AI is really doing," Chase explained. "It's more like a giant filter. It's creating potential links for this name, this photo . . . it's verifying, checking, connecting more and more . . . "

Wen scanned nearby traffic cams—not for the man, but making sure they were still safe, scrutinizing each vehicle.

"Which databases is it searching?" Grimes asked. "I mean, how does it decide?"

"All of them," Chase said. "It's searching everything that has ever appeared anywhere."

"*Everything?*" Shelby echoed. "Wow. Is that even possible? What about all the records that haven't been digitized?"

"There are ways to get into them, too. Just because it's not on the Internet, or even the dark web, doesn't mean we can't find it and see what's going on."

Additional images of the man began appearing on the biggest screen. They seemed to be mostly from various surveillance cameras around the world.

"Incredible," Grimes said. "Those are all photos of him."

"Just wait," Chase said. More photos streamed through, now showing the man with other people. "Are any of them Belfort?" Chase asked.

"Trouble!" Wen announced.

"What?" Chase asked, immediately hitting the keys that would upload all the data to a safe spot in the cloud.

"Men with guns!"

Grab your copy…
vinci-books.com/chasing-lies

About the Author

USA TODAY Bestselling Author Brandt Legg uses his unusual real life experiences to create page-turning novels. He's traveled with CIA agents, dined with senators and congressmen, mingled with astronauts, chatted with governors and presidential candidates, had a private conversation with a Secretary of Defense he still doesn't like to talk about, hung out with Oscar and Grammy winners, had drinks at the State Department, been pursued by tabloid reporters, and spent a birthday at the White House by invitation from the President of the United States.

At age eight, Legg's father died suddenly, plunging his family into poverty. Two years later, while suffering from crippling migraines, he started in business, and turned a hobby into a multi-million-dollar empire. National media dubbed him the "Teen Tycoon," and by the mid-eighties, Legg was one of the top young entrepreneurs in America, appearing as high as number twenty-four on the list (when Steve Jobs was #1, Bill Gates #4, and Michael Dell #6). Legg still jokes that he should have gone into computers.

By his twenties, after years of buying and selling businesses, leveraging, and risk-taking, the high-flying Legg became ensnarled in the financial whirlwind of the junk bond eighties. The stock market crashed and a firestorm of trouble came down. The Teen Tycoon racked up more than a million dollars in legal fees, was betrayed by those closest to him, lost his entire fortune, and ended up serving time for financial improprieties.

After a year, Legg emerged from federal prison, chastened and wiser, and began anew. More than twenty-five years later, he's now using all that hard-earned firsthand knowledge of conspiracies, corruption and high finance to weave his tales. Legg's books pulse with authenticity.

His series have excited nearly a million readers around the world. Although he refused an offer to make a television movie about his life as a teenage millionaire, his autobiography is in the works. There has also been interest from Hollywood to turn his thrillers into films. With any luck, one day you'll see your favorite characters on screen.

He lives in the Pacific Northwest, with his wife and son, writing full time, in several genres, containing the common themes of adventure, conspiracy, and thrillers. Of all his pursuits, being an author and crafting plots for novels is his favorite.

Acknowledgments

Chasing Time . . . This title has multiple meanings for me. To those who have read many of my books, you know the line "Time is a funny thing." I guess everyone can relate to the speed at which life seems to race by. People we've lost, who we've shared too little time with, the ones still with us who there is never enough time to be with, the dreams we seek, the peace we yearn for . . . it feels as if we're all constantly chasing time.

Although this book is a thriller, an action-packed page-turner, the theme of the story is that the clock never stops moving. We must not waste a moment, whether we are trying to defuse a bomb, or find a few moments to enjoy a sunset, or share our time with a loved one.

There is no place to get more time. Spend it wisely.

Thank you to Ro and Teakki, who make me the luckiest man in the world, and who live with the characters in my stories whether they like it or not. (Sometimes it gets crowded, but there's never a dull moment!) We talk about the people and plots in my books quite a lot, but hopefully not too much. And Teakki, an extra thanks for your ideas about the ending!

And to my mother, Barbara Blair. Her enthusiasm for my work is easy to take for granted, because she's my mom, and yet I have so much respect for her. I'm humbled by her high opinions. It's great fun sharing these adventures with her. She has also single-handedly kept certain "fictional" characters alive by her influence.

Joan Osborne and Gil Forbes deserve special recognition for sharing their finely-tuned and experienced minds. I always appreciate Jack Llartin, my copy editor, who has mastered the method of under promising and over delivering, and has a special talent for the final polish.

And, finally, to Teakki, who patiently waited to read me the latest scene he's written on one of his projects, to show me something he's built, or to discuss movies, until I finished writing each day. Best part of my day, best part of the world.

Most of all, I can never express enough gratitude to my readers. To all the ones that have read everything I've published, to the ones who have just finished their first Booker thriller or Chasing adventure, it means the world to me that you've decided to spend your money and time on my stories. Please drop me an email anytime. Responding to reader emails is one of my favorite parts of the day!

There are so many wonderful authors I've had a chance to meet. This is a small group of the ones who've made a difference to me: Robert Gatewood, Mike Sager, Craig Martelle, Michael Anderle, Mark Dawson, Nick Thacker, Ernest Dempsey, John Grisham, A. Kelly Pruitt, Eric J. Gates, Dale DeVino, Phil M. Williams, Jennifer Theriot, Haris Orkin, Brian Meeks, Michelle McCarty, Mollie Gregory, and Zoe Saadia.

There are so many friends of mine who are creatives as well. Their work inspires my work (and my life): Tony Schueller, David Manzanares, Geraint Smith, Michael Hearne, Don Richmond, Lenny Foster, Jared Rowe, Jimmy Stadler, Scott Thomas, Carol Morgan-Eagle, Deonne Kahler, Bart Anderson, Ernest James, Jenny Bird, Angelika

Maria Koch, Brad Hockmeyer, Verne Verona, Brooke Tatum, Markus Kolber, Terrie Bennett, and many others!

And to the readers who, with their reading, complete the book. I'd like to give extra special thanks to the following readers and/or members of the street team for either their support, kindness, reviews (I love reviews), suggestions, and/or encouragement.

(If I left anyone out, I apologize. Please forgive me, and let me know. I can fix it!)

Please don't let the fact that there are so many of you do anything to diminish your importance to me. That this group continues to grow is so amazing to me, it blows my mind and takes my breath away.

In alphabetical order (by first name):

Adam Tanner, Alec Redwine, Amber Hunt, Anne Kaplan, Bill Borchert, Blake Dowling, Bob Browder, Bob Dumas, Brian C. Coffey, Brian Schnizlein, Cara Johnson, Carl Howard, Carol M, Cathie Harrison, Cheryl Olson, Chet Keough, Chis Bond, Chris Tomlinson, Christine Moritz, Christopher Bowling, Chuck Gonzalez, Cid Chase, Consuelo Ashworth, Debra Harper, Dennis Lowe, Derek Redmond, Diane Whitehead, Douglas Dersch, Douglas Meek, Elaine Dill, Ernest Manpino, Ernest Pino, Frank Fusco, Frank Murphy, Gene Leach, Gene Legg, Gil Forbes, Gillian Charlton, Glenda Dykstra, Glenn Legge, Ingo Michehl, Irene Witoski, Jacky Dallaire, Jan Dallas, Janice Gildea, Jean Sink, Joan Osborne, John McDonald, John Nicholson, John Nunley, Judith Anderson, Judy Hammer, Julie Price, Justin Lear, Karen Mack, Karen Markovitz, Kat Heyer, Kathleen Robbins, Kathy Creecy, Kathy Troc, Ken Clute, Ken Friedman, Kyle Dahlem, LA Dumas, Leslie Royce, Linda Loparco, Liz Miller, Marcel Roy. Gerry Adler, Mark Perlmutter, Martha Heckel, Martin Gunnell, Melanie

C. Hansen, Michael Ferrel, Michael Picco, Mick Flanigan, Mike Brannick, Mike Lauland, Nigel Revill, Pam Gilbert, Patricia Ruby, Paul Gyorke, Peggy Gulli, Randy Howerter, Rick Ferris, Rob Weaver, Rob Zorger, Robyn Shanti, Ron Babcock, Sam J. Rhoades III, Sam Rhoades, Samantha Jackson, Sandie Parrish, Sandra Zuiderhoek, Satish Bhatti, Sharon Moffatt, Stephane Peltier, Sue Steel, Susan McGuyer, Susan Norlund, Susan Powell, Terry Myers, Tom Strauss, Tony Sommer, Tricia Turner, Vicki Gordon, Vivienne Du Bourdieu.

Speaking of reviewers, the prolific readers and top Amazon reviewers who have been a great support of my work deserve extra recognition. Thank you so much, and special gratitude to, the remarkable Grady Harp, and to whoever the reviewer "Serenity" is!

There is a goal among some authors to turn readers into fans, fans into super fans, and super fans into friends. I am fortunate to have been able to achieve that goal on numerous occasions.

Thank you.

www.ingramcontent.com/pod-product-compliance
Ingram Content Group UK Ltd.
Pitfield, Milton Keynes, MK11 3LW, UK
UKHW041854120925
462873UK00003B/72